Showdown In The Capital

Showdown
In The
Capital

Rob Shumaker

Cover design by Cormar Covers

Also by Rob Shumaker

Thunder in the Capital

Chaos in the Capital

D-Day in the Capital

Manhunt in the Capital

Fallout in the Capital

Phantom in the Capital

Blackout in the Capital

The Way Out

For Mom and Dad
With thanks for taking me on all those great adventures.

CHAPTER 1

The White House – Washington, D.C.

"'We hold these truths to be self-evident,'" William E. Cogdon mused aloud in the Oval Office. The President's chief of staff let the words of the Declaration of Independence float throughout the room like some invisible smoke ring of which he was most proud. He was apt to read historic documents out loud, pondering what the authors, this time Jefferson, must have been thinking when they put their ink-dipped quill to parchment throughout American history. The fact that he was sitting inside the White House and could look out across the Tidal Basin to see the stately memorial to the Sage of Monticello did not escape his contemplative mind. During his episodes of deep pondering, his boss would usually mutter something under his breath to show he was actually listening.

"'That all men are created equal.'"

"Uh huh." President Anthony Schumacher, a highlighter in one hand and a pencil in the other, was making changes to his first State of the Union address just two weeks away.

"'That they are endowed by their Creator with certain unalienable Rights,'" he said before pausing and looking up to the Great Seal on the ceiling. "'Endowed by their Creator.'" He whispered the phrase again, loud enough for the President to hear.

Another line out by the President, his eyes still perusing the sentences. "Creator, not me."

"Not you, the President," Cogdon responded. "Not the government either."

"Not the government."

Cogdon continued, "'that they are endowed by their Creator with certain unalienable Rights.'"

"Unalienable."

"You can't deny 'em."

"Wouldn't try to."

"'That among these are Life, Liberty and the pursuit of Happiness.'"

"Never gets old hearing that."

The President's life, liberty, and pursuit of happiness had come under assault in the preceding two months. He had been in office for eight weeks without even being elected. The former Vice President, who hadn't been elected to that office either, assumed the position as the most powerful man in the world after the previous President died.

But not before plotting to have Vice President Schumacher killed.

In one of the most sensational stories in the vast annals of American history, Schumacher was the target of an assassination plot by the very man who chose him to become Vice President after the previous occupant of the office died of a heart attack. President Ronald Fisher and his lover Jillian Franklin, who just happened to be the Director of Central Intelligence, conspired to kill Schumacher so Franklin could be appointed Vice President and they could then rule the world for multiple presidential terms. With a rogue CIA hit squad targeting the Vice President's helicopter, their evil plan almost worked. But Vice President Schumacher survived the crash, uncovered the plot, and President Fisher and Director Franklin found suicide was a better end than a murder trial and a permanent residence in a federal penitentiary.

With the rest of the country rallying around him, President Schumacher enjoyed a wave of popular sentiment for his first eight weeks in office. It was a great political honeymoon of peace and tranquility. His poll numbers were through the roof. Hallmark must have been doing a brisk business because the cards of support piled up at a rate of three hundred per day. Americans lined the streets to wave and cheer at his passing motorcade. If any of the left-wing media dared make a disparaging remark about the President, the conservative triumvirate of Limbaugh, Hannity, and Levin would stir up such partisan patriotic passions that the offending party would quickly apologize and retract the remarks.

But the wave of good cheer couldn't last forever. President Schumacher was hinting at reforming the tax code and drastically reducing the growing list of entitlements bankrupting the country. This, of course, made the liberals restless. The Left was preprogrammed to fight any attempt at shutting off Big Government's spigot. This was how they held on to their power. Even though the polls showed attacking

President Schumacher was politically risky, they were lining up their issues ads and talking points.

"He's not a leader."

"He wasn't even elected."

"He has no mandate."

"He's too conservative for the country."

They even trotted out their human props, having an elderly woman or young child tearfully claim they would lose this or that if that "mean-spirited bastard" of a President got his way. The Right always found it interesting that none of the Democrats offered to pay for the props' "this or that" out of their own pockets, but they were ready, willing, and able to take it out of somebody else's pocket.

Along the same lines as the Democrats, the terrorists in every corner of the world couldn't sit still for much longer either, what with the Great Satan in constant need of annihilation. They were lining up their attacks too, plotting and strategizing to win their own battle. But their bombs would not be verbal.

It was time for President Schumacher to govern and prepare himself for the fights that were sure to come.

"Did you see that the Civil Liberties Alliance is suing you again?" Cogdon asked with a great deal of disdain.

The ring of hair around his bald dome had turned white and his tie was already hanging loosely around his neck at ten in the morning. Known as "Wiley" to his closest friends because of his propensity for wild ideas and clumsy Wile-E.-Coyote-like falls back to earth, he had been President Schumacher's right-hand man since the latter's early political career in Silver Creek, Indiana. Schumacher served two terms as state's attorney of Wabash County before Cogdon convinced the former FBI agent to run for a seat in Congress. Following six successful terms on Capitol Hill, Schumacher and Cogdon continued on to the Vice President's office.

Fueled by heavy doses of caffeine, Cogdon now acted as the doorkeeper to the Oval Office and nothing that reflected poorly on his boss or could harm his presidency escaped his watchful eye. Poll numbers, which the President disdained for their lack of reliability and constantly changing nature, were beamed to Wiley's ultra-secure, super-secret General Dynamics BlackBerry on a daily basis. On occasion, he was seen walking the halls with a BlackBerry in each hand and oblivious to all around him.

Wiley was beginning to put the pieces in place for the next presidential election, which was less than ten months away, and his ultimate dream was to choreograph a fifty-state landslide that would top the forty-nine state trouncings by Nixon over McGovern in '72 and Reagan over Mondale in '84. He even wanted liberal D.C.'s electoral votes, too. And with the President's current level of popularity, it was not out of the realm of imagination. Cogdon's ultimate goal was to orchestrate a 538 to 0 electoral vote shutout.

"The CLA just can't stop themselves."

"What did I do now?" President Schumacher asked as he crossed out another word on the first draft of his message to Congress.

"They are suing to remove the cross you put up in the Oval Office."

The President looked up from his reading and over at Wiley. He started tapping his pencil on the desk. His gaze then settled on the hand-carved wooden cross on the wall to the right of his desk. The twelve-inch cross was a gift from a neighbor back home in Silver Creek and it was plainly visible in most pictures that were taken in the Oval Office. The National Gallery had offered to provide a portrait of the President's choosing from its collection but he hadn't gotten around to selecting it. So one afternoon he called in the White House handyman, asked for a hammer and a nail, and hung up the cross to fill the void.

The CLA threw a hissy fit the very next day.

It wasn't the first time the CLA had tried to tear down America's historical religious traditions. The left-wing nuts in the Alliance gave it their best shot to wipe "In God We Trust" off the currency, put an end to "under God" in the Pledge of Allegiance, and prevent any prayers from taking place before sessions of Congress. They were so on the ball that when then-Vice President Schumacher was scheduled to take the oath of office after President Fisher died, the CLA attorneys had filed a petition for a temporary injunction in federal court asking that the Chief Justice of the United States be barred from using the phrase "So help me God" in the presidential oath.

"Separation of church and state!" they fumed.

The federal judge barely managed a yawn at the petition, and by the time the order was entered denying the injunction Schumacher had been President with the help of God for five full hours. Given that the former President Fisher had been a founding member of the CLA, and many of its administrators were closet leftists like him, the Alliance was sure to be a thorn in the Schumacher Administration's side for years to come.

And the President kind of liked the idea of mixing it up with them.

Schumacher looked back over at Wiley, who was shaking his head in disgust and itching to fight. "Why don't we tell them that if they make it into the Oval Office they can take it down themselves."

"It sounds like a good idea to me," Wiley responded, knowing the Secret Service might have a thing to say about any unauthorized entry.

The President sat up in his chair and neatly folded his State of the Union address. "Bring it on," he said with a sly smile. "Now let's get started on revising the speech. America has bigger problems than the CLA."

The President's core political beliefs centered on smaller government and national security. Both were never easy sells to the Democrats in Congress – most of whom thought it best to take money from the Pentagon's budget and in turn expand the latest greatest welfare program. The President may not have been elected, but he had a large swath of America backing him. With an equally divided Senate and a slim Republican majority in the House, his goal of reducing the size of government, or at least putting the brakes on its rate of growth, was attainable. And the State of the Union was his first big chance to lay out his agenda.

"I think we ought to include a line in the speech that the era of free handouts is over," Wiley said.

The sixty-two-year-old Cogdon was as conservative as his boss, and his rants against the welfare state had been known to get him and Schumacher in trouble on a number of occasions during their time in politics. Wiley had once battled a drinking problem and enjoyed the occasional prostitute as well, but Schumacher stuck by his friend even through Cogdon's deepest valleys. When his wild ways almost got then-Congressman Schumacher killed, Cogdon kept his alcoholic palate dry and his zipper high. While antidepressants were no longer necessary, the caffeine helped a great deal. His therapist also told him to freely express his feelings and not keep his emotions bottled up inside. This caused him to say what was on his mind and not let his salty tongue get in the way. Although he paid for it recently after *SNL* lampooned him for uttering an expletive on *Meet the Press*. The President didn't mind, however. Wiley was just referring to some blowhard Democrat. Reporters never failed to crowd around him in hopes of snagging a memorable quote.

"I think we need to start cracking down on those damn freeloaders who always have their hands out expecting their neighbor to pay for their welfare, their health care, their food stamps, and their electric bill. Then they go out and spend their money on fuckin' four hundred dollar iPhones and plasma TVs."

The President sat back in his leather chair and rocked it slowly. The Oval Office probably hadn't heard this much heartfelt profanity since the Nixon Administration. The President got a kick out of Wiley's daily diatribes.

"I heard a story on the radio the other day that a customer went to a Wal-Mart pharmacy and had to pay a three dollar co-pay for her prescription. When the pharmacist asked if she wanted to pay for it right then and there, the lady said no she had other shopping to do. Then she goes and walks out of the store without paying! That's BS! Those cheap bastards think they're so entitled to everything that they don't think twice about screwing over the American taxpayer! And do you ever hear a welfare queen thank her fellow Americans for helping out? Hell no! It's just more bitching that it isn't enough. More, more, more. Why don't we put a few lines about that in the speech."

The President couldn't help but smile. "Let's see," he said in deep contemplation. "Maybe I could get up before both Houses of Congress and the worldwide viewing audience and say, 'You f-ing' freeloaders had better shape up and provide for yourselves because the bank of the United States is now closed.'"

Wiley stewed in his chair, his face red as a tomato. He wiped the sweat forming on his forehead. He knew the President couldn't say it that way, but he thought some blunt talk was necessary. What the freeloaders needed in his mind was a good kick in the pants.

"Or we can say we're going to crack down on welfare fraud so those who truly need it will receive the help they deserve."

Wiley thought that was the politically correct answer but he would defer to his boss.

"All right. Let's move on. We're already going to piss off the Democrats so let's work on ways to piss off the terrorists."

South Suburbs, Chicago, Illinois

The mosque sat thirty five miles south of Chicago, just on the outskirts of the suburbs where civilization met the trees and corn fields. It was an ever expanding area, as people sought refuge from the high taxes and crime ridden streets of the Windy City. Although south of I-80, it would someday be gobbled up and referred to simply as a south suburb. Most of the residents worked in downtown Chicago, and the trains ferried a good portion of them up there every day. With the exodus from the big city came all colors, creeds, and nationalities. Ethnic areas were already beginning to pop up.

The Illinois Center for Islam had purchased fifty acres in increments of ten in hopes of not arousing suspicion. The Center's stated plan was to build a mosque for the growing Muslim population that had been transplanted from Dearborn, Michigan, during the last economic crisis. The mosque's outer facade was low key in nature, no golden domes or spires that would raise the suspicions of county code regulators or any nosy neighbors. Scaring people who knew nothing about Islam would only raise questions. The main building and its accompanying parking lot only took up two acres. The Center didn't even want a sign to beckon all who might want to enter for daily prayers. The membership list would be handpicked and secret. The Center obtained the land relatively cheap, the western border fronting a rock quarry. Other land speculators wanted the land but not the dust and the dynamite blasts. The Center claimed the noise would not be a problem. Its members were used to bombs during prayers.

"Let's go! Moamar, let's go!" The man demanding his underlings pick up the pace was Abdullah Hassani, an American-born Muslim with strong ties to the Middle East. He grew up in Michigan, his parents part of the first generation to leave Saudi Arabia in search of the freedom and opportunity of the West. His dad had been an engineer at General Motors, and his mother kept a small grocery store where Muslims picked up their halal. They worked long hours, forcing young Abdullah to fend for himself during his formative years. Allah became his babysitter, the Koran his afternoon cartoons. He took no interest in American sports; and the girls, those American girls with their makeup, tattoos, and uncovered bellies, not to mention their ignorant belief in equal rights, fanned the flames of his radicalization. He was determined to return to his homeland, his Mecca, and leave this dirty civilization that had been forced on him in the United States of America.

The tipping point came in 1979. Hassani was sixteen and the subject of endless taunts from the white snobs at his high school outside of Detroit. After classes one day, he returned to the parking lot to find his car spray painted with the words "Abdullah the Queer" on its side. Believing the jocks had insulted his name for the last time, he took a hunting knife out of his trunk and sliced the tires of every football player's car he could find. It was a methodical butchering of rubber, and nothing had given him the satisfaction like plunging that cold steel blade into those Goodyears and Firestones. It was feeling he would never forget.

Needless to say, the jocks didn't like it that their cars had four flat ones. Instead of getting even with their own brand of juvenile justice, they resorted to calling the cops, who promptly arrested Hassani. One white officer, who had a son who now needed four new tires, took the long way to the police station. In an abandoned industrial area, the officer took pleasure in giving the "towelhead" a good beating. The baton was whipped out and threatened to be thrust in places where it didn't belong. Hassani's rights were violated, but in that day and age, the real crime would go unpunished. Battered and bloodied, Hassani was thrown into a cell. The officers promised to call his parents when they got around to it. If they got around to it.

His cell mate was Mohammed Hadiq, a local cleric who had been picked up earlier in the day for burning the American flag. Some might call it his constitutional right under the First Amendment. But the First Amendment does not allow the practice inside a federal courthouse. Hadiq practically gutted the first floor men's room. Once handcuffed, he found the nearest TV camera and hurled insults to all Americans. His hatred for the United States centered on its support for Israel.

The date was November 4, 1979. Halfway around the world, the Iranians were rioting and charging through the security fence at the American Embassy in Tehran. The Detroit police officers in the station cursed at the TV as they watched the riot unfold. Hassani had no particular love for the Iranians, but the bandaged and bound American soldiers and Embassy staff being paraded through the raucous crowd as hostage trophies excited him. That was the day the Islamic world took it to the Americans and won. The next 444 days would be a glorious ride for those who claimed to have endured years of oppression under "the boot of American tyranny." The concerned face of that feckless President Carter made Hassani smile. The Americans were cowering in fear, and every terrorist, thug, and despotic regime were laughing at them. Although the arrival of Reagan tamped down his joy, he was not dismayed. That the Iranians backed down was not surprising in retrospect considering Reagan turned the mighty Soviet bear into a cute little grizzly cub. Instead, Hassani decided he would use the Gipper's eight years to learn, to better himself, and prepare for the day when he would take it to the Americans.

But he decided it would not be from abroad.

That was the day Hassani vowed to bring his revolution to America and he went about setting his plan in motion. The Clinton years were the perfect time to strike in his mind. He thought the Clinton Administration seemed more worried about gays in the military and universal health care than the safety and security of the American people. The distractions were endless and Hassani knew terrorists overseas were implementing their jihad. Hassani considered letting off an explosive device in Chicago but why arouse the Americans when they were intoxicated with their excesses of the dot-com economy and distracted with Lewinsky and her blue dress. Instead, he wanted something bigger – more destruction on a grander scale.

Hassani's reticence ended with the arrival of that "Cowboy" from Texas. Oh how he wanted to strike to pay America back for its war against Saddam in Kuwait. But bin Laden beat him to it and the Twin Towers came down. He admired the nineteen hijackers' work, but Hassani wanted more – more destruction and more lives lost.

He wanted to bring down the President. And the current occupant was no more than a clone of the cowboy.

Hassani dropped out of college and studied hard under Hadiq at a mosque in Chicago after the latter was released from prison for his arson. Hadiq spent the years behind bars fueling his rage and, once free, brought his fire and brimstone to the mosque. The rants from within concerned even Hadiq's followers, many of whom wanted jihad but felt it should be done in silence so the surprise would exact a greater blow. But Hadiq was unconcerned. The Americans will scoff at our rhetoric but they will do nothing, he promised. The rising tide of political correctness would protect Hadiq and his followers and allow them to recruit more soldiers for the cause.

Hassani became Hadiq's top lieutenant and begged his master for a chance to strike. He offered himself as a martyr – a bomb strapped to his chest or hidden in his shoe or lining his underwear or a car full of explosives. Anything.

"No. You must wait and learn. Then you will strike like a great cobra."

"But I want to fight now."

"Patience," Hadiq would say. "You will get your chance."

Calm and determined, Hassani took a job at a construction/quarry firm and began learning the business inside and out. Nothing escaped his grasp. Contracts, blueprints, demolition, lumber, steel, concrete. He would become an expert in every facet of the process to gain an advantage on his competitors – his lazy American competitors. Shipping became his specialty. If he needed a load of material, he could find a truck, a train, a plane, a boat, a bicycle, or a mule that could get it delivered. And he knew where the shipment was every minute of the day.

After ten years, the firm became his own and Hassani Enterprises had grown into a Midwestern powerhouse with offices in Chicago, St. Louis, and Kansas City. If a construction project was in progress within five hundred miles of the Great Lakes, you could take it to the bank that the unions, the mob, the politicians, and Hassani had their hands in it.

Every day, Hassani wore a pair of black slacks and a crisp white long-sleeve dress shirt with the outline of a house beneath a crescent moon. His short dark hair was closely cropped, the style of the desert, and his black eyes burned with intensity. He had a perpetual look of anger on his face, and his employees were often on the receiving end of a good tongue lashing if something wasn't right. Although he had learned to be patient, his inner rage against America burned with white hot intensity. It would be a glorious day when his plan could finally be put into operation.

Hassani waved Moamar through the gate and checked the delivery off his list. For the last two weeks, the dump trucks rumbled in and out every thirty minutes from sunup to sundown. The man-made earthquakes brought forth the quarry's gold, fueling the business and the plan. But today's blasts would produce little more than dust and one dump truck would never rumble through the gates again. Business was booming, but the time for jihad was near.

CHAPTER 2

Muddy Rock, Kansas

"Damn Mexicans," the man mumbled to himself as he rolled out of bed and shuffled his white stockinged feet across the wood floor over to his computer screen. The floor creaked and cracked just like his old arthritic knees. It was 2 a.m. and pitch black outside but the buzzer was sounding. It could mean only one of two things.

Wild animals or Mexicans.

A few years after 9/11, the patriotic fervor started to slowly subside. Tattered flags attached to car antennas were properly disposed of, but poles and porches were mostly bare except for the Fourth and Flag Day. All in all, people relaxed, took a breath, and got on with their usual routine. Suspicious happenings were laughed off or quickly forgotten. But one band of brothers would never forget, and they were determined to dedicate their lives to saving their beloved country from those who sought to destroy it. They were rabid patriots who hated terrorists and big-government liberals, not always in that order, with guns on their hips and racks in their trucks. They each fashioned themselves as the modern day Revere, and Hancock, and Adams.

Now with the buzzer still sounding, it was time for this patriot to ride to the rescue. He grabbed the red phone, which provided a dedicated line to the United States Border Patrol station in Nogales, Arizona, some eight hundred miles away. He bought the phone at a flea market. It just looked official, like whoever used it for whatever reason was doing important work. The screen showed nine ghost-like figures, snaking single file along a curvy trail through the underbrush and tumbleweeds. Every so often they would come to a quick halt, crouch down, and then look in every direction but south. They weren't going back. At least not voluntarily. South was the land of despair and out-of-control drug lords. North was the land of opportunity. Relying on the full moon, they carried no light source, and the only thing in their hands was a garbage bag full of their paltry possessions. For three hundred and fifty American dollars, the coyote promised them safe passage until a distance of two hundred yards from the border. They were on their own after that.

"Yes, this is Bo Duncan," he grunted, obviously in yet another foul mood for the late-night wake-up call set off by those trying to sneak into the country illegally. He had made this same call over a hundred times and it pissed him off on each one.

"I've got a pack of nine illegals heading for the border at camera position X9."

He gave the GPS coordinates for good measure. The person on the other end thanked him for the information, but Duncan would not be satisfied until the Mexicans were cuffed, marched into the back of a paddy wagon, and sent back from where they came.

"Hurry up and get on it, dammit," he snapped into the receiver before slamming the phone down.

Binford Orville Duncan, "Bo" for obvious reasons, was the commander of the American Border Brigade, a twenty-person private outfit spread out across the country that monitored cameras fixed on the U.S. border with Mexico. His lieutenants kept close watch over their computer screens in places like Brush Prairie, Washington; Du Quoin, Illinois; Bear Town, Mississippi; and Melville Landing, Vermont. The pictures came from infrared cameras placed on private property by landowners along the southern border who were fed up with illegals traipsing through their yards, urinating in their bushes, stealing their vegetables, and breaking into their houses. Once the cameras were up and running, Brigade members could watch the borders from their remote locations and alert the authorities with a single phone call whenever the ghosts came marching north.

Bo Duncan had fought valiantly in Vietnam and returned home with a Purple Heart and a noticeable limp courtesy of the Vietcong. After making his way back to the states, the communist enemy's tactics seemed tame in comparison to the spit and vitriol of long-haired, anti-war hippies who promoted their sexual revolution, ingested their hallucinogenic drugs, and all in all led a lifestyle of irresponsibility. Disgusted with this segment of American society, he returned to his rural Kansas home halfway between Wichita and Dodge City, farmed his land under the open sky, and cherished the unalienable rights his Creator had endowed him since birth. With every passing year, however, the growing liberal establishment in Washington and across the country with their high taxes, forced dependency, and federal regulations grated at his inner soul. Paying for some lazy ass's welfare just about sent him over the edge. Over time, the lifelong Republican slowly morphed into an anti-government, anti-tax Libertarian. He thought about starting a militia but decided against it. Too old, he thought of suiting up for weekend war games.

After seeing his hard-earned money going to pay for the education and health care of illegal immigrants, Duncan blew a gasket. He started the Brigade and implored pro-American zealots to support his cause with their time and monetary donations. He wrote and edited *Red Alert*, the group's newsletter, recruited new lieutenants, and handled the hate mail from the liberals. The left-leaning pro-immigration crowd lambasted him, calling him a racist and a thug who sent those poor Mexicans back to live their lives of poverty and despair. What about their civil rights! they would argue. He would fire right back, telling all who would listen that if the Mexicans wanted to live in our country and enjoy the rights under the Constitution, they could show up at our front door, knock, and request entry just like every other lawful immigrant had done since the country's founding. Whether he was loved or hated, he had become a national celebrity. *USA Today* had a front-page article on his bombastic rants and Brigade exploits, complete with a picture of him showing his crossed arms and scowling face undeniably indicating he was pissed off at someone or something.

Duncan was once married, but his wife left him after the war and before he hunkered down in his compound. The house was a cluttered mess of books on the Founding Fathers, pro-American heroes, and soldier-of-fortune types. Gun magazines heralded the arrival of the newest must-have weapons. "Don't Tread On Me" banners were numerous, and American flags flew proudly outside next to his "No Trespassing" signs. Two snarling German shepherds, Liberty and Justice, prowled the grounds in a constant state of animated agitation.

Just like their master.

Before heading back to bed, he made a notation of the date, the number of illegals, and the location of their attempted illegal entry. Next month's edition of *Red Alert* would note his tally of "captured" illegal aliens had crossed the fifteen-hundred mark. He also decided he would fire off a letter to his local congressman and both Kansas senators the next morning, yet another constant reminder that they had failed to secure America's borders. He might just personally call them and "give 'em a good cussin'" to make sure they got the message. He thought he'd start another petition to finally finish building the fence between the U.S. and Mexico to help stem the tide. The liberals would no doubt call it the new Berlin Wall. He would call it our last line of defense. He wondered if that President Schumacher would be more receptive to his overtures than the last president.

The White House – Washington, D.C.

The President was beginning to fall into a routine every morning. He would awake at 5:30 a.m., shave and shower, and have a breakfast of cold cereal and toast by 6 a.m. On weekends, he'd indulge and have the White House chef fix pancakes. After eating, he would put on his suit and tie and head downstairs. He would be greeted by the head of his Secret Service security detail, Michael Craig, and they would take a stroll along the Colonnade and enter the Oval Office by 6:30 a.m. The President and Agent Craig had grown close since the latter was on the Vice President's security detail. The two were the only survivors of the Marine Two crash, and the President trusted him with his life. Once inside the Oval Office, the President would read the *Wall Street Journal*, the *Post*, the *Times*, and the *USA Today*. The box scores in the sports section would take at least ten minutes with a good portion of that time admiring the exploits of the great Pujols from the Cardinals game the night before. He would then enter his private study and check the Internet for anything he might have missed.

At 8 a.m., the national security team would file into the Oval Office and brief the President on any threats to American interests. To his constant consternation, there was never any shortage of threats.

"Morning, Mr. President," the black woman said. She wore a dark pantsuit with a red blouse. In her hands she held the highly classified intelligence briefing that her CIA liaison had dropped off at her residence two hours before. She was the newest occupant of Number One Observatory Circle.

The President looked up from his mess of papers on his desk. "Morning, Madame Vice President."

Brenda Jackson was no stranger to the status of being a historical figure. She was the first female Vice President of the United States as well as the first African-American. She grew up in Arizona before heading off to Stanford on a full scholarship. With her brilliant mind, she studied international relations with minors in political science and American history. After graduating, she headed east to work at the State Department under the tutelage of Secretary of State Wallace Swanson, a relic of the Cold War who had served under both Republican and Democratic Administrations. There she learned the intricacies of diplomatic relations with the Soviets, then the Russians, as well as the growing number of despots intent on striking the United States and its allies.

After the end of the Cold War, Jackson returned to Phoenix where she parlayed her considerable knowledge into a successful campaign for a seat in Congress. There, she served six terms in the House and was a colleague of then Congressman Anthony Schumacher, who found her knowledge on foreign affairs especially helpful. With her popularity still on the rise, she returned home once again and ran for governor of the Grand Canyon State. Although she was the second female governor, she was the first African-American and she worked hard to bring together the white retirees, the immigrant Hispanics, the transplanted blacks, and the Native Americans.

Governor Jackson's success in catapulting the booming Arizona economy came as no surprise to many. She was a free-market thinker who thought the people should run the show and government should get out of the way. But what surprised the political establishment, and what struck fear into the hearts and minds of liberals in Washington, was that she was a Republican. And having a popular black female Republican was the worst thing that could happen to the Democrats.

When President Schumacher assumed the office, he needed to pick a Vice President under the Twenty-Fifth Amendment. There were some calls for a military man to help with the President's lack of expertise in that area. Others wanted a stately senator with foreign policy know-how. But the President only had one person in mind – his old Arizona friend from his days in the House. And since his political hero Ronald Reagan tapped the Arizonan O'Connor to become the first female Supreme Court Justice, he thought he'd do the same with the first female Vice President.

His selection of Governor Jackson set off a firestorm in Washington. While the President was treated favorably given the circumstances, that didn't mean the Democrats were going to roll over and concede on every point. How could they brand all Republicans as racists if the President was allowed to put a conservative African-American into such a position of power. With a Republican majority in the House, Jackson sailed through with only a few nicks and cuts.

But the Senate would be a different story.

Democrat investigators searched under every rock, canyon, and cactus they could find looking for some dirt that could be used to prevent Jackson from becoming Vice President. They searched her college transcripts, her thesis on American diplomacy in the nuclear age, her votes in Congress, and her executive decisions in the Arizona Governor's Office. They found nothing. So they resorted to the old standby – make something up and hope it sticks. They called her an "Uncle Tom" and an "Oreo" and polished off the sad pathetic claim that she wasn't a "real black." Nothing stuck, however, and the Democrats were forced to lick their wounds and regroup.

"Mr. President, the world continues to be a dangerous place."

"That it does. Have a seat."

The President and Vice President were joined by National Security Adviser Carl A. Harnacke, a former four-star Army general who fought against just about every communist, jihadist, and terrorist that had taken up arms against the United States in the past thirty years. At seventy-three, he was respected by both political parties. Joining them was Bradley Michaelson, the Homeland Security Director and a former Governor of Florida, President Schumacher picked Michaelson for his ability to coordinate a vast array of agencies in an emergency – which the Governor was experienced in doing in preparing and responding to Florida's many hurricanes.

"I'm sorry I'm late, Mr. President."

"No, that's all right, we haven't started."

The tardy soul was Tyrone Stubblefield, the Director of the Federal Bureau of Investigation and an old friend of the President. Since their days as new agent trainees in the FBI Academy, the President and Stubblefield were nearly inseparable. They started off as partners, which lasted until Anthony took a bullet in the chest from a bank robber. The only thing that prevented his untimely demise was Stubblefield's quick trigger and expert marksmanship in killing the gunman. Anthony would never forget the man who saved his life. They both rose in the ranks in their respective fields, Ty inside the Bureau and Anthony in the political arena. They stayed in touch when both were in Washington, and President Schumacher's first executive decision was to nominate Ty as head of the FBI.

Ty opened up his briefcase and pulled out a folder marked classified. The FBI had been working on the contents for the past week and it did not present a rosy picture of the security of the nation.

"Mr. President," Director Stubblefield began, "we've been tracking two sleeper cells within the country. Our focus has been in Buffalo and in Detroit. The CIA has provided us with intercepted phone calls between Saudi Arabia and a mosque in Toronto. We believe terrorists are trying to smuggle biological weapons into the country via the northern border. We have no concrete evidence but we have been watching a mosque in Buffalo frequented by Canadian travelers."

"Canadian travelers?"

"Yes."

Ty then gave President Schumacher "the look." Only two people who had known each other for thirty-four years would know the meaning of the look. It was almost as if the two could read each other's mind. They might have been mistaken for twins – other than the difference in the color of their skin.

"All right everybody. Pens down," the President ordered.

"What?" Director Michaelson asked, his eyebrows raised. Were they taking a quiz? He didn't understand.

"No notes."

Director Michaelson looked around and saw the rest of the group drop their pens and he felt the need to do the same. If what Director Stubblefield was about to say happened to be made public, all hell might break loose. President Schumacher began his Administration with the demand that there be no leaks. And written memos or notes scrawled onto a piece of paper with a date on it could come back to haunt everyone involved. The Democrats in the Senate would love to subpoena an Administration official and haul his ass and his notes up to the Hill to claim for all the world to see that President Schumacher was violating somebody's rights somewhere in the world. The President, of course, could and would refuse to hand over any documents or allow officials to testify under the umbrella of executive privilege, but those in the opposition would just roundly criticize him for hiding something. Thus, the directive came that no notes be taken in certain instances.

"We really need to get inside that mosque, Mr. President."

The President winced. "I knew you were going to say that," he said with a smile. "Do we have anybody that can get inside as a worshiper?"

"We're working on it. I'm not comfortable sending in an undercover agent just yet."

"What do you want then?"

Director Stubblefield closed his file and folded his hands across the top. "I want to wiretap the mosque."

The President sat back in his seat and crossed his arms. He wanted to make sure he got this straight. "The mosque we are talking about is in the United States, yes?"

"Yes. Buffalo." He also mentioned a mosque in Chicago, but the evidence there was scant and he wasn't about to push his luck just yet.

The President got up, causing all but Ty to stand. "Sit down, sit down," he admonished them with a motioning right hand. Knowing the President like he did, Ty knew he liked to pace the floor in thought. Hands clasped behind his back, the President pondered the ramifications of such an order. The Left would flip out. The CLA would claim he was shredding the Constitution – violating the right of peaceful American Muslims to worship without government interference.

"I can't sign off on a wiretap right now, Ty. I need more. You gotta get someone in on the inside."

"Yes sir." Ty knew the President would say no, but he was planting the seed just in case the order was necessary.

CHAPTER 3

West Bend, Illinois

The quiet stately prison planted amongst the cornfields had barely caused a yawn since its first day of operation in 1980. The four guard towers sprouting from the fields often caused a surprised response from travelers off the interstate who had no idea there was a prison in West Bend. The State of Illinois had built the maximum-security prison to house some of the Land of Lincoln's most hardened and notorious criminals. Most of the prison's residents had brought decades of death and destruction to the streets of Chicago – drug murders, gang shootings, and mob hits were the most frequent offenses. The worst of the worst took up space in the cramped cells, and most would never get out.

Despite its dangerous clientele, the prison was an economic boon to the town and a gift to state senator Joe Marshman who had begged the governor for something to help the struggling economy in the area. West Bend had little else than a highway running through it taking riders to and from Iowa – a mere ten miles from the town. But the creation of the prison did help to sprout two gas stations, a McDonald's, a Motel 6, a new car dealership, a car wash, and – surprise, surprise – a Super Wal-Mart to take the money of those hardworking correctional officers and their families.

Senator Marshman had initially hoped for a community college. He would rather take the chance on irresponsible students and an occasional radical liberal professor than put up with the stars of *America's Most Wanted*. Moreover, unlike manufacturing and industry, a state college rarely went out of business during bad economic times or moved to Mexico in search of cheaper labor. If a college was in need of money, the state legislature would simply raise taxes to pay the bills (or promise to pay when it pried the money out of the hands of the citizenry). No, Senator Marshman didn't get his college. Instead, his constituents received four hundred of the most dangerous men Illinois had to offer. But the prison never had an escape or even one attempted. It was considered one of the most secure prisons in the world.

And for the last five years it had a giant target on its back.

For nearly a decade, the Democratically controlled Illinois legislature gorged itself to obesity on every welfare, health care, and pension buffet it could belly up to. Then, one day, the state found itself mired in a deep economic recession and, to no one's surprise, realized it could no longer pay its bills. The geniuses in the General Assembly, who could not stop spending the taxpayers' money, decided to raise taxes, which caused businesses and citizens to flee to more agreeable tax havens like Indiana, Wisconsin, Iowa, Missouri, and Kentucky and take their hard-earned money with them. Colleges went without funding, public-aid doctors didn't get paid, state troopers were parked, and the Illinois Department of Corrections laid off hundreds of correctional officers.

Unable to print money, the desperate governor decided to sell state cars and office buildings to raise cash. He then went begging to Washington, D.C., hoping for a bailout for the state's irresponsibility. Luckily for the governor, this was near the same time the United States was grappling with what to do with terrorist detainees held at the Guantanamo Bay detention facility in Cuba. Then President William Jackson, a left-leaning Liberal, thought it wise to bring terrorists onto U.S. soil so they could be put on trial in civilian criminal courts. The thought was it would somehow show the United States was giving terrorists the rights and process they didn't deserve and weren't entitled to under the Constitution, thereby satisfying European pacifists and those haughty, self-righteous morons at the United Nations. Republican members of Congress howled in protest, most wanting to keep the terrorists on the island and away from their constituents. Most liberals in the House and Senate were in favor of the move but only if the terrorists weren't transferred to prisons in their states. "Not in my backyard" became a familiar cry.

The governor stepped right up to the plate and announced the State of Illinois would roll out the welcome mat to the terrorists if the feds would be so kind as to send them to West Bend along with a check for one hundred million dollars. Done deal. The feds closed their ultra-secure, state-of-the-art prison at Guantanamo Bay. Illinois got its money. And the American people were not a bit safer.

"Excuse me," the man hollered from his truck. "Can you tell me where Jo Ellen's antique shop is located?"

The request was not out of the ordinary. A male in a dusty pickup truck asking for directions. He probably had something of great vintage value under the blue tarp in the back. West Bend had a charming downtown area which the senior citizens and treasure hunters frequented year round in their search for old forgotten furniture or rusty relics of the past. The county courthouse took up the center of the town square with the antique shops, a greeting card store, a coffee shop, the post office, and five law offices lining the outer perimeter. Although downtown could bustle with activity every now and then, most people had to have a good reason for being there. Those simply passing through West Bend stuck close to the interstate and the McDonald's near the exit.

The man walking down the sidewalk was in a hurry. He was a lawyer with a jury trial set to start in ten minutes, and running late was the least of his worries considering his client was most assuredly guilty and unlikely to pay his legal bills. He had a large black briefcase in one hand and his smart phone in the other. He didn't even make eye contact with the man.

"Turn right at the stop sign. It's in the middle of the next block."

The man in the truck responded with a thank you and rolled up his window. His hands were sweating but his lips were dry from the lack of moisture. He found Jo Ellen's and pulled his truck into the parking spot. Thinking better of it, he put the truck in reverse, pulled into a spot facing the courthouse, and then put it in reverse again and backed across the street so the rear was facing the antique shop. Looking out the big picture window, the proprietor of the establishment wondered what great bounty the man had waiting for her. No doubt a pot of gold that would look great on display and bring a princely sum in the near future. Jo Ellen loved her antiques, and her shop was fairly well known within the surrounding communities. She could barely contain her enthusiasm.

With her gray head of hair and no coat, Jo Ellen came out of the store, the bell above the door causing the man in the truck to look in his rear-view mirror. This wasn't part of the plan. The man opened his door and quickly got out.

"Can I help you with anything?" she asked with great anticipation. She nodded at the bed of the truck.

"I'll be inside in a minute. I just need to make a quick call."

Jo Ellen nodded and backed away. The man didn't look familiar. He was slightly unkempt with a scruffy beard and a dirty denim jacket. His appearance wouldn't cause many females to approach him in the local bar, unless the bar had the lights down low. Jo Ellen knew the man had never brought any junk in as far as she could remember but sometimes the strangers have the best goods to peddle.

The man opened his door and leaned inside. He fiddled with the blasting cap and lit the fuse. The cord ran through a hole in the rear cabin compartment through the truck bed into the seven barrels of ammonium nitrate and fertilizer. Four two-gallon gas cans were filled to the brim with nitromethane. The fuse would burn for two minutes, at least that was what the prior tests had shown. It gave the person lighting the fuse a chance to calmly walk away.

As calmly as one can expect considering he was igniting a half-ton bomb.

The man had practiced the maneuver four previous times, mostly in his garage. He had never experimented with the bomb before, but the Internet bombmaking recipe said it was foolproof.

He shut the door and stepped onto the curb. Two elderly ladies were walking into the store in search of some must-have treasure. Jo Ellen politely welcomed them, but she kept her focus on the man in case he summoned her outside. The man looked at her, brought a cupped hand to his mouth and then pointed down the street, indicating he was going to get a quick cup of coffee. He then held up five fingers and mouthed that he would be right back. He had no concerns of her remembering his particulars.

Jo Ellen watched the man pull his phone out of his pocket and turn left at the corner. It surprised her a bit. The coffee shop was located in the opposite direction. Unable to take the suspense any longer, she pulled open the door, the bell announcing her presence and slightly startling her. Not seeing the man, she hurried to the truck, pulled the blue tarp away to one side of the bed, and then sighed.

"Shoot," she said in disappointment. "I don't need any blue barrels and gasoline."

With the four barrels lining the bottom and three more strapped on top, she didn't see the timer cord reaching its end point. She couldn't have done anything about it anyway. The explosion rocked the town and could be felt ten miles away. The blast tore a twenty-foot crater in the street and demolished the antique shop. The blast and resulting fire would destroy the whole block of businesses. Legal secretaries and waitresses were seen crawling and then running from their burning offices and coffee shops holding their heads after their eardrums had been perforated. The two women inside the antique shop were killed instantly by the flying glass shrapnel and two tons of bricks and mortar raining down on top of them. Bits and pieces of Jo Ellen's body would later be identified but mostly it was incinerated in the blast. Chaos erupted around the square. Women were screaming at the top of their lungs. Every window facing the square was blown out. Lawyers, judges, stenographers, jurors, and alleged criminals, some bloodied and all dazed, stumbled outside the courthouse to gasp at the horrific scene.

With sirens blaring, the fire department arrived and started hosing down the rubble. Car alarms wailed for blocks on end and made it hard for people to talk without shouting. The entire West Bend police force blocked off the streets and wondered what in the hell happened. One fourth of the town square was gone. It would take two days to find all of the bodies buried under the mounds of brick and stone.

The man in the truck was four blocks away, the collar of his denim jacket up near his cheeks to keep out the chilly air. He stepped into the car of his co-conspirator. The traffic was light heading out of town.

Everybody was heading to the square.

The White House – Washington, D.C.

President Schumacher was in the Oval Office having a meeting with Illinois Senator Russ Bender, a Democrat with a tough-on-terrorism bent. Through the open door, the President could see Director Stubblefield talking with the President's secretary.

"Ty," the President said. "Come on in."

It usually wasn't a good sign when the Director of the FBI showed up unannounced. Stubblefield marched in with a scowl on his face and stopped ten feet from the President's desk.

Senator Bender had enough sense to know it was not going to be good news. "Do you guys need me to leave?"

"No, Senator," Ty said. "You'll need to hear this."

"What's up?" the President asked.

"Sir, there has been an explosion in West Bend, Illinois."

The President and the Senator both looked at each other. They then both thought of the West Bend Federal Penitentiary.

"Is it the prison?" the President asked.

"No. There was an explosion in the town square about a half hour ago. A whole block has been destroyed."

The trio left the Oval Office and hurried into the President's private study. Every cable news network was showing the lone helicopter's view of the gaping hole in Broadway Street along with the crumbled remains of the block. Shots of crying locals behind yellow police tape played in an endless loop. Local news reporters had little specifics.

The President walked closer to the screen of the TV sitting on the credenza. He pointed at the hole. "Could it be a natural gas explosion?"

Ty pointed at the hole and shook his head. "No. It was truck bomb."

"Dammit!" The President exclaimed smacking his hands together. "I knew this was going to happen!"

During his tenure as Vice President, Schumacher had pushed to remove the terrorist detainees out of Illinois and back to Guantanamo Bay. He wasn't worried about a terrorist attack on the prison. That would be a suicide mission. The hardened walls and thirty rows of razor wire would prevent any attempt at a land-based attack. The cables crisscrossing the sky above the prison would make a helicopter landing a losing proposition. The prison was secure. What Schumacher was worried about was an attack on the townspeople. A terrorist would have no qualms strapping on a suicide vest and detonating it at the local Wal-Mart or opening fire with an AK-47 at a Little League baseball game. The loss of life would be in the hundreds. Once the carnage was over, the terrorists would demand the immediate release of their brothers in the prison. And if the feds refused to comply, they would take their bombs to the town square and try again. And if that failed, they'd poison the water supply. The citizens of West Bend would become prisoners in their own homes – afraid to venture out in public for fear of meeting a strange face on the street.

Vice President Schumacher's concerns went unheeded. And now eight American citizens were dead.

"I've got FBI teams from Springfield, Chicago, and Des Moines on the way."

Wiley walked into the office and asked the President what he wanted him to do.

"Get the warden on the phone. Tell Rachel to tell the press that we're monitoring the situation and I'll have a statement later in the day."

"Yes, sir."

"What else do we need to do, Ty?"

"The Illinois State Police have set up road blocks at t mile checkpoints. Right now the bridge over the Mississippi has be ed. We'll find 'em."

Senator Bender excused himself so he could catch the first Illinois. Before Ty left to get back to FBI Headquarters, the Pr closed the door to the private office.

"I need you to get someone on the inside. We have to put a s this."

Stubblefield knew exactly what the President wanted. The pla inserting a mole inside a mosque had been ongoing for two years. Tl sworn to protect the safety and security of the American people co wait no longer.

Now was the time.

CHAPTER 4

orthwestern University Law School – Evanston, Illinois

Abdullah Hassani showed up promptly at 9 a.m. In his black briefcase, he carried last year's tax receipts for Hassani Enterprises. The receipts were numerous. It had been a good year at Hassani Ent. Upon entering the law building, he took the elevator to the third floor. He then proceeded down the quiet hallway bisecting the offices of Northwestern's cerebral professors, no doubt preparing to wow their students with their great learned minds. He stopped outside the office of Sharif al-Rashad and knocked on the molding of the door.

"Mr. Hassani," al-Rashad said looking up from his papers. "Come in. Come in."

"Sharif, my son." Hassani whispered as they greeted each other with a kiss on each cheek. Their smiles were wide and long lasting. They both wore dark suits and navy blue ties. A crescent moon lapel pin covered their hearts. They could have been mistaken for father and son. They had known each other for five years, and Hassani personally sought out al-Rashad for his brilliant mind.

Sharif al-Rashad had graduated *summa cum laude* from Northwestern University with a degree in accounting. His summer breaks were spent learning the trade in Chicago's biggest accounting firms and he became an expert in corporate taxation. Following graduation, he was accepted into NU's school of law, where he graduated first in his class in two-and-a-half years. He was highly regarded by the faculty, the editor of the law review, and an award-winning member of the moot court team. Based on his credentials and recommendations, al-Rashad was immediately hired on after graduation as a law clerk to Judge Charles Bond of the Seventh Circuit Court of Appeals in Chicago. It was a sure stepping stone to the ultimate prize for law school graduates – a clerkship with the Supreme Court of the United States.

While working for Judge Bond, al-Rashad also accepted an adjunct professorship at Northwestern where he taught federal income and corporate taxation. His face could be seen regularly in the masthead of scholarly articles and in the pages of the *Chicago Daily Law Bulletin*. He was a rising star in Chicago legal circles.

But his rise to legal prominence did not start out as he hoped. His first experience with fame was broadcast on the pages of the police blotter. Between his first and second years in law school, al-Rashad was working late one night in the offices of the McPherson & Mahler accounting firm, the largest collection of certified public accountants in the Midwest. While driving down Lake Shore Drive on his way back to his apartment in the firm's leased Lexus, al-Rashad was pulled over by the cops for what they claimed was improper lane usage.

Being a nonwhite in an expensive car, al-Rashad believed he was the victim of racial profiling. He refused to cooperate and was eventually hauled down to police headquarters. The bruise on his face and his fat lip were said to have come when al-Rashad became belligerent and refused to go peacefully into the back of the squad car.

It didn't take long for the shit to hit the fan. His battered mug shot was on the front page of the *Tribune* and the *Sun-Times* the next day and the howls of protest came fast and furious. Muslim community leaders decried the violation of al-Rashad's civil rights and called for the firing of the arresting officers. Driving while Muslim was not a crime, they yelled. Local attorneys lined up with their typed complaints and stamped subpoenas ready to sue the cops, the city, the state, and everyone else short of Mrs. O'Leary's cow in seeking financial retribution. The news didn't stop in Chicago. Liberal gadflys in the General Assembly passed a law requiring the police to record the race and ethnicity of drivers and occupants and then send the numbers to Springfield so minority members of the Statehouse could shake their reports of racial profiling in the air and complain at the perceived cause of the injustices – mostly likely those rogue and racist cops, or the old standby – those law and order Republicans.

Prosecutors quickly dropped the charges, not wanting to deal with the protests and the bad press. Hassani, however, took a special interest in the case, what with his experience with racist cops when he was a teenager. He contributed to a legal fund to help Sharif's civil suit in any way. Al-Rashad eventually settled out of court.

Hassani later brought Sharif into his circle of friends. The Muslim community held Sharif in great regard, and the lesser known but more militant leaders were determined to use him to advance their agenda. They wanted his legal expertise – to change laws, to bring lawsuits that would slowly cripple the economy, and to punish America for its discrimination of minorities. Sharif was a slow convert, but his meteoric rise showed him he could bring the fight to levels never before attained by a jihadist. He could fight the war from within the enemy's camp, and they would not even see it coming.

Hassani also brought his firm's taxes to Sharif. He distrusted most accountants, especially the Zionist infidels who were more interested in taking his money than finding ways to keep it from Uncle Sam. Sharif was an expert, and Hassani was reassured that the IRS would not be snooping into the firm's finances. Before they got down to business, the two had bigger things to talk about.

"Can you believe the news?" Sharif asked in a hushed whisper.

Hassani glanced at the door and pushed it shut. He took a seat and they both leaned toward the other.

"I heard eight people were killed," Sharif said.

Hassani could not suppress his smile. "Yes, and twenty more were injured. Some severely. Plus, the whole town is apparently on edge. It is on the front page in every newspaper in the country and the networks have provided wall-to-wall coverage. Someone sent a letter to the *Tribune* demanding the release of all Muslim inmates in West Bend."

"Have you heard who did it?"

Hassani hesitated. He had longed for the day to strike against those "infidels" as he called them. He had mentored Sharif on the evils of the Americans. He never preached that he would be the cause of the violence or that Sharif should do the deed. That would be left to Allah and his chosen ones. But Hassani wanted it to be him so that he would be the glorified martyr for the cause.

"No, I haven't been able to find out."

Hassani kept his ears open in his many business dealings in the Midwest. His friends in St. Louis and Minneapolis had little information to give him. But they were all pleased. Soon the demand would be made to release the detainees, making the feds squirm in their offices. The infidels would have to change their policies of destruction and end their imperialistic drives in foreign lands. The U.S. military would be brought home with its tail between its legs, and the American people would now feel the pain of the collateral damage of terrorism.

"I will keep my ears open though." Hassani gave him a wink. "I have brought the tax documents you asked for."

Sharif shuffled some papers around and took the stack from Hassani. The taxes would be easy and would not take more than a week. He had prepared the firm's taxes for four years now and could do them in his sleep. He was eager to start them because he had just received word that he would soon be moving to Washington, D.C. This was a day of double good news.

"I have something else to tell you," he said. He folded his hands in front of him and looked at his mentor. "I have been chosen to serve as a law clerk to Justice Ali Hussein." His face beamed with pride.

Hassani's eyes widened. His back stiffened in his seat. "*The* Justice Hussein. Of the United States Supreme Court."

Sharif nodded. This was some of the biggest news a recent law school graduate could receive. This was the big leagues – like getting a call up to pitch for the Yankees or signing a contract to shoot jumpers for the Lakers. It was the reason law student intellectuals spent Saturday and Sunday nights in the law library and scratched and clawed their way to the top of the class rankings. Freshly minted lawyers dreamed of landing one of the thirty-six available spots. And most would only step into the marble halls of the Supreme Court if they stood in line as a tourist.

Justice Hussein had served on the Court for six years. A Democrat appointee, he was the first Arab-American on the Supreme Court and a solid member of a five-to-four liberal majority. His nomination hearings had been contentious with the Republicans wondering if he had the temperament to be a thoughtful jurist. Two witnesses had testified to Hussein's volatile temper, and a twenty-year-old police report showed an instance of domestic violence. He also had a radical past, leading demonstrations and protests against Israel that made front-page news. His association with a militant Muslim group while in his twenties continued to raise eyebrows. In the end, the Republicans in the Senate buckled under the attacks of minority groups and Hussein was confirmed by five votes. He stood a lean six-four, and he looked tall even when he was seated at the bench. His opinions were long and verbose and tended to incorporate ideas from around the world, a matter of contention with strict-constructionist conservatives.

A Supreme Court justice is entitled to four law clerks to research the law and help draft the opinions, concurrences, or dissents that will fill up case reporters for the rest of time. Some justices hire clerks with similar political beliefs and legal philosophies, finding them easier to work with as they craft their writings. Others want polar opposites, someone who can argue the opposing side with great fervor, thereby helping the justice understand both sides of the argument.

Justice Hussein liked his clerks to be of the same political mind-set – liberal, progressive, and borderline angry. Hussein and Sharif hit it off during the interview, and their history and background made them feel like kindred spirits. It was a match made in legal heaven.

For Sharif, the clerkship meant the prestige that came with the highly sought after position and a guaranteed six-figure job once his term ended. For Hassani, it meant his protégé was moving to the heart of the United States government. He would continue the fight from the inside.

"Does this mean I will have to find someone else to do my taxes?" Hassani asked as he shook Sharif's hand.

"I leave in two weeks. But don't worry, I will finish the taxes by Saturday."

They hugged again. Life was good, and both thought life would only get better.

West Bend, Illinois

The citizens of West Bend were on edge. Doors were locked at night for the first time anyone could remember. The playgrounds were empty as parents kept their kids locked inside after school. Shotguns were pulled out of the closet and dusted off. The front door of the Wal-Mart contained a note from management that all of the store's ammunition had been sold and a new shipment of ammo was not expected until the day after next. Boxes of Remington UNC .9mm and .40 S&W had flown off the shelves faster than the strawberry Pop-Tarts.

Everyone and his brother were looking for the jihadist right around the corner. A TV station hired a sketch artist and a handful of citizens who had not been out in days came forward to describe a multitude of Middle Eastern men with "beady eyes" and "angry dispositions" on their sinister faces. One of the foreign doctors at the local hospital actually placed a plywood sign on his front lawn notifying those passing by that he was Hindu, not Muslim, with the sincere hope that any gathering mob would get the hint that he was not a terrorist and take their pitch forks and torches and move on down the road.

The FBI took over the investigation with its bevy of agents, forensic experts, and canine handlers. Ten agents could be seen starting on the north end of the street and another ten starting from the south. They moved slowly in a nice tight line, picking up every piece of metal, rock, or anything else, noting its location, and placing it in a brown evidence bag. Camera flashes helped catch every inch of the bombed out crater. Once the collection was complete, they trucked their bags to a warehouse near Des Moines and did their best to put all the pieces of the puzzle back together.

The conference call between Raul Marteno, the Special Agent in Charge of the FBI field office in Chicago and point man of the bombing investigation, FBI Deputy Director William Hunter, and the President took place with the latter two in the Oval Office.

"Mr. President, here is what our investigation has found so far," Martino said. "The bomb was loaded into the bed of a Chevrolet Silverado half-ton pickup. The front axle was found on the roof of the courthouse. From what we can tell the bed of the pickup near the cab had been reinforced with six inches of concrete with a height of twelve inches. This was most likely done to force the blast toward the antique shop. Although, in reality, it didn't matter. That storefront block was built in 1910 and it wouldn't take much to bring it all down. Once the interior walls crumbled, the rest of the buildings fell like dominoes. It's a miracle more people weren't killed."

"What was the bomb made of?" the President asked.

"The forensics lab at Quantico told me this morning it was an ammonium nitrate and fuel oil mixture. It appears the fuel oil was nitromethane. We also found the remains of Tovex, which is a gel-like explosive containing ammonium nitrate and methyl ammonium nitrate, along with a number six blasting cap."

"What about the size of the bomb?"

"I would estimate it at approximately one thousand pounds. To put that into perspective, McVeigh used over forty-eight-hundred pounds of explosives in Oklahoma City, but he was also using a bigger truck."

"Where can somebody pick this stuff up?"

"As you know, Mr. President, the ammonium nitrate is used as a farm fertilizer. It's more difficult to obtain in this day and age with the ID requirements but this amount could easily have been stolen. The nitromethane could have been purchased at a number of locations here in the Midwest. Drag racers and motorcycle racers purchase it all the time."

"What about the Tovex and the blasting cap?"

Agent Martino cleared his throat and leaned into the speaker of the phone. "Those are much more difficult for the public to obtain. The Tovex is used nowadays in place of dynamite. Ski patrols use it to set off avalanches. It is also used in mining and rock quarries."

The report of the bomb didn't surprise the President. If someone wanted to build an explosive device it was pretty easy to do with the right information. And the Internet was unfortunately a treasure trove of how-to manuals. The President wanted to know who was responsible.

"Do you have anything on a possible suspect?"

"Mr. President, it has been slow going. I have agents checking fertilizer and fuel suppliers throughout the Midwest. We're also sending agents to demolition companies and quarries to see if the proprietors have noticed anything suspicious or are missing any type of explosives inventory."

"No eyewitnesses or security cameras?"

"No one has come forward with anything definitive. A lawyer who was walking down the street before the explosion remembered a man in a pickup truck asking for directions to the antique shop but he claims he did not get a good look at the man. A security camera outside the police station that is located on the opposite corner of the square shows what appears to be a male with a denim jacket turning the corner and walking away from the square before the bomb went off. That's all we have as of now."

"What about the letter sent to the *Tribune*?"

The bomber had sent a rambling single-spaced, one-page letter to the *Chicago Tribune* demanding the release of Ibrahim Alar and Mohammed Akbar, the two masterminds of last year's thwarted Fourth of July attack on Washington, D.C. At the time, Vice President Schumacher was in charge at the White House. The Commander-in-Chief was incommunicado because he was off banging the CIA Director on his yacht in the Atlantic. Schumacher gave the order to shoot down two Cessna 210 Centurions headed for the National Mall and loaded with enough explosives to vaporize thousands. The after-action investigation revealed Alar and Akbar had recruited the two pilots and provided the funds for the operation. They pleaded guilty in hopes their death sentences would make them martyrs. The judge thought differently and decided to make them suffer the indignity of wasting away in a federal prison for the rest of their lives.

The letter also demanded the release of Mohammed Hadiq, Hassani's one-time mentor. Hadiq had left America for five years and settled in Pakistan to bring his Islamic radicalism to the cauldron of American hate. There, he would provide terrorist groups with information on everything he knew about the United States, including the layout and possible targets in the city of Chicago. Once his sabbatical was over, he returned to O'Hare where he was promptly arrested by the FBI for providing material information to foreign enemies. He was convicted and sentenced to life in prison. Hassani cried for a week but ultimately traded his sadness for rage. His goal in life became his desire to seek retribution for Hadiq's imprisonment.

"Mr. President, we have checked the paper and the ink. The sender did not use a typewriter but a laser printer. A good many of the laser printers on the market today encode on to the paper a series of dots that can't be seen with the naked eye. Kind of like an invisible watermark. The Secret Service uses the codes to help catch counterfeiters. The dots, which can be viewed with a blue LED light, give the make, model, and serial number which can be cross-checked with the store's scan of bar codes. The person who sent the letter was using an Epson AcuLaser C900. We know the printer was purchased at an Office Depot in Quincy, Illinois, sometime within the last year. We're getting closer, Mr. President."

The President had nothing else to ask. "Okay, thank you, Agent Martino. Keep up the good work."

"Yes, sir."

CHAPTER 5

FBI Headquarters – Washington, D.C.

Director Stubblefield skipped the Oval Office conference call because he already knew the details of the investigation. He also had an important meeting with a man who might become America's most valuable weapon against terrorism. The man had been preparing for his duty for the last two years.

And just yesterday he was released from the federal penitentiary.

Micah Allen "Mac" Carter walked into Director Stubblefield's office without apprehension. He acted almost like he belonged there, not someone who spent the last twenty-four months in an eight-by-ten cell with a convicted murderer as his bunk mate. But that's because he did belong there.

Mac Carter was a special agent with the Federal Bureau of Investigation.

Three years ago, under the direction of the late FBI Director J.D. Bolton, then Deputy Director Stubblefield proposed a plan to use whatever resources available to infiltrate Islamic terrorist groups sprouting up throughout the United States. One idea was to plant undercover federal agents in mosques and businesses in New York City, Los Angeles, Chicago, and Detroit. But devout militant Muslims had grown suspicious of outsiders and a strange face was quickly summoned for an intensive interview. Backgrounds were checked, questions were asked, references were contacted, and if local leaders felt uneasy about bringing the person into the fold, the outsider was politely told to find another place of worship or employment.

Stubblefield knew an unknown man off the street was unlikely to get inside or gain the confidence of those in the know. So, he knew he had to give the man a background to get his foot in the door and enable him to keep it there. And what better place to become immersed in the Muslim brotherhood than in the United States penal system.

For the last twenty years, the vast majority of inmates have entered prison with little or no religious affiliation. Had they been devout Catholics, Baptists, or Lutherans, it would most likely be the case that they wouldn't have found themselves behind bars in the first place. But the prison population had slowly become a bubbling cauldron of black males angry at, not only society, but also "The Man" or the law that put them there. While inside, only so much time could be spent lifting weights or playing cards during the day to pass the time. Besides the gang culture, Muslim inmates and visiting clerics offered their views, welcomed new brothers, and gave them a mental avenue to vent their frustrations. One by one, African-Americans were indoctrinated by those reared in the most radical and militant side of the Muslim faith, which oftentimes resulted in a fervent hatred for America and its promise of freedom and opportunity for all citizens.

Enter Mac Carter.

Stubblefield handpicked three FBI agents – all young, single, and African-American. The plan was to place them in separate prisons in the federal system for two years. Once inside, they would be treated as any other prisoner. Only the prison warden would know their true identity, lest a rogue guard expose the agent and subject him to violent retribution. Upon Carter's release, two agents still remained on the inside.

Special Agent Carter was thirty-five years old and a graduate of the U.S. Naval Academy. He had been a Navy SEAL for two years before a knee injury prevented him from performing his top-secret duty. He left the Navy to join the FBI at age thirty. While at the Bureau's headquarters, he attracted the attention of higher-ups, including Deputy Director Stubblefield, because of his intellect, undercover work, and patriotic devotion. Stubblefield thought he was the perfect candidate.

Carter thought long and hard about giving up his freedom for two whole years. He had no wife and no family. His parents were killed in a car accident when he was a senior in high school. The loss steered him toward the Navy, and the midshipmen became his family. Still, he loved to go to the occasional ball game or down to the local watering hole to enjoy a beer with friends. But that would have to be put on the back burner if he took the assignment. Stubblefield promised that the Bureau of Prisons could place him in solitary confinement or initiate a "prisoner transfer" to give him a week or two of "vacation" every year. But to keep the plan as tightly controlled as possible, he would have to act like every other prisoner. That meant day-in and day-out incarceration. He underwent a battery of tests to determine his ability to withstand the long days of boredom and lack of freedom. The plan had never been tried before, at least not for this length of time. It would be a voyage of unchartered waters on many levels.

The government, for its part, would pay Carter handsomely for his efforts, and Stubblefield gave him a code word if he couldn't take it anymore and needed out. Carter was given a criminal conviction – drug trafficking – and sentenced to thirty months in prison. The Bureau of Prisons was directed to find a cell for him at the West Bend Federal Penitentiary in West Bend, Illinois. He became inmate number 42616-011.

When Stubblefield walked in, they hugged like long lost brothers, one of whom could not believe his eyes that the other was finally out of the joint. Carter was five-nine and weighed two-hundred pounds, up twenty pounds since he entered prison. His head was shaved and his eyes clear. He did have a sense of relief about him though, like he could breathe freely again.

"You finally broke out of that place," Stubblefield said, a wide smile forming.

"I was worried you might forget about me and leave me there, like someone was thinking I was getting what I deserved."

Both took seats in front of Stubblefield's desk. Carter had traded in the orange jumpsuit typical of big house chic for a pair of blue jeans and a dark blue polo shirt. He was slightly underdressed from the other spiffy agents in the building, but he would be given a pass for the fashion faux pas. He had earned it. The tattoos covering his arms were inked on as part of the plan. The two-inch scar on his cheek was from a household knife accident as a child. But in prison, he claimed it was courtesy of a knife fight in the 'hood, a nice touch.

"So what was it like?"

Carter paused and let his gaze settle on the wall behind Stubblefield. He knew this would be the most asked question by anyone who knew the truth of his whereabouts and his mission over the last two years. Maybe someday he could write a tell-all book and express the horrors he witnessed in prison.

"Pure hell."

Stubblefield nodded his head, almost ashamed he put his friend and fellow agent through that hell. But he was not surprised. All his years in law enforcement told him the inside of a prison was not an enjoyable place to lay one's head at night. But this mission was paramount.

"There's an awful lot of anger in there. Seventy-five percent of the men in prison think they're innocent and they wouldn't be there if it hadn't been for the pigs who arrested them, the prosecutors who screwed them, the incompetent attorneys who represented them, and the judge who didn't listen to them. They all think they're going to win on appeal or in a *habeas corpus* petition."

"What about the other twenty-five percent?"

"The rest of those sickos bragged about their crimes, and some seemed to take great pleasure in replaying their violent acts of rape and murder. Part of it was intimidation, to keep people off their backs. Others were just simply evil men."

"What about the food?"

"The food sucked," Carter started off, managing a slight laugh. "Every once in a while, they gave us this crap called 'meal loaf' which is some sort of leftover food menagerie, I think, with ground beef, spinach, carrots, beans, applesauce, potato flakes, and some mysterious something or other all mashed together into a brick like meat loaf. You can go without the ground beef if you request the vegan variety. But all the ketchup in the world wasn't going to help wash that down."

"What would you do all day?"

Carter kept shaking his head. "Get up and wait for breakfast. Then we would sit around and play cards until lunch. I think I have perfected my Spanish, courtesy of my new amigos in cell block H. Some of us were lucky enough to get jobs in the laundry or the kitchen, but that work went mostly to inmates who had been around five or more years and had shown they could be trusted. In the afternoon, we'd get an hour or two of yard time. Most lifted weights, played basketball, or ran laps around the yard."

"You look like you hit the weights pretty hard," Stubblefield said, leaning over and tapping Carter on his bulging biceps.

Carter flexed his right arm but then grew quiet.

"But the worst part, the absolute worst part, was the persistent god-awful stench of sweaty human beings. It would never go away and the humid air hanging over the cells almost suffocated you. Then there were the beatings at night in neighboring cells. I even heard a few rapes. Some of the men in there are like caged animals. The smell, along with the horrifying sound of a man raping another man, can drive a person crazy. And I think some of the prisoners in there are teetering on the edge of insanity."

Carter's eyes drifted to the floor. Stubblefield thought he might be tearing up. But remedying harsh prison conditions would have to wait for another day. A secretary interrupted the meeting to announce lunch was on the way. Subs and chips were on the menu, hopefully better than prison meal loaf. Carter asked for a Coke, his first in two years.

"All right," Director Stubblefield said, wanting to get down to business. "How do you think the mission went?"

"I don't think I'll have any problem getting in wherever you want me." Carter told of how he befriended Sherrod Amir, who was serving a life sentence for murdering a Chicago police officer during the turbulent sixties. Amir was born and raised in the militant Muslim faith, and when Carter presented himself in the prison lunch room as a black male angry at all things American, Amir took the potential convert under his wing. He told him the ways of the brotherhood and the new fight that was brewing between Islam and the religion of the West. Amir invited Carter into the circle of brothers within the walls. They dined together and talked in the yard. Amir even gave Carter his first copy of the Koran. Carter had taken a crash course in Islam prior to entering prison, but Amir's tutelage provided a first-rate education. When Carter told Amir that he was being released, Amir gave him a list of old friends to contact once on the outside. They would provide him needed instruction and offer him an avenue of release for his anger.

"What about in Chicago?"

"Absolutely. There's a vibrant Muslim community in and around the city. Amir wrote down three names in the Chicago area." He took out a scrap of paper from his pocket containing a list of names he had already passed off to the Bureau for investigation. "Bashir, Bandar, and Hassani."

"What about the recent bombing in West Bend? What was the talk inside the prison?"

"Surprisingly little. I mean, several men were overjoyed. You could see it in their eyes that it gave them great pleasure, the sick freaks. They ranted that the victims got what they deserved. But then they would whisper to each other and ask who did it."

"What about the terrorist detainees?"

"I never saw them. They have them hidden away in their own building."

West Bend, Illinois

The sign outside the Qik-n-EZ indicated a gallon of unleaded with ten-percent ethanol was $2.45. It was fifteen cents cheaper ten miles to the west across the border in Iowa. Consumers were known to make the twenty-mile round trip to fill up on gasoline and cigarettes, the latter also being cheaper than the Camels and Marlboros sold at home in the land of high taxation. While in Iowa, the consumers would also pick up a gallon of milk and a loaf of bread, causing Illinois state-line businesses to wage a constant battle to keep their clientele in the state.

The man in the white pickup truck pulled into the one of the open gas islands and turned off the engine. Upon exiting, he flicked his cigarette on the ground and mashed it with his boot. He noticed a young mother in the car on the other side of the island filling up her Toyota Corolla with a baby wrapped in a pink parka and strapped into the car seat in the back. The woman was jabbering into her cell phone, oblivious to the warning sticker on the island instructing drivers to turn off their engines, extinguish all cigarettes, and hang up the phone. Two other cars were parked across the way, and their owners were busy watching the price on the screen click up at a quick rate.

The blue tarp covering the truck bed hid ten four-gallon gas cans all filled with $2.45/gallon unleaded. One was empty. The man unhooked the hose, pushed up the lever, and hit the button to pay inside with his glove-covered finger. He ran the hose into the truck bed and inserted it into the empty can. It would take ninety seconds to fill it to the brim. He had timed it the day before. He clamped the nozzle to run wide open. With a glance to his left and then to his right, his hands were hidden by the bed of the truck bed. He was slightly startled when the young mother walked by to go into the station to pay her bill, her phone still stuck to her ear, and her crying baby left alone in the locked car.

The man ripped off the cap of a signal flare, its fiery white hot flame sparking in the dark confines of the tarp-draped bed. The flare would burn brightly for two minutes. The man pulled the tarp back over the bed. He could hear the gasoline flowing through the hose and the giant sparkler's heat hissing at full strength. The man then walked into the gas station, passed behind the mother who was standing in line, and out the other side. He continued on beyond four other patrons filling their tanks.

When the mother walked out with her giant size Mountain Dew, she noticed some sort of liquid seeping out of the truck bed. She was then almost overcome by the overpowering smell of gasoline. She gasped at the sight of the hose snaking out of the bed. She turned to yell at the attendant inside but nothing ever came out of her mouth.

When a spark from the still searing flame hit the overflowing gasoline, the entire truck exploded into a ball of fire. The remaining forty gallons brightened the night sky in a giant mushroom cloud of orange and red flames that could be seen in eastern Iowa. The fire also ignited the fuel flowing out of the open gas hose, whipping it around like an out-of-control sprinkler spewing a stream of fire before it finally ignited the underground fuel tank. That blast set off a chain reaction of exploding fuel tanks in the ground and in the surrounding cars. West Bend residents thought they were experiencing an earthquake. The young mother was blown into small fiery bits, her infant daughter incinerated in her melted car seat. Those fueling their cars on the other side of the building simply left the hoses in and ran away as fast as they could before their cars would become two-thousand pound roman candles. Ten people would not survive the night. One would manage to hang on for a few days but the burns over ninety percent of his body would finally take their toll.

The man who stopped his truck to fill his gas can was two blocks away with a phone to his ear, almost oblivious to the carnage taking place behind him.

CHAPTER 6

The White House – Washington, D.C.

The President and the First Lady's private dining room is located on the second floor of the White House right across the hall from the President's bedroom. The Schumachers were known to be light eaters – sandwiches and salads – so most dinners were not elaborate affairs. There were no nightly forays into three course meals of Kobe beef and caviar for the First Couple. After a long day of national security meetings, the President's best release from the pressures of the office was a nice quiet evening with his beloved Danielle.

The former Danielle Marie Sexton had grown up next door to the future President of the United States since they were five years old. Anthony had fallen in love with her at an early age and spent twenty years of his life trying to sweep her off her feet. It was a tough sell but his persistence finally paid off. It just couldn't be any other way, he thought. He once told a crowd of locals that Danielle was his shooting star – someone who took his breath away every time she passed through his life and made him pray to the God of the Heavens that He would send her back just one more time.

"Hey Sunshine," the President said as he entered the dining room. "Sunshine" was Danielle's Secret Service code name and it was appropriate given her flowing blonde hair and sunny disposition. He gave her a kiss on both cheeks, always starting with the dimple in her right, then the left, and a quick peck on her cherry red lips. It was always three kisses. And there would be three more before they turned the lights out in the evening. That's just the way he had always done it. "Sorry, I'm late."

"No, it's okay. I just finished the salads."

They sat down at the table, the stillness of the evening always surprising them after the hustle and bustle of their days in the White House. Gone too were the days when the Schumachers had to corral three children for dinner before heading off to a ball game or dance practice. Their oldest daughter, Ashley Jewel, who was affectionately known as A.J. after her father's favorite race car driver and four-time Indianapolis 500 winner, A.J. Foyt, Jr., was a third-grade teacher in a suburb of Indianapolis and preparing for the arrival of a little bundle of joy with her ER doctor husband. The Schumacher's middle child, Michael, who was named after seven-time Formula One world driving champion Michael Schumacher, was studying law at Indiana University. Last but not least was Georgetown University junior Anna Julia, who was also referred to as A.J. by her parents, Junior by her older sister, and Indy by her older brother. The kids' father did not demand their names be racing related, but coming from the home state of the Greatest Spectacle in Racing no one was surprised. Danielle, however, was determined to draw the line if her husband had wanted to name a fourth child Mario or Dario or Helio.

"Anna called me today," Danielle said, passing the salad dressing to her husband.

The President smiled at the thought of his littlest blonde angel and wondered what she wanted now. She always seemed to want something and, being the baby of the family, she usually got what she asked for.

"Was she complaining about her Secret Service detail again?"

It had been a subject of discussion since Schumacher became Vice President. The children couldn't go anywhere without Secret Service protection. It was just too risky in the age of terrorism to let an offspring of a President or Vice President walk around unprotected and become a target of hostage takers. Notwithstanding the dangers, it was not surprising that some growing young adults didn't like their dad's bodyguards keeping an eye on them or restricting their movements.

Danielle laughed. "Oh, just a little this time. She keeps saying Walter is too old. She says it's like being followed around by her grandfather."

"Well, his gray hair would stick out a bit on a college campus."

For a whole thirty seconds, the President of the United States forgot about terrorists killing innocent American civilians or planning to cause destruction somewhere in the world. No thoughts about Democrats and their tax-and-spend, big government political platform. Just hearing about his youngest daughter's complaint about something so minor brought great relief to his mind.

"I'll see if I can do something about it."

"She also said she wants to work at the National Archives this summer."

This pleased the President greatly. Anna had become a connoisseur of American history and the Founding Documents just like her dad. She hoped to be a docent, and a decent one she would be. Plus, what group wouldn't love to have a personal tour of the National Archives by the President's very own daughter.

"I don't know," the President said, wincing a bit. He wondered how that would work. "I'm sure the Secret Service might have something to say about it."

"Maybe she could work behind the scenes in the Archivist's office as an intern or a volunteer."

The dinner with his Elle had brightened the President's mood considerably. Perhaps too he could smell the fresh baked chocolate chip cookies the White House chef was personally delivering. "I'll see if I can make some calls. How about we take these cookies and go watch a movie?"

No sooner had the President spoken those words than Wiley made an appearance in the doorway. Danielle knew by the look on their old friend's face that there would be no movie on this night. The President took notice.

"What's wrong?"

"Mr. President, I'm sorry to interrupt but there's been another explosion in West Bend."

The President sighed. Fun time was over. It was time to get back to work. He gave his wife his usual three kisses, in order as always, just in case he didn't make it back upstairs before she went to bed.

The Vice President and the National Security Advisor were already in the Situation Room when the President arrived. Director Stubblefield was monitoring the situation from FBI Headquarters down Pennsylvania Avenue. The inferno was playing out on the screen on every broadcast network and cable news show. Firefighters in ladder trucks were hosing down the area as best they could but it would be several hours before the fire burned itself out.

The President was furious, pounding the table and repeating that these innocent citizens did not have to die. And it would not have happened but for the spineless politicians and their desire to cozy up to leftists leaders around the world. He was matching Wiley in a dueling barrage of expletives.

"I am sick and tired that the safety and security of the American people are subordinate to the Liberal Left in this country or the self-righteous demands of the President of France or the General Secretary of the United Nations!"

Vice President Jackson nodded her head vehemently in agreement. She was just as angry as the President. She was never in favor of housing the terrorists in the United States and had voted against the move while she was a member of the House of Representatives. "Mr. President, I think it's time for you to move those terrorists."

The President had wanted to do that since he came into office but the federal government did not move as speedily as he had hoped. He paced back and forth, shaking his head and cursing under his breath.

Wiley was writing it all down and wondering how it would play out politically for the President. He sometimes thought out loud. "Mr. President, will the terrorists think they have won if you move their brethren? I mean, will the bloodshed continue in some random town even though the terrorists are back at Gitmo?"

The President stood facing the wall, hands clasped behind his back, trying to think it all through. "Well, if they're going to attack then they're going to attack. But we can at least take away their magnet and maybe disrupt their operations."

"What about the trials in New York City?"

Vice President Jackson chimed in. "That's the biggest stage in the world. It could attract a lone wolf or a whole pack of terrorists."

The President was no fan of the trials either. The terrorists were not American citizens, they were sadistic killers who did not adhere to the laws of war.

The President made his decision. "All right. This bloodshed has to stop. Tomorrow we start working on moving the detainees back to Cuba and reestablishing the military tribunals. We'll get the ball rolling and announce it at the State of the Union the day after tomorrow. Make it happen, Wiley."

"I'm on it."

CHAPTER 7

West Bend, Illinois

The FBI could almost sense that they were going to get a break in the case. Agents were chasing down leads and not leaving any stone unturned. Another letter to the *Tribune* promised more attacks in the future if Alar and Akbar weren't released. This only pushed the FBI to work harder. Agents worked rotating twelve-hour shifts, and the parking lot of the Motel 6 looked like a convention for government vehicles.

A sleep-deprived Agent Marteno headed up the conference call with the President and Director Stubblefield in the Oval Office.

"Sir, we checked the surveillance tapes from the Office Depot and found a white male buying an Epson AcuLaser C900 printer believed to be the one used to print off the demand letter."

"Did you say *white* male?"

"Yes, sir, Caucasian male. We also got a good picture of the suspect at the gas station. He looked right up at the parrot camera."

The President and Stubblefield gave each other quizzical looks. Both wondered if they heard correctly. The President even mouthed the words to the man sitting across from him. "I'm sorry, say again, Agent Marteno. The *parrot* camera?" the President asked.

Agent Marteno knew he would have some explaining to do on this one. In all his years of law enforcement, he had never come across a parrot camera.

"Mr. President, I know you have a law-enforcement background. As you are aware, your typical gas station robber will oftentimes enter the building with a hat pulled down near his eyes to hide his face from the security cameras. Well, inside this gas station was a mechanical red macaw sitting on its perch that was bolted to the wall. It looked liked the real thing. When a customer entered the building, the parrot would flap its wings and squawk 'Hello, friend, thanks for shopping at the Qik-n-EZ.' This would, with amazing success I might add, cause the customer to look up at the bird, and a hidden surveillance camera would take a picture of the person's exposed face and send it to the computer hard drive in the office and another one off-site. It's just human nature to look up at the distraction and, unless you were prepared for it and had the wherewithal to resist its call, it's almost impossible to ignore."

"I've never heard of such a thing."

"I haven't either," Stubblefield added.

"Mr. President, I've investigated a lot of bank robberies in my day, and I can tell you I have never seen any such technology. Of course, a talking parrot would not fit the decor of most banks. But this gas station sold a lot of kitschy trinkets. Everything from Indian art, angel statutes, and turquoise jewelry. It was not out of place. One of the off-duty attendants we interviewed said the station owner was tired of the stickups and had a friend come up with a solution. It drove the attendant crazy because the kids would run in and out just to set the bird off."

"Well score one for American ingenuity," the President said, "but what did our parrot friend get for us?"

"Sir, it is a white male, brown hair, scruffy stubble. I'm faxing you a copy right now. We have a news conference in one hour and we will release the photo to the general public. Our sketch artist also has made several variations to take into account dark hair, full beard, etcetera. None of the local police recognize the man, and given that he looked at the camera, he might be from outside the area. Or he could have forgotten about it in the heat of the moment."

"Okay, good work, Agent Marteno. Keep us posted."

South Suburbs, Chicago, Illinois

Mac Carter showed up at 9 a.m., thirty minutes before his job interview. He drove a faded black 1991 Chevy Caprice, and the large amount of rust and lack of hubcaps made it look like it had just been saved from the clutches of the car crusher at the salvage yard. But Carter was playing the part of a poor black male just released from prison. He couldn't show up in a gleaming new Ford F-150 or a tricked-out Cadillac with flashy twenty-fours and gaudy spinners. His old clunker would look right at home in the housing projects on the South Side of Chicago.

A job in construction was one of the few opportunities ex-cons have to make something of themselves after they get out of the joint. Just released inmates have a hard time sitting behind a desk for eight hours a day, and a suit and tie remind them of their uniform prison jumpsuits they were required to wear. Construction allowed them to use their strength. More importantly, it kept their hands busy and away from guns and drugs and off the bodies of nonconsenting women. Fast-food establishments were also known to employ many with criminal backgrounds. Most worked in the kitchen, tending the grill or washing the dishes. Their bosses would usually keep them off the registers – a drawer full of cash sometimes proving to be too big a temptation. Other than those two areas of employment, newly freed inmates had better hope for a self-employed relative or a government-assistance check. More than half returned to their life of crime.

"Yeah, I'm here to meet with Mr. Hassani about a job."

The secretary looked Carter over. He was wearing a clean pair of jeans and a shirt with a collar. He looked presentable, the tattoos notwithstanding. He didn't bring a resume but job hunters rarely did in this line of work. Their work history was passed on by word of mouth. If they were asked if they could hammer a nail, their answer was yes. Install drywall? Their answer was yes. Lay bricks? Yes. Shingle a roof and pour concrete at the same time? Absolutely, did it all the time.

"You can go on in," the secretary said.

Carter walked in to find Hassani standing up from his chair behind his desk. "Mr. Carter, good to meet you."

Carter had never met Hassani and the background report from the FBI didn't provide much detail. His instant reaction was one of a dedicated businessman. He wore dark pants and a white dress shirt with the company logo on the pocket. The wood-paneled office was filled with blueprints and papers and work schedules, but it was not a cluttered mess. But Carter could not take his focus off Hassani's dark penetrating eyes, which seemed to be peering into Carter's soul to determine what type of man was appearing before him. Hassani trusted few people, and he kept most outsiders at arm's length. It would be Carter's first time on the wrong side of an interrogation.

"Thanks for meeting with me," Carter said, his big muscular hands giving a firm shake. "I really appreciate it."

Hassani made all of the company's hiring decisions. If he was going to run an operation, construction or otherwise, he was going to be the one controlling it. He wasn't going to let one of his construction bosses be responsible for looking into the eyes of a future worker and decide whether that person was worthy of working for Hassani Enterprises.

With his rising militant mindset, a hiring decision could mean the difference between a glorious victory or an untimely defeat.

"Amir tells me good things about you," he said softly, his eyes narrowing. The tone in his voice indicated what Amir told him might not be all that good. It certainly was not great things that's for sure. Hassani was, of course, dealing with a man that had just been released from prison. "He says you're a hard worker."

"Yes, sir."

"Tell me a little about your past employment history."

Carter had it all memorized. He knew this day might come, and the long days and nights behind bars gave him plenty of time to rehearse.

"I did a lot of odd jobs, you know what I'm saying, like if someone in the community needed a job done I'd be there, you know what I'm saying, fixing things. Everything from plumbing, roofing, painting, you know what I'm saying. I'm a fast learner too."

When Carter normally spoke, people knew what he was saying. He was highly educated and spoke three languages. He didn't need to ask the listener if they understood. But he was now playing the part, and some might say his performance could win him an Oscar one day. He claimed to have been educated through the eighth grade and he was proving it with his questionable grammatical skills. He told Hassani he ditched high school and ended up being harassed by the police, which he pronounced "po-lease." His daddy died when he was fifteen and his momma worked two jobs so he joined a gang and started smoking dope. Prison had made him clean however, and he just wanted to work hard and make a decent living. He was also tired of getting hassled by the cops and Amir told him a job at Hassani would help him stay out of trouble with the law.

Hassani never took his eyes off of Carter's. He was slightly turned off by the man's lack of education but Carter showed no love for the police or the American system that sent him to prison for two years. Hassani didn't mind if Carter loathed the police so long as he understood that Hassani was the authority around here. He expected his laws to be followed. Amir had written to him that Carter could be trusted and was mostly a quiet individual. Carter would not let him down, Amir promised. Hassani trusted Amir, and he would take a chance with the malleable man begging him for a job.

"Can you start working on Wednesday?"

"Absolutely."

Hassani stood up from his chair and extended a hand "Good. Call in Wednesday morning to see where we need you. I can't promise you work every day of the week, but I will do my best to find something when I need you."

"Thank you, Mr. Hassani."

The White House – Washington, D.C.

The President's afternoon schedule focused entirely on national security. American citizens were dying in the streets, and he had to do something about it. The CIA, now back in the President's good graces considering the former Director's involvement in the plot to kill him, briefed him everyday on increased chatter from terrorist groups around the world.

Schumacher had nominated James A. Olsen to be CIA Director. Olsen had been in the spy agency for twenty years before he became National Security Director under two Republican presidents. Ty Stubblefield said Olsen had solid credentials and was a trusted member of the intelligence community. Given his background, Olsen was quickly confirmed by the Senate. During his meetings with the President, Olsen told him something was brewing, but he could not pinpoint what the terrorists were planning or how they intended to carry out their murderous ways. Afghanistan and Pakistan were hotbeds of anti-American sentiment, and the CIA was monitoring suspected terrorist hideouts with unmanned drones. The intelligence also indicated Yemen, whose chief export appeared to be terrorism, was becoming a magnet for those wanting to strike at the United States and its interests around the world. He suggested the President continue to pressure America's allies to take a strong stand against any country harboring terrorists.

Olsen heard nothing as to who might be committing the West Bend bombings, although no known terrorist organization was disavowing the attacks as of yet. For its part, the FBI had increased their surveillance in New York, Michigan, Illinois, and Arizona in response to the growing rash of terror. The Department of Homeland Security was also on high alert, and orders were given to ratchet up passenger screenings at airports and armed patrols in the subway systems. The focus on national security never seemed to be very far from President Schumacher's mind.

"All right," the President said, "who's next?"

Wiley looked at the schedule. "The Mayor of New York City. I'll go get him."

Wiley walked out of the Oval Office to greet the Mayor and escorted him inside.

"Mr. Mayor, good to see you," the President said, standing up behind the Resolute Desk. He walked around to greet him.

"Mr. President, always a pleasure. Thank you for inviting me."

"Would you like some coffee?"

"No, thank you, sir."

Crandall Foxworthy took a seat to the right of the President's desk. His slicked back hair looked as if it was stiffer than usual, most likely caused by the frigid temperatures outside. He was sixty-two years old and was starting to show the strain of leading America's largest city. He was charismatic and tough, more Giuliani than Bloomberg, and dapper like the days of old, more LaGuardia than Koch. Still, his fine tailored suits were beginning to stretch with his growing waistline and the hairline was slowly making a retreat.

The moderate Democrat had won his second term with 51% of the votes, the majority of the NYC populace happy with his conservative fiscal policies and tough-on-crime agenda. There had been no terrorist attacks under his watch, and he was determined to keep it that way. But it was a constant battle in the city that never sleeps.

"So, how are things in the Big Apple?"

The Mayor cleared his throat. "Fine, as of now."

"But?"

The Mayor had held his tongue in public for two months now. The last thing he wanted was to disparage the new President after the assassination attempt and his move to the top office after Fisher's death. Anyone who did so was roundly criticized no matter the strength of their arguments. It was a time for the people of America to rally around their President, to give him the support he needed to do the job.

But the Mayor had a problem that wasn't going away. "Mr. President, I have been reluctant to discuss this publicly and that's why I asked to meet with you personally." He pulled out a list of talking points from the pocket inside his suit coat. "Mr. President, I want you to call off the trials of the terrorists in federal court in New York City."

The President looked beyond the Mayor and cast his gaze out the Oval Office windows. It had been billed as the "Trial of the 21st

Century" – *United States of America v. Abullah and Mohammed.* The two men had been arrested in Pakistan ten months earlier and the depth of their sinister plot to harm America was still being uncovered. Former lieutenants inside bin Laden's al-Qaeda, they had started out small with coordinated attacks at U.S. Embassies in Karachi and Baghdad. Two American diplomats were killed, and al-Qaeda leaders considered it a success. But Abullah and Mohammed were not satisfied. They wanted destruction and mayhem on a grander scale than 9/11. The number 2,973 ran through their heads constantly like a strobe light. That was the number of Americans killed on that fateful Tuesday in September 2001. Abullah and Mohammed dreamed of eclipsing that mark, as much as Pete Rose hustled after Ty Cobb's famed career hits record. They wanted to strike a crippling blow on those evil Americans.

And they would not be satisfied unless they could double the carnage.

After getting a tip from one of the rare Pakistani government leaders who was not in al-Qaeda's back pocket, CIA operatives captured Abullah and Mohammed in the dark of night in northwest Pakistan. Word of the capture was kept silent from all but the top leaders in the federal government. If word got out that two of the FBI's most wanted fugitives were in secret custody, howls of protest from the Left, foreign governments, and the Civil Liberties Alliance would inundate the airwaves in an attempt to paint the U.S. as some bully violating the rights of the scum of the earth.

But the information was kept quiet for months. And the CIA utilized every trick in its handbook to extract information from the two terrorists. The waterboarding proved to be very effective. Abullah broke after only five rounds, and he informed his interrogators that a plot had been set for an attack on Washington.

Then, a Democrat Senate staffer overheard a conversation between two members of the Senate Intelligence Committee. Something about waterboarding and secret CIA prisons. Since Washington leaks like a sieve, the *Post* found out about it and ran with it. Once the public opinion polls told the Democrats it was safe to trot out the need for civil rights and liberties for the terrorists, they started demanding President Fisher do something about it or risk having it become a political issue.

Fearing claims that he was violating someone's rights, President Fisher ordered the terrorist detainees held at Guantanamo Bay to be tried in federal court as opposed to a military tribunal. He had received millions of dollars in donations throughout his numerous campaigns from the likes of the Civil Liberties Alliance, whose arsenal of attorneys was ready to offer *pro bono* services to ensure the terrorists received the constitutional rights they didn't deserve.

The President decided the site of the trials would be New York City, since Abullah and Mohammed had their hands in the first World Trade Center bombing, the second, as well as a few other attempts that had been thwarted by law enforcement. The New York City Police Department, the FBI, the U.S. Marshals, and the Department of Homeland Security had begun setting up plans to prevent any attempts to disrupt the trials, which would be the center of the world's attention for weeks and even months on end. Mayor Foxworthy had warned that the Trial of the 21st Century would bring the Big Apple to a screeching halt and plunge it deeper into the fiscal abyss. But nobody in the Fisher Administration listened. He hoped President Schumacher would be amenable to other ideas.

"Mr. President," the Mayor started respectfully. "I don't know if you're familiar with the federal courthouse in Lower Manhattan. It's just off the Brooklyn Bridge near City Hall and not too far from Wall Street and the World Trade Center site." The Mayor stopped suddenly and his eyes moistened slightly. They always did when he discussed the World Trade Center. He had been a federal prosecutor in Manhattan on 9/11 and saw the planes flying into both towers. In his office closet, he had kept his ash-covered suit coat and blood-splattered dress shirt in a plastic garment bag to forever remind him of that tragic day. He was determined not to let anything similar happen again.

"I have had endless discussions with the New York City Police Commissioner, the U.S. Marshal, the Circuit Court Security Inspector, as well as the FBI and Homeland Security Department. They assure me the courthouse can be made secure for the trial. The judge, jurors, and courthouse personnel would be protected twenty-four hours a day if necessary. But, Mr. President, Lower Manhattan would essentially have to be shut down. Residents are already complaining they won't be able to park their cars on the streets during the months' long trial. Shopkeepers fear no one will get anywhere near the courthouse during the trial. The cost will be astronomical. The police overtime alone will be over fifty million dollars. Look at what's happening in West Bend and multiply that by a thousand. The skyscrapers, the subway system, the bridges. Then there's the . . ."

The President held up his hand and cut him off. "Mr. Mayor, the trial is not going to be held in Manhattan."

The Mayor was ready with an alternate plan if the President demanded it. He had hoped the President would consider Plan B or Plan C, anything but holding it in Lower Manhattan. But if the Schumacher Administration wanted to continue the prior administration's desire for public trials in the Big Apple, he would do his best to oblige. "We could put the trial on Governors Island, which is a Coast Guard facility just east of Liberty Island."

The President rocked in his chair. He thought of Lady Liberty's lamp in the background of the year-long terrorist circus. She would no doubt shake her head and cover her eyes at the farce – terrorists ranting and raving in the courtroom while their lawyers demanded the government hand over every last bit of information that was used in the discovery and apprehension of their clients. The terrorists' lawyers would love to shine a light on CIA tactics and expose its operatives, and if al-Qaeda happened to find out about them and change their murderous strategies in response, well that's just America's fault for being the world's big bad bully they would claim. The President gave a slight shake of his head at the thought.

"Sir, I've even looked into having the trial on a cruise ship. The federal government could commandeer a cruise liner and sequester the jury right in the cabins. Almost like a vacation. The jurors would have three square meals a day. Their families could even come in on weekends. The defendants," he rattled on.

"Terrorists," the President interrupted.

"Yes, sir. The terrorists could be shuttled in every day via helicopter. We could put the ship out in the Atlantic if necessary with a military escort. It would keep Lower Manhattan from being shut down and people would be able to go on with their lives."

The President stopped rocking in his chair. "Mr. Mayor, we are *not* going to have a trial on a cruise ship."

The Mayor was just about to throw up his hands. "Sir, I just don't know what else we can do. We're gonna go broke trying them in the City."

"Mayor, the trial is not going to be held in civilian courts." The

President let the statement sink in. He then reached over to the left side of his desk and took a sheet of paper out of a leather folder. "And it's not going to be held in New York City, or on a cruise ship, or in the middle of the Hudson or East Rivers. This is an executive order that I will sign tomorrow before the State of the Union. We're going back to military tribunals."

The Mayor's eyes widened. The fiscal and security nightmare he had endured for the past six months had just been erased from his memory, the great burden lifted from his shoulders. He could have kissed the President. All the work, all that worry, was now gone.

"The terrorists will be tried at Guantanamo Bay. Unless you object."

The Mayor practically jumped out of his chair. "No, sir, Mr. President. I will stand wholeheartedly behind your decision."

The President stood, reached out his hand, and smiled. "Good. I hope you will convince your fellow Democrats that it's the right one."

CHAPTER 8

The United States House of Representatives – Washington, D.C.

"Mr. Speaker!" the House Sergeant-at-Arms bellowed. "The President of the United States!"

The hearty welcome for the new President cascaded through the House Chamber as President Schumacher made his way down the center aisle. The packed chamber had raised the temperature five degrees and made the air stuffy. Members of Congress from both political parties reached out for a handshake or a pat on the back. There was Congresswoman Moeisha Robinson from Michigan, a longtime thorn in the President's side from his days in the House, grinning from ear to ear and showing her constituents and the TV audience that she could pretend to be bipartisan for even a couple of seconds. On the other side, Congressman Andrew Totten from the Eighth District in Indiana even got a hug and a hearty handshake from the President. Totten had taken over for Representative Schumacher when the latter became Vice President. They were old friends from their days together in the Wabash County State's Attorney's Office and to this day they argued over who was the most conservative prosecutor.

According to Article II, Section 3, Clause 1 of the United States Constitution, the President "shall from time to time give to the Congress Information of the State of the Union." Jefferson decided not to make a personal appearance and instead thought the written form would suffice. Lincoln did the same for his Annual Message, as it was then called. The American public heard Coolidge's address for the inaugural time on radio in 1923 and first saw Truman in black and white in 1947. But with the advent of the digital TV age, no President would dare to simply send a copy of the State of the Union up to Capitol Hill for congressional perusal. No sir, it was prime time on the major broadcast networks and cable news outlets for millions of Americans to sit back and enjoy. It's the reason presidents primped their hair, whitened their teeth, and put on their best suits.

And with the new President making his first foray to the House Chamber since his elevation to the Executive Office, tens of millions around the country and around the world were tuned in.

With the thunderous ovation still at full force, President Schumacher reached the end of the aisle and was greeted by the Chief Justice of the United States, Raymond J. Shannon, the man who had sworn him in just over two months ago. The Chief Justice had been on the Court for twenty-two years, the last ten in the middle chair. He was a states' rights conservative from the Lone Star State, and the Texan oftentimes used his country-boy charm to wrangle the two more moderate justices on the Court to agree with the conservative bloc. He was a skilled administrator and his boundless energy belied his age of seventy five.

"Mr. Chief Justice," the President said warmly. "Good to see you again."

Chief Justice Shannon took the President's hand with both of his. "Always a pleasure, Mr. President." He gave him a wink in support.

Given the President's deep respect for the judicial branch since his days in law school, he made sure to shake the hands of all eight associate justices, each nicely attired in their black judicial robes, who decided to make their presence known during the annual confluence of the executive and legislative arms of the government. News anchors could not remember when the entire Court showed up for a Presidential address.

After four minutes of handshakes, the President finally reached the podium where he greeted the Vice President, in her capacity as President of the Senate, and the Speaker of the House and gave each of them a manila envelope containing a copy of his address. He turned toward the gathered assembly, gave a quick glance and a wave to his wife in the First Lady's box in the gallery, and then raised both hands in appreciation. When the ovation failed to subside, he pulled back the cuff of his shirt and tapped his watch. Feeling slightly embarrassed by the generous welcome, he turned to the House Speaker and twirled his finger.

Speaker Spencer banged the gavel on the rostrum, the members of the House and Senate finally relenting and taking their seats. "Members of Congress, I have the high privilege and distinct honor of presenting to you, the President of the United States."

This, of course, caused the chamber to erupt again in thunderous applause. The Republicans tried to keep from jumping up and down. The President didn't let it go on too long. He needed to get to work. After a quick sip of water from the glass to his right, he cleared his throat.

"Thank you, Mr. Speaker. Madame Vice President. Members of Congress, Mr. Chief Justice and members of the Supreme Court, distinguished guests, and last but not least, my fellow Americans."

President Schumacher began by thanking all those who sent their good wishes to him and his family over the previous two months. The ordeal had been a harrowing experience and he said it had only made him stronger and more willing to serve. He mentioned the First Lady, his beautiful Danielle, and the entire chamber graciously acknowledged her. Even the Supreme Court justices stood to politely applaud. It had been a trying time for him and for the country, he said, but it was time to put the business of the people back into the spotlight.

The address was entitled "The Responsibility Society." The country was trillions of dollars in debt – its credit rating was on shaky ground and a large portion of its treasury securities were in the hands of foreign governments. FDR's New Deal had turned into the "Raw Deal" for generations who came long after the Great Depression but were now stuck with the Liberal promises that couldn't be kept. Likewise, LBJ's Great Society became little more than a "Welfare Society" and the war on poverty a six-trillion-dollar failure. It was an economic path that could not continue. The economic well-being of America and future generations depended on a return to fiscal responsibility.

"But it is a shared responsibility," he said. "The American people have a responsibility to provide for themselves and their families in their food, housing, and health care. The days of asking your neighbor to provide for you cannot continue. In the upcoming budget, I will propose a ten-percent reduction in all domestic welfare spending."

The Democrats sat stoned faced and stunned at the President's words. The look in their eyes made it seem they were listening to an alien talking complete gibberish. Their jaws fell to the floor in disbelief. How dare he talk to them like that! How dare he take away their money! That was their lifeline to power! But the Democrats just couldn't get it through their thick liberal skulls that it wasn't their money. It was the American people's money. And frankly, the Dems hadn't been very good stewards of the people's money.

"While we will continue to provide assistance to those who cannot help themselves and to those who have put on a uniform in service of our country, I intend to get the federal government out of the people's way so they can enjoy the endless opportunity that this great nation can provide."

The Republicans could not stay seated. They were practically jumping all over themselves at what they thought was the greatest speech they had ever heard in their lifetimes. Two conservative representatives seated in the back of the chamber were so giddy with delight they were slapping high-fives after every sentence. The President's mention of tax cuts, spending freezes, and entitlement reform just about brought down the right side of the aisle.

"My fellow Americans, we in the government also have a responsibility to you. Our job is to provide the citizenry with that which individuals cannot do for themselves. And the greatest responsibility of the government is to keep the people safe."

The Republicans continued their cheering, the Democrats finally relenting and putting their cold hands together.

"This evening at the White House, I have signed two executive orders. One, I have ordered the removal of terrorist detainees awaiting trial at the West Bend Federal Penitentiary in West Bend, Illinois."

The House Chamber fell to a hushed silence. The recent loss of life was no clapping matter. The debate would wait until tomorrow. Or at least until the President's speech was over.

"The American people endured another act of terrorism this past week. Regrettably . . .," he said reading off the names from both attacks, ". . . and Jo Ellen Dawson lost their lives." The President's jaw clenched, and he could not keep his eyes from drifting to the left side of the aisle. "And they need not have died."

The President mentioned his prior opposition to the transfer of the terrorists to Illinois, and his new plan to ship them right back to the friendly confines of Guantanamo Bay. "Because I will not permit a peaceful American community to remain in the crosshairs of the terrorists."

The Republicans let loose a full-throated roar, many wanting to charge out of the chamber and string up the first terrorist they could find. The Democrats applauded as well, but only because the television cameras were on.

"Two, I have signed an executive order reinstituting the military tribunals for the terrorist detainees. They will be given a fair trial. But they will not receive the rights they are not entitled to just because some in this world believe they should."

The cameras panned the chamber scanning the crowd. The Republicans didn't know how much more they could take. Schumacher was too good to be true. Finally, an American President promising to kick some terrorist ass. The Democrats looked at each other. Many wondered how they could take on the new President – one who had nearly been murdered by the previous President and was now in full command following two terrorist attacks on the country.

One camera shot picked up the justices of the Supreme Court in the front row. The Chief Justice and the eight associate justices sat motionless, their hands politely folded and lying on the black robes draped over their shoulders. They all knew a legal fight would soon break out, and the brawl wouldn't end until it reached their courtroom across the street.

The political commentators would later discuss the complexity of the arguments and the uneasiness the justices must feel while sitting in the chamber. A few eagle-eyed reporters would point out one justice could not restrain his emotions. It was not a boisterous display at all. But the unmistakable furrowed brow, the squinting eyes, and the two shakes of the head indicated one justice would not be a rubber stamp to the President's authority.

And that man was Justice Ali Hussein.

CHAPTER 9

Muddy Rock, Kansas

Juanita Dixon peered out the cracked front windshield of her rusted Ford Tempo, a relic from the early ‘90s that had 158,000 miles on the odometer. She hoped to someday buy a new car; well, a nice pre-owned car would suffice. But the single African-American mother of two young boys had been unemployed for six months and putting food on the table and a roof over her kids’ heads were her top priorities. She had utilized a temporary employment agency in Wichita on several occasions – supplying resumes and filling out applications, but the pool of workers always seemed to outnumber the jobs available. She tried everything she could think of – babysitting, house cleaning, dog walking, and even cutting the grass on occasion. But then one day her eureka moment hit after seeing an advertisement in the local newspaper. She could earn fifteen bucks an hour for the next ten weeks. That’s two-plus months of good money, she thought. Plus, her unemployment benefits wouldn’t be affected. She already met two of the job’s requirements. She had a driver’s license and the use of a vehicle. Yes, that’s what she wanted to do.

Juanita was going to become a U.S. Census worker.

Article I, Section 2 of the United States Constitution requires the Census to be taken every ten years. Doing its decennial duty, the U.S. Department of Commerce floods mailboxes across the fruited plains in hopes of counting every man, woman, and child in the fifty states. In return, adjustments, if necessary, are made to the number of representatives each state would send to Congress. Also, number crunchers in Washington determine how much each state receives from the federal treasury for highway projects, schools, and health-care programs.

To the Commerce Department’s dismay, not all Americans fill out and return their Census forms. The success rate is about 67%, which is well below the 97% of Americans who follow the law and mail their tax forms back to the IRS. The disparity might have something to do with the fact that the IRS sends out its agents with their pocket protectors, calculators, and, if necessary, their loaded weapons. When reminders in the mail fail to elicit the return of the Census form, the government recruits citizens like Juanita Dixon to go "address canvassing" to count heads.

With a million temporary jobs available, the government seeks double that amount in candidates to fill the field. Some applicants are weeded out because of their status as convicted felons, and some are told that instead of filling out the application they should have been filling out their Form 1040 (which they had apparently forgotten to do for several years). Others are hired but fail to show up for work, claiming they expected to receive a federal welfare check without the requirement that they actually do anything. A few are even delicately told that they wouldn't be hired in light of the fact that they never learned how to count.

With her two forms of identification, Juanita was first in line at the Wichita Public Library for the Census examination. The multiple choice test would examine her clerical skills, reading and math proficiency, ability to interpret information, consider alternatives, and navigate maps. After thirty minutes in the hot seat, she passed with 80%. Good enough for government work. The guy next to her wasn't so lucky but was pleased to know he would be allowed to retake the test the next day. Dixon was told to promptly report for duty on Monday morning.

She did, and her supervisor gave her a list of names and addresses. She was to locate the household, explain the Census to the occupant, and after a brief interview, record the needed responses on the form provided. Easy enough, she thought.

Now she was on the road and her first stop looked like it would be quick work. Ninety-two-year-old Gertrude Kladis implored Ms. Dixon to come inside for a chat. Kladis hadn't had a real visitor in three months and rarely got out of the house any more. Her food was delivered by Meals on Wheels, and her son only stopped by on Sundays long enough to pick her up and drop her off at church. When Dixon inquired about the Census form she should have received in the mail, Kladis was unsure of what happened.

"Oh dear," she fretted with genuine concern.

She received about as much mail as she did visitors, and if the envelope didn't have a picture of Ed McMahon or Billy Graham on the front she probably just threw it away. She apologized profusely. She would never fail to do her duty as a citizen. She voted in every election, and always for GOP candidates as she came from a long line of solid Republicans. Her father even campaigned and voted for Alf Landon. She paid her taxes every year and twice was called to serve on jury duty. Nowadays, she spent most of her time knitting and listening to the Royals on the radio. Like most Kansans, she was a big fan of George Brett. There was even a faded picture of the Hall-of-Famer hanging on the wall amongst the grand kids that she rarely saw. She rattled off their names and where they lived.

"How many people live here, Ms. Kladis?" Dixon dutifully asked.

"Just me," she said softly. Now comfy in her favorite rocker, Kladis proceeded to tell Dixon her life story – how her family survived the Dustbowl, endured cold winter nights scurrying to the outhouse in the backyard and banking the coal furnace, and raised ten kids in that little ol' house. Her husband was in the War, where he lost an eye. He returned home and ran the farm, where he lost an arm. He loved God, his country, and his family. And George Brett, too. After a cup of coffee and a couple pieces of fresh baked banana bread, Dixon was out the door with a plea to come back any time.

She had spent two hours and thirty taxpayer dollars counting one person. Once back on the road, she craned her neck out the window trying to maneuver down the dusty roads of rural Kansas. She hoped the next stop would go quicker than the last. She didn't want to get fired for indolence and sloth. The name on the list read "Binford Orville Duncan."

"Who in the hell names their kid Binford Orville?"

West Bend, Illinois

"Agent Marteno, I think you need to hear this."

Agent Marteno had been on the phone all day with Washington while his Joint Terrorism Task Force team was hard at work beating the bushes in search of clues. Needless to say, people were getting antsy. The President had wanted to make an announcement at the State of the Union, one that could let the people of West Bend breathe a sigh of relief after the terrorist in their midst had been captured. But no dramatic note was passed to him at the podium. Now, the Illinois governor was contemplating issuing an order to send out the National Guard to protect

West Bend if the attacks continued. News organizations had sent out the face of the FBI's suspect over the airwaves and tips were pouring in. Some people thought it looked like their long-lost brother, or their angry neighbor, or the weird farmer down the road. It was taking time for the FBI to track down all the leads. The big break, however, came not from a person recognizing the individual but from the FBI supercomputer in Washington, D.C.

FBI Special Agent Brent Crawford had spent the previous day scouring a list of numbers that had been faxed to him from Headquarters. On the twenty-page printout were thousands of phone numbers made in the greater West Bend area within thirty minutes prior to and after the two attacks. Two numbers stood out.

"As I was telling you yesterday," Crawford said with the list in front of him. "The computer indicated the person with this particular phone number made a call to the same person within thirty seconds of each attack. The cell-phone tower records indicate the person making the call was within a four-block radius of the truck bomb at the antique shop and a three-block radius of the gas-station explosion. If this is our suspect, it's possible he was calling his co-conspirator for a ride. One number is a cell phone, the other a land line. The owners of the numbers share the same address."

"Did you get the overhear?"

"Yes, we contacted a judge last night and he signed off on the authorized overhear for those two numbers. Our guys have been listening in and a female called a male at the suspect number. The male told her he would call her back in five or ten minutes. That's why I called you in."

An agent in the other room raised his hand and gestured for Crawford and Marteno. The man was on the line. All three agents put on their headsets and hoped for the break they had been waiting for.

"Hello." The voice was female. The phlegm was noticeable. No doubt a chain smoker. Maybe in her late forties.

"Yeah, it's me." A male, also a smoker. The tone was hushed. "I need you to go buy some more gasoline."

The woman didn't seem to question the man's request. "I thought you were going to use the fertilizer and the barrels again."

Agent Marteno raised his eyebrows to Crawford. He sat down and opened up a yellow legal pad. The affidavit for a search warrant was going to be written quickly.

The man hacked up what sounded like half a lung. “No, the gasoline is easier. But I need six gallons quickly. There’s a basketball game at the high school tonight. I’ll park the truck near the front entrance, go inside and pull the fire alarm, and walk out the back. There will be hundreds of people waiting outside for the fire department to come.”

Agent Marteno slapped Crawford on the shoulder and told him to get moving. The FBI had all it needed for the warrants.

CHAPTER 10

Office of the Civil Liberties Alliance – Washington, D.C.

The ink-jet printers were humming at full strength as they had been throughout the night. The smell of hot soy ink and warm recycled paper filled the humid office air. The attorneys had been working since last night's State of the Union speech and the petitions were rolling fast off the presses. Most of the attorneys were in a foul mood, and it wasn't because they had no sleep for the past twenty-four hours. They were angry at one man, and their leader was the most angry of all.

"That bastard Schumacher!" The phrase went without disagreement in the office and to no one's surprise, considering a similar sentiment could probably be heard in terrorist caves and Democrat offices all over the world.

Art Brennan's cherubic face was as red as the Big Apple from whence he came. He was mad as hell and liked to let anyone within earshot know the reasons why. The stocky New Yorker was old-school Liberal – a cigar-smoking, in-your-face Democrat who relished a good brawl – in the courtroom, in a back alley, it didn't matter. He had the personality of a cornered warthog, which was probably the reason he had never married. Most CLA types were single, with no kids, and no life outside of the office. Their evenings at home usually consisted of stewing in silence at the thought of Republicans running the show. There was always some Republican in power somewhere that would fuel their perpetual anger. The mere mention of the word "Cheney" used to send them into convulsive rages.

Brennan was the chairman of the Civil Liberties Alliance and he oversaw fifty attorneys who made it their business to represent the most minor of minorities, no matter how dirty and rotten those clients might be, and kick the other side's ass.

If 99% of Americans were opposed to a certain group, the CLA would be available to take up that group's cause. But only if their cause was of the anti-American variety. The members of the CLA did not like how America had become the world's only superpower – raping the world of its resources and bombing civilians in countries it did not belong. The only difference between the CLA and a terrorist organization was the former waged its brand of warfare in the judicial system. Those in the Alliance planned to dismantle the American way of life one lawsuit at a time.

The client list included a group of ex-child molesters who claimed the fundamental right to marry teenage boys. If an atheist was offended by others saying "under God" in the Pledge of Allegiance in schools or public gatherings, the CLA would file suit claiming a violation of the atheist's constitutional rights. That America was founded on Christian principles and values was a historical fact conveniently forgotten. The American flag was also a frequent topic of CLA litigation. The Alliance would gladly stand behind some idiot who wanted to piss on the Stars and Stripes, smear it with horse manure and call it art, or dip it in gasoline and light it on fire. But a retired veteran who wanted to fly his flag in contravention of his condo association rules? Well hell's bells, the CLA wouldn't lift a finger to help him.

"Let the old man fend for himself," the CLA would scoff. "It's a free country."

The CLA depended on donations to fund its operations and considering the previous President had started the Alliance, the money from big city liberals had been flowing in at a steady pace. But once President Schumacher took office, the checks came rolling in from like-minded and angry left wingers intent on putting the new President in his place. They wanted to go back to the days where presidents apologized for America's misdeeds and promised to submit to the utopian ideals of the United Nations. Who is America to think it was better than anyone else? they ridiculed to all who would listen.

"Who is it?" Brennan barked into his phone. His secretary was not taken aback at his angry tone. It was not out of the ordinary.

"It's the House minority leader."

"All right. I'll take it."

Rosita Sanchez was just as angry with President Schumacher as Brennan. She was destined to be the Speaker of the House until it was discovered the former Democratic Speaker Catherine O'Shea had known about a plot to kill then-Representative Schumacher and didn't do anything about it. O'Shea was a classic East Coast liberal, a scion of a long line of Massachusetts political big shots who promised to take other people's money and spread the wealth around. During her rise to power, O'Shea brought her trusted lieutenants along with her, including the up-and-coming Sanchez. But Sanchez was not born into political power. She was raised in a dirt poor section of Los Angeles, where the law was laid down by the local gangs and drug lords. She managed to escape and worked her way through law school. She ran for Congress and won the election on the backs of the large Hispanic population in her district. After O'Shea was expelled from Congress, Sanchez had to get used to being in the minority party in the House. She routinely found reason to praise the CLA, especially its work on pushing for amnesty for illegal immigrants. She was also determined to get back the power that was destined for her. If she played her cards right, she thought she could be the next Speaker of the House. But her new roadblock was President Schumacher.

Before Brennan could even say hello, Sanchez was cursing the President. "He is *not* going to get away with this!" She was talking about the President's economic plan and the reduction in government welfare payments. She knew Brennan would be focused on the terrorist detainees but their like-minded hatred gave them an equal opportunity to vent their anger. "He is going down!"

"We're already on it. The petitions to stop the transfer of the detainees and the New York City trials will be delivered to the federal district court within the hour, Rosita."

"Good! I'm thinking about filing articles of impeachment right after that!"

Brennan gave a slight chuckle to Sanchez's anger. "Don't you think it's a little early for that?"

"I don't care. Some Democrat always files articles of impeachment when a Republican is in the Oval Office. It's like a rite of spring."

She was correct about that. One Michigan representative in Congress had been around long enough to vote or file articles of impeachment against every elected Republican back to Nixon. It was just something that Democrats did to pass the time considering they rarely had anything productive to add to the debate other than call for higher taxes and bigger government. President Schumacher was next on their hit list.

"We need to forge a two-pronged attack," she fumed. "You blanket the airwaves with the President's plan to violate the rights of the detainees and I'll make sure we hit him with everything we got on the economics issue. I'll call my union friends to get their signs and pickets and we'll put an all-out stranglehold on the President's message. Before you know it, he won't even think about running for a full term."

"I like it."

Sanchez let loose a calming exhale. She thought it was a brilliant plan. "The next election is ours!"

West Bend, Illinois

The FBI SWAT team was suiting up on the top floor of the parking garage at the West Bend Memorial Hospital. It was the best place in town to coordinate the plan as it was covered by a ceiling and no unauthorized personnel would know what the dark government vans were hiding upstairs. The target was a one-story residence near the trailer park on the east side of West Bend. Twenty agents in black BDUs and Level IV body armor were strapping Colt 1911 .45-caliber pistols to their thighs and loading their MP-5 submachine gun magazines to the brim. Two hulking agents stretched and twirled battering rams around like two-liter bottles of pop. They were the breachers and would be the first to hit the doors. Agent Crawford, less of a hulk but still six-two and two-forty, stashed the warrant in the zippered pocket of his vest. He would be the first to enter, and four more would be following right behind him. Each of the twenty agents had an assignment – some would be entering, some would be covering the rear, all would be ready. Their well-choreographed assault needed no practice run. Practice was for off-days and weekend drills.

It was game time.

Agent Marteno, himself fully loaded and attired, had taped a map of the residence and surrounding streets to the back window of an FBI van. His team of agents stood behind in silence, their eyes focused and the pulse steady.

He made one last call to his eye in the sky.

"Sierra One, do you have a visual?"

Sierra One was Special Agent D.A. "Duke" Schiffer, one of the FBI's most decorated marksmen. He was perched on top of a three story apartment building two hundred yards from the suspect house. The veteran sharpshooter was keeping close watch on the suspect through the high-powered scope of his Remington 700P .308 sniper rifle and providing up to the minute intel to those on the ground.

"The target is lying on the couch, facing east and watching TV," he reported, the pulled-back curtains providing a clear view of the interior of the residence.

A curious man, Agent Marteno had another question. "What's he watching?"

"The Price is Right."

The balaclava masks worn by the members of the SWAT team could not hide their smiles.

"Ten-four," Agent Marteno responded. "He's going to think he's watching an episode of Jerry Springer in about ten more minutes." He then turned to the map. "Team A will come in from the west on Pulaski Street. Team B will come in from the north on Broadway. The house is on a corner. It's a single story. There's a detached garage on the north side and an alley running along the east. Agent Burdette is keeping an eye on the rear of the residence while he pretends to change the tire of a rusted Ford Tempo. We're gonna hit the back door first then the front. It's a no-knock search warrant, so we're barreling on in."

One hulk spoke up. "How many subjects are we expecting?"

"Just one male inside at this time," Agent Marteno said before his shoulder-mounted walkie-talkie squawked to life. "Yeah, go ahead."

The scratchy voice on the other end came in clear enough for all to hear. "I've got the target female loading a gas can out at the station near the interstate, over."

"Ten-four. As I was saying, one male inside. We believe this woman will also be heading back to the residence. This is her third stop to fill gas cans in the last twenty minutes. As soon as she gets inside, we're going in."

"Agent Marteno," the voice on the walkie-talkie said, "she's heading in the direction of the suspect house. ETA five minutes."

"Okay, let's go," he told his team. He then gave the order over the walkie-talkie. "All units prepare for departure."

The two black Econoline vans packed with large armed men drove under the raised arm of the parking garage entrance and turned right. Two Suburbans followed closely behind. The lights were off and the sirens were silent. Two more vans were on their way from the West Bend police station. A police helicopter was hovering outside of town ready to swoop in when the entry was made to give those on the ground a bird's eye view if necessary.

"ETA two minutes."

Agent Marteno shifted in the front seat of the van and held up two fingers to those in the back. He then grabbed his walkie-talkie. "All right. Close the roads."

FBI agents and West Bend police officers proceeded to close off the intersections within three blocks of the suspect house and stopped all vehicle traffic. The woman drove the rusted Chevy truck into the alley on the east side of the house and then made a quick left onto a patch of gravel between the house and the garage. Surveillance teams saw her exit the vehicle and discard a cigarette before she opened the back door of the house and walked inside.

"Female suspect is inside," Agent Burdette announced, trading the tire iron for his concealed sidearm.

"Sierra One, is the price still right?" Marteno asked.

"Affirmative. Come on down."

"Teams A and B are clear to engage."

The doors to the van were open before the vehicles came to a complete stop. From his rooftop perch, Agent Schiffer had his crosshairs on the suspect's chest as the SWAT teams silently snaked their way toward the house. The shock and awe that was about to follow would be a matter of excited discussion amongst the neighbors for weeks to come. The toothless woman who lived next door would later tell reporters that she thought there had been a natural gas explosion. When she looked out the window, she claimed "all hell was breaking loose."

Team B's barrel-chested breacher busted down the back door at the same time the flash-bang grenade shook the house. Agent Schiffer could see the suspect raise his head up from the couch and look toward the kitchen wondering what in the hell was going on. Distracted by the commotion at the back door, the man didn't even see the second flash-bang grenade Team A rolled toward him. The blinding flash of light and concussion it brought with it caused the man to fly off the couch like a scared cat. That, along with the rolling thunder from five heavily armed men hurtling toward him, literally scared the shit out of him. He was quickly apprehended without resistance. The only casualties – the broken doors, the blown out living-room windows, and the suspect's pants, which took the brunt of his involuntary bowel movement.

Team B found the woman in the bathroom flushing something down the toilet with great determination. She too offered no resistance. The entire entry and apprehension took fifteen seconds.

The area outside the house was soon swarming with a tight phalanx of federal and state law-enforcement agencies. The police chopper broadcast the view from a thousand feet – the area below lined with yellow tape and surrounded by police cars, black and whites, unmarked, SUVs, the whole arsenal. A bomb disposal team came in with their robots and blast suits to check the truck and the garage for explosives. They found nothing but gas cans and flares, six each in the garage and four in the bed of the truck.

In their khaki pants and dark pullovers with FBI emblazoned on the back, agents were later observed carrying out a printer and a computer, along with evidence bags containing cell phones and a ream of paper. The house was a dump, and it was obvious to even the most junior of agents that the occupants were in the business of methamphetamine dealing. There were bags of pseudoephedrine pills on the table along with lithium batteries, coffee filters, rubber tubing, and enough Coleman fuel to make it through a month's worth of winter camping in the Alaskan wilderness. The woman, who had been hustled out the back, said she was forty but she looked twenty years older. Her eyes were hollow and her mouth showed a fine collection of rotten teeth and canker sores. Her brain was so fried she barely knew what was going on.

The man, identified as Benjamin Conrad, was handcuffed and taken to the police station. After Agent Marteno was able to get out of his tactical gear, he entered the interview room where the disheveled Conrad was sitting stone-faced in his chair. He still smelled like crap. A quick check of his criminal background indicated he had a conviction for methamphetamine manufacturing and delivery, possession of a controlled substance, and assault on his girlfriend. He had spent two years as a guest of the government in the Illinois Department of Corrections.

"I'm Special Agent Marteno, FBI," he said. He showed Conrad his badge and flipped open a yellow legal pad. "I'd like to ask you some questions about what has been going on the last couple of weeks."

Conrad nodded his head once. Marteno proceeded to read him his *Miranda* rights and had him initial the waiver form.

"I think you know what I want to talk about."

The smug look on Conrad's face indicated he wasn't afraid.

"Sandra's not involved in the meth production. She's just a user."

Marteno pulled his chair closer. "I'm not here to talk about the meth."

Conrad was well aware of that. The feds don't send in a small army of agents to raid a low-level meth house.

"I want to know about the bombings."

"I don't know anything about them."

Agent Marteno wasn't one to beat around the bush so he grabbed Conrad's attention with a few tidbits of evidence the investigators had collected. "The letter sent to the *Tribune* was printed off using the Epson printer you purchased at the Office Depot." He handed over the surveillance photo of Conrad buying the printer. Martino noticed Conrad's eyes widen at the sight. "Cell phone records indicate you made a call to Sandra shortly after each of the explosions. We've got you on the surveillance tape walking into the gas station and out the other side just before your truck exploded into a ball of fire. We also have you on tape telling Sandra to purchase gasoline so you can blow up the high school tonight. We've got twenty dead people out there, and you're in a hell of a lot of trouble, Mr. Conrad."

The man turned his steely gaze at Agent Marteno. "My name is not Conrad," he huffed. "It is Mohammed Islam."

Marteno sat back in his chair and took a breath. Great, one of these guys, he thought. "You've converted to Islam?"

"Yes."

"Who are you working with?"

"I work alone."

"Don't you bullshit me," Agent Marteno snapped.

"I tell you the truth. As a soldier of Allah, I am bringing jihad to America so that the citizens will know the true meaning of Islam."

"And your brand of Islam calls for the murder of innocent women and children?"

Conrad snickered. "It is simply collateral damage. Just like when American soldiers kill innocent civilians and claim they are fighting terrorism."

"That's where you're wrong, my friend. We are targeting terrorists who are trying to kill us and destroy our way of life. You are targeting innocent civilians to advance your sick and twisted agenda."

Conrad/Islam reared back his head and spit in Marteno's face. "You will die with the rest of the infidels! My brothers will make sure of that!"

Agent Marteno stood up and wiped the saliva running down his nose. It took a great deal of self-control to keep from slapping the sick and twisted idiot sitting before him. Two agents appeared at the door to take Conrad/Islam back to the cell. They cuffed him behind his back and put a surgical mask on his face. That way if he decided to hock a wet one he'd be spitting in his own face.

Agent Marteno huddled with the U.S. Attorney on the charges that were being drawn up and would be filed within the hour. He then made the call to Director Stubblefield to tell him the Midwestern terror scare was over.

The White House – Washington, D.C.

The warm spring air of the Nation's Capital provided a nice opportunity for President Schumacher to make his statement on the arrest of the terrorist suspect from the Rose Garden. Behind the President at the podium were Attorney General Claire M. Donovan and FBI Director Stubblefield. Neither one of them was smiling but they did have a great sense of relief about them.

The President stepped up behind the microphone above the presidential seal and read his statement. "This morning, agents with the Federal Bureau of Investigation arrested Benjamin Conrad in connection with the two bombings in West Bend, Illinois. I want to thank the hard work and dedication shown by the FBI, Director Stubblefield, and Special Agent Ruben Marteno, who headed up the Joint Terrorism Task Force. The matter will now be dealt with in a court of law, and I have full confidence in Attorney General Donovan and her team of lawyers at the Department of Justice. Also, I want to assure the American people that the fight against those who seek to harm our way of life will continue unabated. Thank you."

The questions came fast and furious as the President stepped back from the microphone on his way back to the Oval Office.

"Mr. President," a reporter shouted. "Now that the suspect has been apprehended, will you stop the transfer of detainees out of West Bend?"

The President stopped in his tracks. "No, the transfer will continue."

"What about the criminal trials in New York?"

Again another no from the President, taking a step back closer to the pool of reporters.

"The West Bend suspect is an American citizen and he will be afforded all the rights he is entitled to under the law. The terrorists have been captured on the battlefields and will be treated as the enemy combatants that they are. Thank you all."

CHAPTER 11

South Suburbs, Chicago, Illinois

Mac Carter called in as he was told and showed up at Hassani Enterprises right on schedule. Not knowing which construction site to go to, he walked into the main office and told the secretary he was waiting on his instructions from Mr. Hassani. The secretary seemed flustered, like she had been yelled at that morning. She politely told Carter to have a seat.

"Mr. Hassani might be a while."

With his thermos full of coffee and a brown bag containing a ham sandwich, a bag of chips, and an apple, Carter sat down in one of the plastic chairs in the outer office. He picked a homebuilding magazine from the nearby table and thumbed through the pages. He didn't read a word, but his ears were wide open. Even though Hassani was yelling in a combination of English and Arabic, it didn't take much straining to hear the anger behind the boss's door. What he was saying exactly wasn't entirely clear.

Hassani was on the phone with Sharif al-Rashad, who had taken up residence in D.C. and was now buried up to his armpits in legal work in the Supreme Court chambers of Justice Ali Hussein. Sharif had to close the door to his office, fearing Hassani's rants could be heard by the other clerks and the secretary in the Justice's outer office.

"Did you hear that bastard's speech the other night!?"

"Yes, I was in the chamber up in the gallery," al-Rashad whispered into the receiver. "I was only twenty feet from the First Lady."

"He's going to reopen Gitmo and force our brothers in front of a military tribunal! He must pay for his dastardly acts! We need jihad now more than ever!"

Sharif covered the phone with his hand. He just knew the others in the office could hear what he was hearing. While he agreed with everything Hassani was saying, he was in the initial stages of his dream job and feared he would be shown the door if someone spread the word.

"You must stop him, Sharif! You are part of the solution with your new job. You must convince your boss to put that Schumacher in his place! The Muslim brotherhood must not be treated like this!"

Sharif shuffled a stack of papers on his desk, trying to make some background noise to soften Hassani's angry words. He promised Hassani he would do his job. "I need to get to work, my friend," he said, not even wanting to say Hassani's name out loud. "I will do my best to work hard and I'll keep in touch."

Hassani slammed down the phone and hurled a cardboard tube full of blueprints across the room. The thud on the wall startled both the secretary and Carter sitting outside the office. The secretary didn't make eye contact with Carter but kept her focus on the phone. When she saw the light blink red on the base, she knew Hassani was making another call.

"It's going to be a little while longer," she whispered to Carter. He nodded that he understood and grabbed another magazine.

There were only fifteen seconds of silence until Hassani continued ranting into his phone. Carter had learned a little Arabic while in prison but it was difficult to catch what was being said with Hassani's profane Arabic slang. He was sure to have heard something about "that bastard Schumacher."

After ten minutes, Hassani had thrown all of the objects within arm's reach and the volume began to fall to a more reasonable level. He tried to control his breathing but it was difficult. President Schumacher's speech and his proposed treatment of those innocent soldiers for the cause reminded him of his beating at the hands of the police. The police had caught their suspect, their *white* suspect, and they dared to continue their war against Muslims. The President was bringing out America's baton to force the Muslim community to submit to the demands of Western Civilization. He was thumbing his nose at Islam and must pay for his transgressions. Hassani told himself he could not wait any longer. He was not willing to wait for Sharif to work his magic in the Supreme Court. If al-Rashad did come through, then all the better. But that would take time. Hassani had to implement his plan if he wanted to keep Schumacher from running for election during the upcoming campaign. The time had come. Let the floodgates be opened, he told the man on the other end.

"And let the blood flow."

Muddy Rock, Kansas

Juanita Dixon had searched for the Duncan residence for fifteen minutes, which included two harrowing turnarounds in a couple of still muddy farm fields. She was beginning to think Muddy Rock only had two citizens. The sign outside of the mostly abandoned town said "Population 10," but even that might have been in its heyday. There was an old broken down gas station that sold no gas, only cold sandwiches to farmers during the planting and harvesting seasons. Seeing an implement plowing the nearby field and a pair of rusted Fords out front of the station, Dixon stopped to ask for help. The bell atop the door announced her arrival, and she could not have looked more out of place.

Five overall clad locals stopped their meaningless chit-chat and looked at the woman. She was petite and nicely dressed in a pantsuit. She looked like a young executive and would have fit right in in the hustle and bustle of white-collar workers in downtown Chicago or St. Louis. She was definitely out of place in Muddy Rock, Kansas. The men around the counter didn't ask what she wanted. They just stared at her like some alien space invader.

"Could you direct me to the home of Binford Orville Duncan?"

The farmer behind the counter repositioned the tobacco in his lip and glared at her. None of them liked outsiders. "Who wants to know?" His inflection conveyed the sense that Dixon better have a good reason for her query.

"I'm Juanita Dixon," she started proudly, "and I work for the Census Bureau of the United States Government."

The five were not impressed. Flashing government credentials was frowned on in these parts. The locals liked their freedom, paid their taxes, and expected Uncle Sam to leave them alone. They didn't need any health care, welfare, or any other "-are," other than the kind they breathed and God provided. Their leathery faces indicated they spent most of their lives facing the winds of the Great Plains, their calloused hands showing years of tilling the Midwestern soil. They were old-timers with names, all proudly supplied at birth, like Butch and Bump and Bubba and Joe Billy.

"He lives alone," the large one grumbled, hoping the woman would get the hint. Mark it down and move on.

Her instructor had prepared her for this. Be assertive but polite. The Government was counting on her to do her job. She gave her memorized reply. “It’s important that we accurately count our fellow Kansans so we can receive our proper allotment of tax dollars. We don’t want to miss out on our fair share.”

“Let me tell you about our fair share, Missy,” the small one hissed. The patch on his chest indicated his name might have been Buckshot. Or maybe that’s what he sold for a living. He adjusted his soiled hat with the confederate flag that had faded over the years. There weren’t any racists in Muddy Rock and the Stars and Bars recognized the rebel in their blood not an affinity for slavery. They didn’t need slaves anyway. They had a pack of pickers named John Deere, Allis Chalmers, and Massey Ferguson.

“Our tax dollars never make it back here anyway! If those idiots in D.C. give some to Kansas, it gets wasted in those big city schools that don’t educate nobody. Then we got those damn illegals! The Government’s going to give them amnesty and make them Americans even though they broke the law and can’t speak English!” Buckshot’s face was growing redder by the minute. This could get ugly. “I’ll tell you what to tell your bosses, Missy.”

The big one slapped the ranting Buckshot on the arm. He didn’t want to hear any more of it. Buckshot’s short stature was accompanied by a high-plains bravado that even his friends found annoying.

“Take a right at the stop sign and go one mile north. It’s on the left.”

Dixon gave a nod of her head and politely thanked them for their time. Buckshot grumbled something about Washington and higher taxes but he eventually cooled down. The quintet’s mood lightened with the thought of hearing Duncan’s side of the story when the United States Government showed up on his property.

When she made it a mile north, Dixon didn’t have to guess the location of the Duncan residence. The big guy at the counter should have said look for the numerous “No Trespassing” signs adorning the fencing. It would probably be classified as a “compound” in some books. There would be no welcoming committee, and if the signs were to be trusted, the owner is ready, willing, and able to exercise his Second Amendment rights. Dixon nudged the Tempo beyond the rusty barbed wire fences and stopped far enough away from the snarling dogs tethered to the house that she felt safe. The American flag on the pole was whipping something fierce. A great Midwestern storm would soon be barreling down on Muddy Rock. The horizon was already flashing with light and the ground rumbling under foot. Dixon exited her car and straightened her blouse. She grabbed her questionnaire and notes and took a deep breath.

"I'm an employee of the United States Census Bureau," she whispered quietly with great courage. She thought of her two little boys and reminded herself that she was going to buy them some nice school clothes with her first paycheck. "You can do this, girl," her inner mind told her.

She stepped cautiously toward the house, Liberty and Justice yelping like mad in hopes of breaking their chains so they could maul the poor woman. The sign at the right of the front stoop warned that trespassers would be shot. To the left of the stoop, a makeshift tombstone with the letters "IRS" painted bloody red with "Rest in Hell" scrawled underneath. The wooden floorboards creaked in their old weathered state and Dixon took two gentle steps forward. Her mouth was dry and a drop of sweat was beginning to slide down her powdered cheek. She reached out her trembling hand to give a good knock.

She never saw the shadowy figure coming around the corner.

"Who the hell are you!?" the man bellowed with fully loaded shotgun aimed at the intruder.

Dixon screamed in horror, the papers she was carrying now falling to the porch. Her hands were as high as the Kansas sky.

"Who the fuck are you!?" It was louder and angrier than the first time.

"I'm a Census worker! I'm a Census worker! Please don't shoot!" she cried.

She turned her back to the door and watched with wide eyes as the man limped around to the front steps, gun aimed, finger on the trigger, and never taking his eyes off her. The snarling dogs begged their master to let them at her and tear her to pieces.

"What do you want?" he asked in a low growl. His jeans were muddy and his plaid shirt was showing its age. A few strands of his thinning gray hair blew in the wind. His nose, flattened by years of fighting in his youth, flared at the nostrils. His gnarled hands gripped the gun like they had been molded around the stock and barrel.

Dixon licked her dry lips. "Please, sir. I'm just a Census worker."

"I don't like government types on my property." He once chased off the county tax assessor with a pitchfork. Few came to see Duncan unless invited. In fact, Kansas had more tornadoes than he had visitors, and that's just the way he liked it.

"Are you Binford Orville Duncan?" Her voice was becoming weaker.

"Don't nobody ever call me that anymore."

Dixon bent down and picked up her questionnaire, not once taking her eyes off the nut with the gun. "Please, I just need to record how many people live at this address."

"Why?"

"That's my job. It's for the Census."

Duncan lowered the gun to his waist. It was still pointed at her though. His right index finger still on the trigger.

Dixon remembered her instructions. Her sweet voice perked up. "The Constitution calls for a Census every ten years."

"I know damn well what the Constitution calls for. There is only one lawful American at this address. And that's all you need to know."

Dixon nodded in agreement. She wasn't going to argue, and if her boss at the Census Bureau didn't like it he could come out there and take it up with Duncan himself. She decided to wait until she got back in the car; no, until she got back to Wichita to mark the Duncan address as having one occupant. She shuffled cautiously between Duncan and the attack dogs and got in her car. She backed out of the drive as Duncan watched her all the way. She then floored it to get the hell out of Muddy Rock.

The rumbling thunder grew louder by the minute.

CHAPTER 12

E. Barrett Prettyman United States Courthouse – Washington, D.C.

Whether Sharif al-Rashad would have a part in stopping the trials depended on what happened in the courtroom of U.S. District Court Judge Warren D. Barnhart. When the President entered the executive order removing the case from the federal court in New York City to the Nation's Capital, the D.C. legal eagles went to work to prosecute and defend the case. A decision in this court would most assuredly wind its way up Constitution Avenue and make the short drive south to One First Street – home of the United States Supreme Court.

After 9/11, Congress gave the President the authority to "use all necessary and appropriate force against those nations, organizations, or persons" who committed or aided the attack on that fateful Tuesday in September. During President Fisher's Administration, Congress passed a law establishing the military commissions for the trials of enemy combatants who were detained at Guantanamo Bay. President Fisher, however, buckled under the protests of civil-rights watchdogs and not only moved the detainees out of Gitmo but into civilian criminal courts. Now that the detainees were being rounded up for a return trip to Cuba, the CLA was determined to put a stop to it with its multi-count civil suit.

Brennan and his team of CLA lawyers showed up outside the courthouse with great fanfare. Each carried oversized black briefcases stuffed to the gills with motions and filings under which they intended to bury the government's lawyers. Brennan led the charge through the sea of reporters and their microphones.

The team of government lawyers was equally impressive – two assistant attorneys general, the U.S. Attorney for the District of Columbia, and three assistant U.S. attorneys. Their briefcases were likewise stuffed with the law they believed they had on their side. They, however, entered the courthouse through the rear entrance, leaving the strutting and preening to the defense lawyers.

U.S. District Judge Barnhart entered the courtroom at precisely 10 a.m. He was a stickler for promptness and ran his courtroom like a well-oiled machine. Having been around D.C. federal court since the Reagan Administration, he was not overwhelmed by being in the spotlight. He had once presided over the trial of a terrorist who tried to blow up the Capitol. The man was found guilty, and Judge Barnhart sentenced him to life in prison. A CIA mole who was put on trial for espionage provided Judge Barnhart with the greatest amount of intrigue, what with the participants ranging from the Russian mafia, Israeli counter-terrorism operatives, as well the Secretary of Defense and his alleged dominatrix of a mistress. The sketched face of Judge Barnhart made it on the nightly news practically every day during that case.

The benches of the courtroom were packed with media types from around the world – *The U.K. Telegraph*, *Agence France-Presse*, along with *al-Arabia* and *al-Jazeera* television. The alleged terrorists sat at the front defense table with Brennan while the rest of his legal team was relegated to a temporary table behind them. Abullah and Mohammed, dressed in orange prison jump suits, had their hands cuffed at the waist and their feet shackled and secured to an eye bolt in the floor.

"Cause comes for hearing now on *Abullah, et al. v. Anthony J. Schumacher, President of the United States*, number 18-0119," Judge Barnhart announced. "For the petitioners, lead counsel Mr. Arthur J. Brennan. For the United States, lead counsel Deputy Attorney General John W. Darnall. Counsel, are we ready to proceed?"

Both attorneys stood and indicated in the affirmative.

"Mr. Brennan," Judge Barnhart said, looking down with disdain from his perch. "I see you have filed a flurry of last minute motions much to my chagrin."

U.S. District Court judges are known in legal circles as the bad asses of the federal judiciary. Down in the trenches as opposed to their robed brethren in the appellate courts, they come face to face with some of the most vile criminals brought to trial in the United States – drug lords, not simple high-school dope heads; turncoat spies, not Peeping Toms; and billion-dollar Ponzi schemers, not mere petty thieves. With a lifetime appointment, they are not afraid to piss off someone who doesn't follow the rules. Some come off as cocky, others employ a more friendly directness. But all of them are in control of their courtroom.

"Your Honor," Brennan said as he stood. "I faxed copies to the Attorney General's office last night."

Judge Barnhart's icy glare was noticeable by all in the courtroom. "Did you happen to fax a copy to my office so I wouldn't have to read this at the last minute?" He picked up the stack of papers on the bench and plopped them down again.

"Sorry, your Honor."

Judge Barnhart sighed his discontent. "First up today is Mr. Brennan's motion to stay the removal of the petitioners' cases to the military tribunals at Guantanamo Bay. Mr. Brennan, you may proceed with your argument."

"Thank you, your Honor."

Brennan rose from counsel's table and placed his yellow legal pad on the lectern in the middle of the courtroom. Some people have a fear of public speaking. An old trick used by many is to look out into the audience and imagine those looking back as wearing nothing but their underwear. It is supposed to relax the speaker and calm his nerves. But Brennan was not in the mood to be calm. He had worked himself into a frenzy earlier that morning just by thinking of that SOB down the street at 1600 Pennsylvania Avenue. No, Brennan didn't need to picture Judge Barnhart in his underwear. He just used the American flag behind the bench to light his fuse.

"Your Honor, the petitioners contend the military commissions that President Schumacher has just reinstituted are unconstitutional under the U.S. Constitution as well as illegal under the Geneva Conventions," he said, the blood in his veins slowly beginning to boil "The President of the United States is attempting to deprive these men, these innocent men, of their rights as human beings! And they deserve better than to be treated like a couple of mangy dogs!"

Judge Barnhart shot forward in this leather chair. "Mr. Brennan, there is no need to yell in this courtroom. I hear you just fine."

Brennan's chest moved up and down. He always felt his argument went better if he worked himself into a lather. "Your Honor, the President has no right to take these men out of the federal criminal courts!"

"Mr. Brennan, what about the President's authority as Commander-in-Chief of the United States military under Article II, Section 2 of the Constitution?"

"The President cannot prosecute these men in a military tribunal. Congress has not provided adequate procedures to protect their rights."

"Who am I, a federal judge, to tell the President of the United States how best to run the war? You will concede, Mr. Brennan, that the United States is a country at war?"

"Your Honor, it is an unjustifiable war! The President of the United States is the one who should be on trial!"

Judge Barnhart rapped his gavel on the bench. "Mr. Brennan, I am not going to put up with your theatrics. That might work in some other courtroom but not in mine. I have read your petition and the law is not on your side. Let me hear what Deputy Attorney General Darnall has to say."

Darnall said very little. He reiterated the long-held notion that the President is the Commander-in-Chief and has wide latitude in his prosecution of the war. Further, military tribunals had been used throughout American history and will provide the petitioners with the due-process rights they are entitled under the law as enemy combatants.

"Mr. Darnall, has the government's position changed at all in light of the arrest of the West Bend suspect?"

"No, your Honor. The President intends to proceed as stated."

Judge Barnhart had heard enough. He wasn't going to let Brennan yell and scream in rebuttal. "The petitioners' motion to stay the removal of their cases to the military tribunals in Guantanamo Bay is denied."

"This is bullshit," Brennan mumbled with disgust under his breath to his two clients. The court reporter's transcription would read "unintelligible."

But Judge Barnhart's ears worked just fine. "I will pretend I didn't hear that, Mr. Brennan."

Brennan nodded and mouthed the word "whatever."

Once outside the courthouse, Brennan readied himself to put on a show for the assembled media. Without cameras in federal courtrooms, it was difficult for his side to show their emotions with only a transcript or a reporter's notes offering a recitation of what happened. But once the cameras were rolling on the sidewalks, he went to work.

"What went on in the courtroom today was a national tragedy. The President of the United States and Judge Barnhart have done great damage to the Constitution." He then pulled out a copy of the Constitution, one of those fake parchment copies you can buy at museum gift shops. "This is what the President is doing to the Constitution." He then held the copy up and ripped a straight line down the middle in dramatic fashion. "The presumption of innocence, the right to a fair trial, the right to an attorney, the right to due process. All gone!"

With his face reddening, Brennan managed one last peroration on the day. "The President will not get away with this! King Anthony the First may think he rules this country with an iron fist, but the United States Constitution requires that he follow the law. His crimes will not go unpunished!"

Muddy Rock, Kansas

The good ol' boys around the counter at the gas station had finished up their lunches and were back in the fields massaging the dirt of America's breadbasket. The truck rumbling by the station was not out of place – the patches of rust, the caked on mud, the faded blue oval. It turned right at the stop sign and crept slowly north, the driver looking for the home of Bo Duncan. While the truck fit right in with the surroundings, the driver did not. He was Middle Eastern with dark hair and even darker eyes. The truck had been purchased on the cheap at a salvage yard in Kansas City. The plates were temporary and registered under the fake name of Rasoul Mularah, the part played today by the driver, who was also one of Hassani's most trusted lieutenants. He had known Hassani for over twenty years, first working for him in Chicago and then moving to head the construction firm when Hassani branched out into the St. Louis area. He started off driving a dump truck then moved on to dumping bodies of those who crossed Hassani. Like many in the construction business, he wasn't afraid to get his hands dirty.

The script had been written in haste but the overall ending to the story would not be complicated. Mularah was to purchase a truck in Kansas City. If anyone asked, tell them you are in the business of selling old clunkers to foreigners, he was told. Mexicans were always in need of cheap pickups to haul their wares here and there, and a profit could be made selling them if you're willing to put in the effort of getting them across the border. Don't tell them you're a farmer, the script went, and definitely don't say you're a hog farmer. Too many red flags. Mularah carried with him two sets of paperwork, one containing the documentation of the fictional business of Worldwide Cars, Inc. If stopped by a police officer, those were the documents to hand over and rely on.

Mularah pulled to a stop on the dusty road short of Duncan's driveway. He reached behind the seat and pulled out a leather folder. This contained the second set of documents, which were only to be used when meeting with Duncan. Mularah exited the truck, its engine still idling noisily in the rising heat of the day, and walked back to the rear bumper. He got down on one knee and felt the backside of the bumper, where he found the butt and barrel of a gun still attached. He kept it there in case the police stopped him, a quick search of his person or the interior of the vehicle would reveal nothing. A cop would be less likely to snoop around the bumper if the driver's story checked out. He grabbed the gun and walked back to the cab. He unscrewed the false bottom of his sixty-four-ounce Mountain Dew barrel and out dropped a silencer. Once in place, he secured the weapon in his back waistband. The final act of this drama was about to play out.

Mularah put the rumbling Ford into gear and chugged his way to Duncan's driveway and pulled in. After their quick nap, Liberty and Justice sprang to life and welcomed the intruder with a fierce round of salivating snarls and vicious growls. They hadn't experienced such exciting activity in years. Mularah shut off the engine and stepped out. He grabbed his leather folder and headed for the front door, keeping clear of the barking dogs. He gave a good hard knock on the door. There were no beads of sweat running down his forehead and he exhibited none of the nervousness Juanita Dixon had shown two hours earlier.

"Who the hell is it!?" came from a male voice unseen through the screen door.

"Census Bureau."

Duncan was at his computer watching his collection of cameras scanning the Mexican border. He had caught three more Mexicans last night, and he had discovered the illegals liked to come in groups. Some, the sacrificial lambs, would be sent forward to the border. If they made it across, the next wave would follow. If they got caught, those in the queue would hunker down until the authorities were distracted with processing their new catch. It was a waiting game that Duncan relished, like a fisherman waiting for that red-and-white bobber to sink below the surface so he could rear back and hook whatever was on the end of the line

"Who!?"

"Census Bureau!" Mularah said louder. He could hear a wooden chair being angrily pushed back from somewhere, its legs scratching the hardwood floor in disgust.

"I already told you idiots that I'm the only person who lives here!" The thumping footsteps grew louder until Binford Orville Duncan appeared in the flesh behind the screen. "And the government doesn't need to know how many damn toilets I have in here!"

"Sir, if I could ask you a few questions."

"I already talked to that black lady that came earlier!" Duncan's face was growing redder by the minute. The veins in his neck bulged with intensity. One of his fine collection of shotguns was leaning up against the wall to the left of the front door. It was fully loaded and well oiled, just in case Duncan needed to give someone or something another reason not to be on his private property.

"Are you Mr. Binford Duncan?"

Duncan angrily replied in the affirmative. He then told the Census taker that he had thirty seconds to leave his property or he was going to introduce him to the business end of his shotgun. Feigning shock, Mularah dropped the leather folder on the ground, a Census questionnaire flying out. When Duncan looked down, Mularah pulled the gun out of his waistband with his right hand. Duncan's last act on this earth was to glance left to his gun. In one seamless motion, Mularah fired one silent shot through the screen door and into the left side of Duncan's brain. Duncan fell backward to the floor, the thud of two-hundred-and-thirty pounds of flesh causing the barrel of the shotgun to fall to its right and land harmlessly at his feet. Out of Mularah's left pocket came a latex surgical glove. He looked around and saw no activity other than the dogs. With his covered left hand, he opened the screen door and then the right hand sent another bullet tearing through the right side of Duncan's brain. Mularah closed the door and picked up his leather folder and the two shell casings. He was not in a hurry because no one came out to these parts, and if anyone did, Mularah would just kill them too.

That's what Hassani had trained him to do.

He pulled out the cell phone off his right hip and made the call. The person on the other end was expecting him and picked up on the first ring.

"The gate is open."

He said nothing else. He clicked off the phone and lit a cigarette. He looked out across the flat prairie and saw nothing but dirt fields and blue sky. He liked the peaceful landscape. It reminded him of the desert back home minus the sand. The silence, however, would be unimaginable to city dwellers. Nothing but the wind and a few cardinals singing in the trees.

The mailbox next to the door was stuffed with that day's bounty from the Postal Service. Wanting to know what someone like Duncan received through the mail, he opened the box and thumbed through the letters and magazines – a fundraising letter from the NRA, a copy of *Field & Stream*.

The return address on one letter caught his eye though. It read:

The White House
1600 Pennsylvania Ave.
Washington, D.C. 20500

Mularah couldn't resist the temptation. He slid his finger under the lip of the envelope. A screeching hawk startled him slightly. He glanced back inside the house to make sure Duncan's lifeless body was right where he left him. It was, and the flies wouldn't be too far behind. Mularah opened the letter and read it to himself.

Mr. Duncan,

Thanks so much for writing me about immigration reform. Your thoughts are welcome, and they will be considered carefully. I am committed to making sure America's borders are secure. I appreciate your interest in this issue. Please do not hesitate to contact me again in the future.

Sincerely,
Anthony J. Schumacher
President of the United States

It was a standard reply, something the President could send out to everyone who took the time to complain about illegal immigration. The signature was fake too, most likely a preprinted form or an autopen that Presidents utilize to sign the millions of letters that go out of the White House on a yearly basis. Mularah smiled at the letter. He folded it neatly and placed it with his documents. He wanted to keep it and present it to Hassani as a souvenir.

As he walked back to his truck, he thought about putting a bullet in the brains of Liberty and Justice, both of whose necks were starting to strain as only their chains held them back. Mularah thought better of it. If someone did drive by, they might notice the motionless dogs and wonder what was going on. If they saw two angry German shepherds prowling the grounds, they'd keep right on going. Given Duncan's reclusiveness and uninviting nature, it could be days before anyone inquired as to his whereabouts.

Mularah entered his truck and turned the key. The Ford rumbled to life and he backed it out of the driveway. Over the barking dogs, the faint sound of a buzzer could be heard. That could only mean one thing.

The ghosts were on their way north.

CHAPTER 13

U.S./Mexican Border – Nogales, Arizona

The man with the cell phone to his ear went by the name of Juan. Nobody knew his last name and few asked. The only people who sought out Juan were those looking to bury a corpse or ferry illegal goods or immigrants into the United States. His pockmarked face showed the strain of living years in the criminal underworld of Mexico's northern desert. When he was sixteen years old, Juan involuntarily became a part of the infamous Sonoran drug cartel after his father, the owner of a chain of grocery stores in northern and eastern Mexico, was kidnapped and held for ransom. When Juan's mother paid the million-dollar bounty, the cartel leaders shot his father and then killed his mother. The cartel decided that Juan, with his athletic build and no where else to go, would be of service to them. If it didn't work out, they'd just kill him like they did his parents.

After four years of involuntary servitude, which entailed running drugs, burying dead bodies in the desert, luring Mexican police into back-alley death traps, and even overseeing the cartel's cockfighting operation, Juan's Stockholm syndrome began to take over. The men who killed his parents became his new family and their way of life became his. The cartel treated him well, and the more he succeeded the higher up he climbed in the chain of command.

Now forty two, Juan had become the Sonoran drug cartel's chief transportation officer. For the right price, he would coordinate the transport of marijuana and cocaine through various border crossings under his control, at least on the Mexican side. He knew by heart every dirt trail, mountain lookout, and river crossing within two hundred miles of Nogales. He had at one time or another experimented with every known mode of transport he could think of. He had cartel laborers burrow a tunnel underneath the border, he used planes and ultralights to drop bundles of drugs in the deserted lands of southern Arizona, trucks, ATVs, horses, whatever it took. His much talked about late-night escape on horseback from the American federales and the bullets whistling by his head earned him the nickname "El Caballo de la Noche" – the Night Horse. Tried and true Mexicans, some of whom revered their local drug lords as much as Americans love their sports heroes, sang folk songs about "El Caballo's Midnight Ride."

Herding illegal immigrants through the various crossings proved to be a lucrative and relatively simple business for Juan and his cartel. The price of admission was high, but the immigrants were more than willing to pay the steep fare in light of El Caballo's success rate. Moreover, pushing human beings across the border proved to be less problematic than the occasional drug runs into the U.S. Most Americans didn't like the large amounts of Mexican marijuana and cocaine showing up on their streets and in their children's schools. Law and order types on the left and the right sought to crack down on the importation of the poison into their communities. But the immigrants were a different story. While the conservatives wanted strict controls on immigration, the liberals welcomed the illegal aliens, or as they were known in the politically correct world, undocumented workers, with open arms. To the liberals, illegal immigrants meant poor workers who would be in desperate need of government assistance. With Democrat promises of free handouts, the immigrants, once they received their amnesty and became full-blown American citizens, would then become proud supporters of the Democratic Party. Juan sometimes wondered why the DNC didn't just send a bus down to pick up the illegals and then welcome them to the United States.

Juan, however, had no love for America. He viewed the intrusive hand of Uncle Sam as a threat to his way of making a living. He lived a life of lawlessness, and didn't take kindly to rules and regulations from the authorities. Plus, recent events on the American side of the border had made business a lot tougher. That upstart Border Brigade and their infrared cameras gave Juan a headache and cut into the cartel's profit margin. Juan could usually count on lax enforcement from the Border Patrol, mostly because the lack of funding from Washington prevented having eyes and ears at every mile stretch of the border. Once the officers moved on down the road on their patrols, Juan could send the packages or immigrants northward. But the Brigade member's phone calls to the Border Patrol acted like a giant spotlight that shined twenty-four hours a day, seven days a week. To get his business back on track, he needed to find a way to blind those watching the cameras.

Enter Abdullah Hassani.

With his expertise in transportation known by many in the less than upright business world, Juan caught Hassani's eye, who at times went searching for cheap labor and black market goods. They became fast friends. Hassani could call Juan on a moment's notice and the latter almost always delivered on time and on budget. There were no contracts, no corporate lawyers, and little negotiations. Hassani would call with an order, Juan would quote a price, and Hassani would pay the bill once the goods were delivered. They had made hundreds of deals over the years.

But the last order even raised Juan's antennae.

The call came two months ago shortly after President Schumacher took office. Hassani had come to the conclusion that he must strike at America. Now was the time because the Schumacher Administration would push back hard against the terrorists and, Hassani thought, Muslims in general. Hassani wanted two rocket propelled grenades. Not a problem, Juan said. He didn't ask why Hassani wanted them. That was none of his business. It wouldn't be traced back to him anyway since there would be no paperwork. RPGs were easy to obtain too. The drug cartels were better armed than the Mexican police and military combined. The big weapons usually came up from South America – Columbia and Venezuela especially.

Hassani also wanted a smaller package. This would require a little more deft on Juan's part. Hassani wanted six vials of anthrax. Again, Juan did not ask why. But he did point out that such a request would come at a higher price than normal. Hassani said he would pay whatever it took. To see if Hassani was serious about the request, Juan asked him to pay five hundred thousand dollars up front and then another half million on delivery. Hassani agreed and made the deposit.

For Juan to get the anthrax, he put on his best suit and headed for a university in Mexico City. With a suit case full of cash, he visited an old friend in the research sciences department. Dr. Miguel Hernandez balked initially, saying the government tightly controlled the transport and use of hazardous materials and poisons. Too risky, he lamented. Never one to take no for an answer, Juan pointed out how Dr. Hernandez's life could be made more difficult if he couldn't make things happen. For Juan, the "encouragement" was second nature to him – just like mafia bosses threatening to fit the hesitant someone with a pair of cement shoes or a union thug bringing out the baseball bat to push that someone to "play ball."

Or else.

Juan then started throwing down pictures of Dr. Hernandez's family on the table and commented how beautiful the young children were. Dr. Hernandez was a family man and wanted to live out his retirement spoiling his grandchildren, and the shocked looked on his face indicated he was worried whether he would ever see those days if he didn't comply. He complained about his paltry pay from the university, and Juan was quick to open his suit case. Dr. Hernandez smiled and told Juan to meet him behind the research building at 6 p.m. At 6:15, Juan was on his way back north.

With the anthrax and RPGs ready to go, Juan wanted to make sure he got the delivery right. With such explosive cargo, in terms of the political and security ramifications if the items were discovered, Juan was not going to take any chances of discovery. If the Border Patrol picked up a smuggler with anthrax and RPGs hidden in the trunk of his car, the United States Government would close down every border to Mexico and make it next to impossible for Juan and his cartel to do business with fellow criminal comrades north of the border.

From his contacts in the United States, Juan readily knew the Nogales border crossing was under the ever watchful eye of Bo Duncan and his Border Brigade. Juan thought about taking out the surveillance cameras, but a blackout would only raise Duncan's suspicions in Muddy Rock. Along with the money, Juan told Hassani he would do the job only if Hassani silenced Bo Duncan for good. It would give Juan just the time he needed to make the delivery.

Hassani sent Mularah to do the deed and then pick up the goods. Once the job was done, Juan made his way north. The RPGs were strapped to the back of two ATVs that rumbled through the terrain. El Caballo hopped on his trusty steed – a Yamaha dirt bike – with the anthrax canister strapped around his midsection. If he spotted the Border Patrol, he could outrun them back across the border and live to smuggle another day. The packages were delivered to their intended recipient just west of Nogales in the Coronado National Forest, and Juan would soon be counting his vastly increasing wealth.

The White House – Washington, D.C.

The months of April and May had flown by. The President told Wiley to start thinking about kicking off the campaign for this year's election. The Democrats were in a state of disarray, fighting amongst themselves in hopes of taking back the White House. It would be a difficult campaign for any Democrat running against the popular President. But the libs thought they could portray the President as unprepared to lead or so trigger happy as to be a danger to the world. They thought they might bring out Daisy and her mushroom cloud and make people think Schumacher was just as dangerous as, if not more so than, Goldwater was portrayed to be back in '64.

For weeks, Wiley had been laying the groundwork for the announcement. Knowing this campaign could help cement his status as a great political strategist, he was working twenty hour days to make it happen. He was trying to cover all his bases, preparing talking points, setting up campaign offices in all fifty states, and preparing for the expected Democratic onslaught. He promised himself that there would be no October surprise to derail the campaign. Although he had a room across Lafayette Square at the Hay-Adams Hotel, he spent the last two weeks sequestered in the Lincoln Bedroom just down the hall from the First Family's quarters. Secret Service agents on the night watch reported they heard one man who appeared to be having a conversation into the wee hours of the morning. When asked about it, Wiley readily stated he was talking to Old Abe's ghost. What the Great Emancipator may have had to say, Wiley refused to divulge.

On the last Saturday in May, the President and Wiley met on the Truman Balcony overlooking the South Lawn of the White House. They had had a similar meeting on eight previous occasions when Wiley ran the President's two campaigns for Wabash County State's Attorney and six for the congressional elections. Campaigning in some of the reddest areas of a red state, the campaigns were decidedly conservative – pro-life, pro-gun, and pro-America. The Eighth Congressional District of Indiana comprised roughly 7,100 square miles. Now Wiley would be in charge of a campaign comprising more than 3.7 million square miles of territory. Sure there would be the hard-core conservatives in Texas, Oklahoma, and Utah that would be easy sells. But he wanted the President to appeal to everyone – from the rock-solid liberals in Boston and San Francisco to the middle-of-the-road moderates in Des Moines and Concord.

"I think we ought to continue with our responsibility theme from the State of the Union," Wiley said. The view from the balcony was one of the most beautiful in all of America – the Washington Monument and Jefferson Memorial looking sharp in the late evening May sunshine. There were no tourists lining the fence, courtesy of the Secret Service who kept the gawkers away from the fence when the President was on the balcony or strolling the South Lawn.

"I agree. We send the Vice President out to talk up smaller government and lower taxes. While she's doing that, I'll hit the national security issue."

"I'd really like to get Danielle and the kids out there too."

The President thought it over. He knew Danielle would be up to it, but he didn't want to put the kids on the public stage if they didn't want to. Plus, he always was concerned for their safety.

"You know, I hear Minority Leader Sanchez might be the front runner for the Democrats."

"She could make things interesting. I never really got along with her when I was in the House."

"No kidding," Wiley laughed. "You got her boss kicked out of Congress."

"Don't remind me."

"She can be really nasty if she wants. And it wouldn't help our cause any in reaching out to the Hispanic community."

"Well, we'll worry about that when we find out who's the nominee. Let's get the ball rolling and show people we can lead this country and run a campaign at the same time."

The next morning, President Schumacher exited the White House and strolled across the South Lawn to the waiting Marine One helicopter. He was right on schedule. A second chopper was already in place 575 miles west of Washington, D.C. Air Force One was being fueled for the day's destination. His nearly six months in office had exhausted him, his brown hair even showing some gray around the temples. He hadn't slept in his own bed in his own beloved house since he became the Leader of the Free World. But given that it was the Sunday of Memorial Day weekend, and considering the President hadn't missed a certain 500-mile race since Johncock beat Mears to the line in 1982, there was only one place penciled in to his itinerary.

The Indianapolis Motor Speedway – Speedway, Indiana

"Attention race fans," the announcer bellowed over the world's largest public address system. He had no time to practice because the powers-that-be hadn't written it into the schedule of events. Moreover, the Secret Service had only given the go-ahead just five minutes before. "We have a special treat in store for you today. For the first time in Speedway history," the voice boomed, echoing across the sprawling thousand acres and adding to the drama, "the pre-race flyover will be from a Boeing 747-200B from the 89th Airlift Wing out of Andrews Air Force Base near Camp Springs, Maryland."

With a growing murmur from the crowd and sounding like the voice of God, the track announcer timed it just right so the crowd's gaze turned to the north end of the course to witness the final approach of a gleaming Air Force One roaring over the grandstands at two-thousand feet, shaking the ground and rattling residential windows with its four massive General Electric CF6-80C2B1 turbofan engines.

After landing at the airport, President Schumacher ordered the pilot of Marine One to make a flying lap around the two-and-a-half mile oval. The three hundred thousand strong clapped, whistled, and hollered their approval, their vocal vibrations felt even in the belly of the chopper as the President waved to his fellow Hoosiers and race fans. Landing was precise in the infield. The seat in the Pagoda was waiting. Jim Nabors was taking the microphone. Ms. George was about to give the command to start engines. The green flag was about to fly.

And the President of the United States was back home again in Indiana.

CHAPTER 14

The home-state Hoosier adulation was not reciprocated in some parts of the U.S. or around the globe. The CIA was reporting increased chatter among its many channels in the Middle East. Terrorist groups in Yemen and Afghanistan had called for a new holy war against the United States to strike back against that "evil President Schumacher." The United States military had captured a band of Iranian fighters trying to smuggle arms across the desert of Iraq for transport to various terrorist outfits in the region.

At home, Mac Carter was technically walking the unemployment line. The construction boom had dropped off dramatically and, although there were signs of life in the economy, Hassani Enterprises had not been taking on any new projects. Carter reported to the FBI that Hassani had been in and out of the Chicago office on a more frequent basis. If Carter asked to speak with the boss, Hassani's secretary would always state he was too busy, talk to the foreman if you've got a problem.

With little construction work to do, Carter started attending the Illinois Center for Islam near Hassani's Chicago office on a daily basis. There he met a man who claimed he had been a member of the ISI, Pakistan's intelligence agency. The man was on a recruiting mission to bring new believers to Pakistan to undergo "religious training." The man told Carter that only men dedicated to the brotherhood would be accepted. When Carter expressed his interest, the man told him to get his passport in order.

Silver Creek, Indiana

Wiley's campaign kickoff was a master political stroke. An overflowing crowd surrounding the Silver Creek County Courthouse on a sun splashed Memorial Day Monday. Radio ads had saturated the airwaves extolling all who could make it to show up outside the courthouse plaza at high noon. Parents had the day off, kids were out of school, and veterans were out in full force planting American flags in the hands of every man, woman, and child. One radio ad told all those weary race fans in their campers and RVs to stick around an extra day and stop off in Silver Creek before heading back home. What the hell, they said. Another night of partying!

It was a lively bunch of revelers when President Schumacher took the stage to announce his plans to run for election. He was the first native Hoosier to become President, although the Kentuckian Lincoln spent his boyhood in Indiana before splitting rails and practicing law in Illinois and the Ohio-born Benjamin Harrison served Indiana in the U.S. Senate before becoming President. The latter currently rests in peace in Indianapolis. Being in his home state, and Indiana's red political history, President Schumacher did not shy away from offering his supporters some conservative red meat.

"My friends, there once was a man who occupied the Oval Office by the name of Clinton," the President said with sly smile.

The crowd hooted and hollered in mock outrage at the mere mention of a Democrat. And an impeached one at that!

The President held up his hands as if to calm the frothing masses. "He once said that 'The era of Big Government is over.'"

The crowd gave the quote a round of applause, as if to say to no one in particular, "See, we can be bipartisan too."

"Well, let me take that one step forward to say that not only is the era of Big Government over but it is never coming back!"

People were pumping their fists in jubilation. The Tea Party and the right wingers had the man they wanted leading the charge. Wiley was off the stage marking down which lines scored the best political points. He would make sure to slip them in future speeches.

"The federal government has far too often let us down, bogged us down, and kept us down. But I assure you I will do my best to get the government's bureaucratic boot off the necks of the American people and let the people decide how to run their lives."

The liberal media in attendance were borderline apoplectic. Some of the Big Three news anchors could be seen shaking their heads in disgust. They knew that come the next evening news broadcast they would have to hit back hard with the talking points faxed over to them by the Democratic National Committee. Their live Twitter feeds ran out of room deriding the President for being too right wing and out of touch with mainstream America.

But the crowd surrounding the courthouse wanted none of the media spin.

"I have been in and around Washington for almost fifteen years. The capital can change the way people think and how they look at everyday life. But I can promise you that my political beliefs have not changed and they have no expiration date. I am still the same person who was your neighbor here in Silver Creek. And I will not change when I take the oath of office in January. Daniel Webster once said 'I was born an American; I will live an American; and I shall die an American.' I wholeheartedly agree with that statement. But let me add a slightly different version for you here today. My fellow Americans, I was born a conservative, I will live a conservative, and I shall die a conservative!"

The gauntlet had been thrown down. The American people knew what they were going to get if they elected Anthony J. Schumacher. Whether the Democratic opponent could derail the conservative juggernaut, time would only tell.

"Before I close I want to recognize and thank a few people on stage with us. You'll be seeing a lot of them on the campaign trail over the next several months and I hope you'll give them your full support."

The President's mere mention of his beloved Danielle brought a great cheer from her hometown admirers. Many of the young adults had been students in her third grade class at Silver Creek Elementary. She smiled and waved. Her flowing blonde hair, red dress, and youthful beauty caused more than one commentator to gush that she may be the most beautiful First Lady in history.

The Schumacher children were on the red-white-and-blue stage, along with their first grandchild, Ashley's son, Aaron Joshua, a third generation A.J. The President continued on down the line with Vice President Jackson, both Indiana Senators, the Governor, Congressman Totten, the Mayor, and the Sheriff.

"I want to make sure I don't forget Floyd Revson."

Revson was west/central Indiana's donut king with shops in Terre Haute, Covington, Crawfordsville, and Silver Creek. He was also the former boss of the current President of the United States when the latter worked at the Donut Palace during his high school and college years. Revson's business acumen provided the President with great insight on the trials and tribulations of small-business owners. And considering small businesses employed a majority of the people in the U.S., the

President always took seriously the concerns Revson and other business owners brought to him. Plus, Revson always provided donuts and coffee at the campaign stops. Hungry staffers, volunteers, and Schumacher supporters loved the man.

With his finger pointing down to the end of the stage, the President gave the crowd what they wanted.

"Floyd's promising every customer a free glazed yeast donut if we win the campaign!"

Slightly startled, a wide-eyed Revson smiled and started running the numbers in his head. Then, figuring it would be good for business if he became known as the unofficial donut supplier to the President of the United States, he cupped his hands together and yelled something unheard by the cheering crowd.

"What's that, Floyd?"

Revson held up two fingers. The President did the same.

"Two if it's a landslide!"

The President's right fist shot into the air to the delight of the supporters, their miniature American flags waving back and forth.

"Who's hungry for victory!?"

North Scottsdale, Arizona

The dry desert of Scottsdale was beginning to bake in the early June heat. The snow birds had flown their Phoenix, Scottsdale, and Tempe coops to return to the more seasonable weather back where they spent the other nine months of the year. The wealthy retirees got in their rounds of golf well before 10 a.m. and spent the rest of the day visiting the air conditioned art museums and ice cream shops. Transplanted athletes from the NBA and the NFL tooled around town in their Bentleys, Aston Martins, and Lamborghinis that they had plopped down big bucks for at the local high-end Penske auto dealership. The area in and around Camelback Mountain was growing as fast as construction workers could put up the houses and hotels. Despite the intense heat, tourists flocked to the Phoenix area on their way to Las Vegas or on their way back from the Grand Canyon. It was not surprising to see any and all nationalities coming into Sky Harbor Airport – on business or for pleasure.

Rasoul Mularah had made his way west from Muddy Rock after pumping hot lead into Bo Duncan's brain. After El Caballo made the delivery, Mularah was detailed to get the goods back to Hassani at the South Chicago headquarters. Mularah and Hassani had thought long and hard about the transportation of the RPGs and anthrax. A passenger truck would not offer much privacy in the bed. Mularah would look out of place in an RV. A moving truck was an easy possibility but it may be prone to police suspicion. Where was he going? What do you have in the back? Do you mind if we take a look? An on-the-ball officer would certainly be suspicious if Mularah refused or appeared to be nervous.

But Mularah had a brain storm on his way south through Phoenix to pick up the goods. It was all around him, like a giant hand waving at him and enticing him to take a closer look. He did and liked what he saw.

The saguaro.

The saguaro littered the desert landscape like the oaks and maples of the Midwest or the high palms of Southern California. The white waxy blossom of the *cereus giganteus* won the honor as Arizona's state flower. The saguaro cacti, as emblematic of Arizona as the red rocks and the great canyon, were everywhere and of every size – two arms, three arms, prickly outer skin. And they were much in demand. It's a felony to steal one off another's land or state property. The state has even set up a hotline for people to call if they see their native plants being removed illegally. Those who were willing to part with their own saguaro made a small fortune in selling them. Ritzy hotels bought them for their landscaped pool areas. Saudi princes had even been known to fly them on private jets to plant them in their million-dollar backyards.

And Abdullah Hassani decided the new climate-controlled, mega-outdoors store in Chicago needed two for its hiking display. The paperwork was drawn up – two large saguaros to be purchased from a saguaro farmer north of Scottsdale and rush delivered via flatbed truck to Chicago. But these saguaros would never stand tall again to be admired by those looking for their Columbia jackets and Rockport hiking boots. The plan was risky, but only officials knowledgeable in the removal and transplantation of saguaros would raise an eyebrow. If a state trooper pulled Mularah over in eastern Colorado, odds are he wouldn't know that the saguaros had little chance of surviving the trip.

Mularah picked out the two largest he could find and the workers used their tree digging equipment to shovel beneath the root line. With a couple of rubber straps and a hoist, the cargo was carefully placed on the flatbed. With all the necessary permits, native plant tags, and seals,

Mularah drove the truck to a storage facility unit that he had purchased in cash and under a fake name. The facility was brand new and no doubt filled with the belongings of fresh retirees who could not fit their possessions into their condos and bungalows. The RPGs and anthrax were on the floor in their boxes labeled "dishes" and "books" and covered with a tarp. It was a risky gamble that someone, maybe the owner, would snoop around to see what Mularah was storing inside. Drugs? A dead body? But he had to hide the goods somehow.

After placing the RPGs and anthrax in the unit, he bought two bags of flour and layered the floor with the contents. It was the poor man's security system. Just in case someone picked the lock to look under the tarp, the flour would give them away.

Upon his return with the saguaros, the flour was undisturbed – no footprints, not even from a mouse. He backed the rear of the flatbed into the shadows of the unit and went to work. Out came the chain saw and in quick fashion he sliced off the root end of each twenty-inch round cactus. He then hollowed out the middle like a shady major leaguer corking his Louisville Slugger. The plastic wrapped RPGs were placed in separate saguaros and he had enough room to fit the anthrax near the bottom of one. He jammed nails into the end of each and rammed the chopped off end back into place. He threw two tubes of sand around the bottom of the stumps and concluded that none would be the wiser. Nobody looks at the stumps anyway.

In less than four hours, a perspiring Mularah was back on the road. He drove north out of Scottsdale, got lost and turned around, and then got lost again. The air conditioner in the flatbed stopped working shortly thereafter. He wasn't going to risk asking a cop for directions so he pulled into the nearest establishment he could find.

The Buffalo Chip Saloon.

At four-thirty in the afternoon, the saloon parking lot was surprisingly full for a Monday with a large collection of Harleys and Fords. The outside of the place looked like a remnant of the Wild West – minus the horses tied to the wooden posts out front. Inside, waitresses brought the patrons their bottles of beer and buckets full of peanuts – the shells of which were expected to be thrown on the floor. The ringing iron triangle signaled to someone that more red meat had been prepared and was ready to be chowed down on. Hungry vegans usually moseyed on down the road from this joint. There wasn't any tofu on the menu.

A sweat-drenched Mularah peered inside the dark establishment. The music was at a reasonable level, and ESPN ran silently on the TVs attached to the walls. No doubt this place could get rocking when the down-home country types made their way up north from the city looking for a good time. Mularah was almost afraid to walk in, like the place might be full of bikers with bad attitudes or cowboys with burrs under their saddles. His Middle Eastern look wasn't that out of place considering the large population of Hispanics in the area. People probably wouldn't even think twice. He took a step closer to the door before stopping at the sight of a couple heading out the door. They didn't look like locals. Definitely tourists. They saw his concern.

"Go on in," the man said. "They don't bite. Plus, the food's good too."

Mularah entered and quickly found the waitress at the register. "I'm lost. Could you tell me how to get to Interstate 17?"

"Sure," the lady said. She had another bucket of peanuts ready for table five. "Get back on this road and take a right at the stop sign. That'll take you back to Scottsdale where you can catch Interstate 10. Follow it west until you hit 17."

Mularah nodded and looked around. Nobody seemed to be watching him. A quick thank you and he was out the door. As he hurried to his truck, he looked at his watch. He was already behind schedule and that worried him. Hassani was not a man who people kept waiting.

What Mularah saw next nearly stopped his heart. Five men were standing around the flatbed and inspecting the cargo. He thought about running. They hadn't seen him yet. Maybe he could head back into the saloon and ask the waitress to call him a cab. If they even had cabs in these parts. He hid behind the cab of a Ford and peered through its back and front windshields. The men were dressed in dirty jeans and short-sleeve button downs. They looked like they had been out rolling around in the desert dirt. They had to be locals. They couldn't be cops, Mularah thought. Unless they were undercover in which case they were doing a darn fine job of concealing their profession.

Mularah wanted to get the hell out of there. He had killed his fair share of men in his life, but Hassani told him to travel without his gun in case he got stopped by the police. He was now regretting that decision. He decided to just take the chance that the men were simply admiring the saguaros. Just act cool, he told himself. Be friendly. Upon approaching the flatbed, he read the name on the shirt of the man imploring the group to get inside so they could get something to eat.

The tag read Buckshot.

It was none other than Muddy Rock, Kansas' Buckshot Barnes himself. And right along with him were Butch, and Bump, and Bubba, and Joe Billy, too.

"She's a beaut', isn't she?" Mularah said, pointing to the saguaro closest to Butch.

"She sure is. They're a lot bigger than we thought."

"Gotta take these two to Chicago."

"Well, I'll be."

The men stood and marveled at the cacti some more. The native plants they were accustomed to were usually harvested with a combine.

"Where ya'll from?" Mularah gave the "ya'll" as much drawl as he could.

"Kansas," Butch said.

Mularah flinched slightly, his eyes focusing squarely on Butch. He had just come from Kansas. Lived there part of the year. "Never been there," he said. It sounded believable.

"You're not missing out on much," Buckshot huffed.

The Muddy Rock boys had just spent the day in downtown Phoenix where a pro-immigration rally was held so a pack of liberal activists could yell and swear at the Maricopa County sheriff and his crackdown on illegal immigration. Butch and the gang, all members of Bo Duncan's Border Brigade, made the trip in two pickups to protest the protesters and offer their support to the sheriff. The trip had been on the schedule for some time. Bo was really looking forward to it so they could raise some old-fashioned American hell. Unfortunately, he couldn't make it. Buckshot found him two days after he was killed.

The group was tired and a little cranky – Bubba and Bump especially. But that was to be expected since they had to ride halfway across the country with Buckshot jabbering away in the extended cab. A good western meal would perk up their spirits though. Then they could discuss the more solemn duty they had planned. Tomorrow, they would take Bo's ashes and spread them out over the Grand Canyon – one of Bo's favorite American treasures.

Unable to control his hunger pangs, Buckshot kept prodding them to move inside. "Come on, let's go."

“Well guys, I better hit the road,” Mularah said, heading to the driver’s side of the flatbed.

“All right,” Butch said. “Take ‘er easy.”

The urn carrying Bo’s remains was sitting just over Mularah’s left shoulder in the cab of Butch’s Ford. They all took a last look at the man and his saguaros.

And none of them knew that Bo Duncan’s killer was standing right in front of them.

CHAPTER 15

The Dwight D. Eisenhower Presidential Library and Museum – Abilene, Kansas

President Schumacher exited his armored limousine outside the Eisenhower Presidential Library and Museum on a sun-splashed June 6th Friday morning. It was eerily quiet, the only sounds heard were the footsteps on the steamy asphalt and the idling engines of the government's fine collection of bulletproof Cadillacs and Suburbans. The Secret Service had cleared the rear entrance of all nonessential foot traffic and the protective cordon around this President seemed to get bigger and bigger.

The President of the United States receives threats everyday – by mail, phone, the Internet, and even a few nuts who walk right up to the gates of the White House and proudly announce their intention to the nearest uniformed guard. Every threat to every President is taken seriously by the Secret Service, which does not want to lose another protectee. Agents took JFK's assassination hard, and the attempt on Reagan gave them another wake-up call that they had to be right 100% of the time.

With President Schumacher, the Secret Service stepped up its game. He had already survived one assassination attempt as Vice President and the higher-ups in the Secret Service pulled out all the stops to make sure America's new leader was protected. Thus, the usual eight-man team surrounding the President became sixteen. Onlookers lucky enough to get within twenty yards of the President could barely see him through all the suits. The counter assault team looked meaner than usual, their bulging biceps and automatic weapons on full display. Long lines and magnetometers greeted all visitors with bar-coded tickets to events. Local media outlets would tell those going to see the President to arrive early at the venue and refrain from taking backpacks, large purses, and umbrellas. Bottles of liquid were confiscated as well as all kinds of fruit – anything that could hide explosives or become a flying projectile at the

President's head was discarded. People who objected were politely told they could keep their items, but the only place they would see the President was at home on their television sets because they weren't getting in.

The event was billed as the President's tribute to all those Americans who served the country in World War II. Wiley wanted an open air event with a flag-draped backdrop and as many vets as he could find. Some in the media wondered why the President wasn't going to France. Was he snubbing the elitist French snobs? Some penned articles that failed to hide their dismay of being deprived of the chance at a short vacation in France. Don't worry, Wiley reassured, the President would go to the American Cemetery next year. After he won the election, the smiling chief of staff would say with a wink.

But this D-Day remembrance would be spent on American shores, in the heartland, and at the final resting place of the Supreme Commander of the Allied Expeditionary Forces during World War II and the 36th President of the United States. Two thousand people crowded the grounds of Dwight Eisenhower's Presidential Library to wave their flags and cheer the current President of the United States. Some in the audience had voted for Eisenhower and dusted off their "I Like Ike" buttons. Ever the political thinker, Wiley had "I Like Schu" buttons made, and the one vendor working the crowd and the other in the gift shop were doing a brisk business. When the President was announced, the crowd responded with great approval. Except two men scowling in the back.

Abdullah Hassani and Rasoul Mularah.

The two had snared tickets off e-Bay for fifty dollars a piece from an enterprising local who was looking to make a few bucks off some rich Republicans who just had to be there. Hassani had gone to the campaign kickoff in Silver Creek. His digital camera was filled with pictures of Secret Service agents, limousines, and snipers. He watched their movements and their steely-eyed gazes. He took notes on where he could go inside a secured event, what he could take in, and how to blend in. He wore an American flag cap and carried a Sharpie and a picture of the President.

"I'm hoping to get the President's autograph," he told the uniformed Secret Service agent after being told to empty his pockets.

"Good luck," the agent said. He really meant to say "fat chance of that happening."

After leaving Silver Creek, Hassani met Mularah at the Kansas City office after the bleary-eyed Mularah had driven straight through to make it back with his cacti load from Arizona. The RPGs and anthrax were carefully removed and stored. The cacti weren't so lucky. They met the business end of a wood chipper. After scoring the tickets, Hassani and Mularah had scoped out the grounds. They took pictures like tourists do and watched as the construction crew made the final preparations for the presidential stage.

Hassani was getting impatient. He wanted to act. They loaded the RPGs into a construction pickup and headed toward the museum. But their plans changed when they were diverted to the parking lot of the Abilene Municipal Airport some two miles away. From there, they and a load of sweaty and obnoxious Schumacher supporters were shuttled to the site in an overloaded trolley. The purses, backpacks, umbrellas, and RPGs were left behind. Hassani and Mularah decided they would use it as a training run.

"Thank you very much!" the President began over the cheers from the crowd.

He started off by thanking the young Boy Scout who had led the crowd in the Pledge of Allegiance and the Girl Scout who sang the Star-Spangled Banner. Next, the veterans were asked to stand to receive the thanks for their service. Some doffed their caps, others raised their canes. But when the Commander-in-Chief of the United States military gave them a salute in appreciation, all raised a snap salute in return.

"We come together today not just to honor one man who commanded the forces of the Normandy invasion back in 1944, but for all men who stormed the beaches in pursuit of tyranny, flew the planes into the mouth of evil, and pursued the armies of darkness to the greatest depths."

The President used no TelePrompTer, something he had not gotten used to during his short tenure in the Executive Branch. He and Wiley had written the speech during a day of relaxation in Silver Creek and it sounded good. Wiley was beaming offstage.

"On that fateful day, General Eisenhower spoke these words: 'Soldiers, Sailors, and Airmen of the Allied Expeditionary Force: You are about to embark upon a great crusade.' That you did. A crusade for freedom against those who sought to impose their will on the powerless. A crusade for good against those who brought evil to the lives of the innocent. A crusade for human dignity, and for life, and for liberty."

The liberal columnists the next day would report with disdain the President's use of the word "crusade" in the speech. Four times it was used, one left-leaning blogger would dutifully note. The political-correctness police would scoff at the insensitive remarks, derisively reminding the President that "crusade" was verboten in this day and age. Some would call for him to retract his remarks and apologize. It conjured up images of Christians on the warpath, something greatly frowned upon by the Left. Some radical Muslims might get offended!

And they were right about that.

And two who did take offense to the remarks were standing at the rear of the crowd. Mularah and Hassani glanced at each other when they heard "crusade" pulsate from the sound system. The hair on the back of their necks stood on end, their skin tingling in white hot rage. They knew it was intentional. No Democrat or fence-sitting moderate Republican would dare utter such a word. But this President was different, and they knew he meant to put "crusade" in his speech.

And they were right about that.

"Today, my fellow Americans, we are confronted by a power as evil as Hitler's Nazis. Terrorists in every corner of this earth seek to destroy America and her founding ideals of freedom and liberty. Many of you in this crowd fought the fight so that we might live in that freedom. And it is up to this generation and future generations to continue the fight for all mankind."

Mularah couldn't stand much more of it. He kept pounding his right fist into his left palm. The words "son of a bitch" rolled off his lips much too loudly, drawing a stern rebuke from Hassani.

"Now is not the time!" Hassani whispered.

"He is declaring war on Muslims!" Mularah responded in Hassani's ear. The rage in his eyes bordered on maniacal.

"But now is not the time, you idiot," Hassani ordered right back. "Do you want to cause a scene?"

"He must die!"

The sweat forming on Hassani's brow was not a result of the mid-morning sun. He glanced around at the crowd to see if the two men had attracted more attention than they should have. If he wasn't careful, they would blow the operation before it even got off the ground.

"He will, but we must make sure we do it right."

Mularah relented for the time being. There wasn't much they could do anyway other than rush the stage. They would be patient and wait, he told himself.

"My fellow Americans, today I learned President Eisenhower's favorite motto was '*Sauviter in modo, fortiter in re,*' which because I didn't take Latin in high school was translated for me as meaning 'Gently in Manner – Strongly in Deed.' Let us commit ourselves to emulating that belief. Let us live our lives in loving kindness to our neighbors, whether they be black or brown, Muslim or Jewish, Democrat or Republican. But let us also be resolved to doing what is right for our God, our country, and our family. Thank you very much!"

Mularah and Hassani skipped the trolley ride to the airport parking lot and walked back. They needed time to think and figure out their plan of attack. While Mularah stewed in silence, Hassani kept repeating one phrase under his breath.

"He's a dead man."

Office of the Civil Liberties Alliance – Washington, D.C.

Art Brennan and his team of lawyers were finishing up their petition for writ of certiorari to the United States Supreme Court. Normally the appellate process would go to the Federal Court of Appeals for the D.C. Circuit, but Brennan took a shot at bypassing the intermediate level because of the "imperative public importance" of the case. Why waste time when everyone knows the case won't end until it's decided by the Supreme Court? There's no need to develop the case or the law, Brennan thought, so he went straight to the Highest Court in the Land.

The petition for certiorari ran on for forty pages and included an appendix of federal and foreign law that filled up another thirty. Review before the Supreme Court is not a matter of right. One must petition for the right to appear and argue a case before the nine justices. And the reason for review had better be compelling because the Court receives ten thousand petitions a year and typically grants review of only a hundred or less.

"Art, it's Rosita Sanchez."

Brennan leaned back in his chair, his work on the petition now done. "Congresswoman, how are you?"

"I'm good."

"We just sent forty copies of the petition for writ of certiorari via courier to the Supreme Court. It won't be long now."

"Are you sure they'll take the case?"

"I'm positive."

Whether the Supreme Court decides to hear a case depends on the so-called Rule of Four. If four justices decide the merits of the case are worth hearing then it gets placed on the docket. The rule allows for a large minority of the Court to have their voices heard on which cases will be decided.

"The four liberals on the Court will vote to hear it," Brennan said, thinking of each justice as he tallied the numbers. "I'd even bet that the four conservatives would vote to hear it too so they could try and find a way to get five votes and rule in favor of the President."

"People on the Hill keep asking me for our odds on winning."

Brennan threw a cigar into his mouth. He had just spent the last week in the trenches firing up his troops as they searched for every case or law in their favor. He stopped short of declaring total victory just yet.

"We know we'll get the four liberals," he said. "It'll all come down to Justice O'Malley. He's the deciding swing vote. If we get him, we'll win."

"Wasn't he appointed by a Republican President?"

"Yes, but he has steadily come to his senses and moved to the Left over the last twenty years. Don't worry, we'll get him on our side."

Associate Justice Thomas P. O'Malley had been on the Supreme Court for twenty-five years. At eighty-eight years of age, he was the third oldest to serve on the Court, only looking up at Oliver Wendell Holmes, Jr., and John Paul Stevens, both of whom served after their ninetieth birthdays. He had been raised in an Irish-Catholic family in New York City just after the Great Depression. After serving his country in World War II, he worked his way up the judicial ladder – first in the U.S. District Court for the Southern District of New York and then on to the Second Circuit Court of Appeals. Although he was appointed by a Republican, it was a moderate Republican, and his old-school liberalism started showing up in his opinions shortly after he reached retirement age. Although he did not have the prestige of occupying the middle chair reserved for the Chief Justice, he sat to the immediate right. Plus, considering he was the crucial swing vote in most five-to-four decisions, some legal scholars called him the most powerful justice on the Supreme Court.

"What makes you so sure?"

"Trust me," Brennan said, beaming from ear to ear. "I play poker with him every Monday night."

"Really?" Sanchez was not aware of that juicy tidbit.

"Absolutely. Been doing it for the last ten years."

"So, you think we're in good shape."

"We are in great shape. And once the Court restores the constitutional rights of the detainees we are going to take the fight to President Schumacher. Come November, he won't know what hit him."

"I like the way you think."

"Congresswoman, I have a line of reporters ready to fuel the fire that President Schumacher is trampling on the rights of innocent men and perpetuating the belief of American arrogance throughout the world. We're going to put him in his place, and I would dare say that you should start measuring for drapes because you are going to be the next Speaker of the House when the Democrats take back Congress this fall."

CHAPTER 16

St. Louis, Missouri

Before heading back to Washington, the President wanted to make one last stop. Like many Americans enjoying the summer season, he wanted to take in a ball game and maybe enjoy some peanuts and Cracker Jack. Wiley was salivating over the photos of the President throwing out the first pitch that would surely follow. It had become a rite of passage going back to President Taft for the "First Fan" to show up at a ballpark and fire off a strike to salute the National Pastime. After a few calls, the game was put on the President's schedule.

Once word got out that the President was coming to the Gateway City, the Secret Service went right to work. The agents in the St. Louis field office were well-versed in the security plan, what with the city playing host to visits from Presidents and even His Holiness the Pope himself on prior occasions. Manhole covers were sealed shut, newspaper and postal boxes were carted away, flashing construction signs warned drivers that certain streets would be shut down from noon until thirty minutes after the final pitch. The not-so-subtle message was that if you didn't have business being anywhere near the ballpark, stay away.

But Hassani and Mularah had different plans. This was the time to strike. St. Louis was nothing like Washington, D.C., what with the surveillance cameras and agents from umpteen federal law-enforcement authorities walking the streets of the capital. St. Louis has a reputation for being populated by friendly citizens obsessed with their Cardinals. If you walked down the street with the "Birds on the Bat" across your chest and an "STL" covering your forehead, you were just as much family as blood relatives. Given the laid back lifestyle of the city, Hassani thought the Secret Service might also relax. And the RPGs would be the biggest surprise anyone could imagine.

The plan called for Hassani to head out to the airport with one RPG and await the President's arrival. If he had a clear shot of Air Force One at low altitude, the pilots might not have enough time to deploy their countermeasures or take evasive action. If security was too tight, Hassani would radio Mularah that the President was on the ground and headed toward the ballpark downtown. Mularah would then be waiting for the kill. Hassani left it up to him where to set up.

"Just get it done," he told Mularah.

Mularah drove his pickup truck underneath the shadow of the Arch at 8 a.m. The truck was only a year old, and Mularah spent a good deal of money making it look good. The chrome pipes sticking out of the truck's bed near the cab looked like they had been pulled off an 18-wheeler but they were just for show. He loved it when people gawked at the pipes as he sat at the stoplights.

He had thought about the plan all night and wanted to get a good spot in the public parking garage. The attendant on duty told him the cost was ten dollars, and Mularah's mood suddenly turned foul.

"What if I'm not going to the game?" he protested.

"Sorry, sir, it's ten bucks for everyone."

Mularah handed over the sawbuck and stomped on the gas. Up the spiral ramp he went until he reached the last floor beneath the roof. There were a few cars already up there, probably guests of the nearby hotels. Mularah then found what he was looking for – a spot facing west – with a nice view right into the stadium. He figured he would have two shots to get the President – once when he was on the mound for the first pitch and the next up in the press box when the President made the rounds of the TV and radio announcers.

He locked the truck and decided to look around. As he made his way down the stairs of the garage he saw a bomb-sniffing dog on floor two running its nose around all the cars. Mularah thought now would be a good time to make himself scarce while the Secret Service swept the garage. If Hassani hit his mark out at the airport, Mularah might not even need to go back to his truck until after the shock of the President's death had set in.

He headed north for a cup of coffee at the Hilton Hotel. With a few hours to kill, he walked around the Old Courthouse and then across the street to the park with its water fountain dyed Cardinal red. The Cardinal fans were out in full-force, even at this early hour. They had pre-game pep rallies in June, no doubt a warmup for their inevitable postseason run still four months away. Mularah was wearing blue jeans and a white T-shirt. He tried to blend in. He even thought about buying a Redbird hat but the prices at the souvenir stands turned him away.

The ringing phone in his pocket brought a smile to his face. It was almost time to play ball.

"Hello."

"It's me," Hassani said. He was out at Lambert Airport waiting for the President. He was on the west end of the field where airplane enthusiasts go to watch the in-bound and out-bound flights. There was only one other car out there, and the old man inside looked like he had fallen asleep.

"I can't believe they don't have more security out here," Hassani whispered into his phone.

"Are you ready?"

"If Air For . . ." Hassani said before stopping abruptly. He wasn't going to take the chance that someone monitoring a scanner might pick up his mention of the President's plane. "If he comes in from the west, I'll get him." He was almost giddy with excitement.

"What do you want me to do?"

Hassani could not resist the trash talk. "I suggest you find a TV because I'm about to change the world."

"My friend, this might be the last time we talk to each other. Your name will live forever in the annals of greatness."

"Thank you, Rasoul. Now get to a TV."

Mulurah clicked off his phone and bounded across the street to the Hilton. Surely the bar would have a TV he could watch. He waded through a pack of fans outside on the patio enjoying their three dollar brats and two dollar Buds. Mularah made it inside the bar and found the TV over the bartender's head. The screen showed a cloudless blue sky with the graphic at the bottom blaring "Awaiting the President's Arrival."

"What can I get you, my friend?"

Mularah didn't hear a word he said, his eyes transfixed on the TV. When he looked at the bartender and his curious looking eyes, he said, "What?"

"What's your pleasure?"

Mularah wasn't thirsty, and he didn't even drink alcohol. But he thought he'd better try to fit in. Without thinking about what he was saying, he blurted out, "Miller Lite."

The bartender gave him a good laugh. No one dared to order a Miller

Lite unless the Brewers were in town. For goodness sakes, Anheuser Busch had its home brewery right down the street. The Clydesdales could have hitched up their wagon and delivered the beer fresh that morning. Being the friendly type, the bartender played the part of concerned St. Louis citizen.

"That sounds awfully suspicious if you ask me," he said.

Mularah's TV trance snapped in a heartbeat. His black eyes narrowed at the man behind the bar. The man thought he was acting suspicious. Would he derail the master plan? Would he try to call the cops?

"Miller Lite? Really?"

Mularah's pulse lowered slightly. "Oh," he said, "stupid me. Bud Light, please."

"That's more like it," he said, handing over a long neck. "Where are you from?"

"Kansas City," Mularah said. He was from a lot of places, and one home could be dropped one day and another one added the next. He didn't like all the questions.

"Oh, a Royals fan, huh?"

Mularah couldn't stand much more hounding from The Great Inquisitor. He didn't follow baseball or any other sport. He was beginning to work up a sweat between dealing with the bartender and glancing at the TV.

"Has the President's plane landed yet?"

The bartender grabbed a towel, dried off his hands, and turned his eyes to the TV. "He's supposed to touch down any second now."

Mularah's neck seemed to stretch toward the TV, his eyes darting across the screen looking for the blue and white Air Force One entering the picture. He envisioned Hassani holding that shoulder-fire RPG and firing his flaming dagger into the hearts of all Americans. His right hand began to shake slightly. He reminded himself to remain calm when Air Force One fell to the earth in a great ball of fire. The celebration of the President's death would wait until later. Not only did he want to see it happen, he wanted to hear it too, like the old newsreel of the flaming Hindenburg and the cry of "Oh, the humanity!" that went with it.

"Could you turn up the sound please?"

"Sure." The bartender reached up to the TV and adjusted the volume, the little green bars increasing in number.

The part of the screen without the green bars caught Mularah's attention. He blinked his eyes at the words but was unsure of their meaning. "What does that Scott AFB refer to?" he asked, pointing with his finger.

"Oh, that's Scott Air Force Base across the river in Illinois. That's where the President is flying into. Apparently, the Secret Service didn't want to disrupt a half day's worth of flights with Air Force One sitting on the ground so they're going to land over there. It's only about a twenty-five mile drive."

Mularah put his shaking right hand into his left. The perspiration was trickling down his temple at a faster clip. The President wasn't going to land at Lambert, and Hassani wasn't going to get his shot at Air Force One. A cold chill enveloped Mularah. He took a deep breath.

Killing the President was his responsibility now.

His thoughts were interrupted when the reporter gushed with enthusiasm. "There it is! Air Force One on final approach," she said, as the plane roared over Interstate 64 and touched down on the runway. "The President of the United States has arrived!"

"All those fans going to the game better hightail it down to the ballpark because the President's going to be here in about thirty minutes," the bartender said. "Are you going to the game, Bud?"

When the bartender turned around, the bar stool in front of him was empty. There was a five on the bar but no sight of the man he had just spent the last five minutes with. Mularah was out the door and heading for the parking garage. The phone buzzing in his pocket had to be Hassani.

"Son of a bitch!" Hassani had learned about the President's arrival on his truck's radio. His perfect plan had gone awry.

"I'm getting into position," Mularah said, weaving through a crowd of scalpers on the corner. "Can you get down here?"

"I'm on my way."

Mularah tried not to run. He told himself to relax. The game didn't start for another hour and that's when he had planned his attack. He walked up the stairwell of the parking garage and exited on the fifth floor. The place was packed with cars, all of them empty. He could see no movement on the floor. He stopped behind his truck and looked through the slats of the garage wall. The stadium was filled to its capacity, and Mularah had a good view of the pitcher's mound and the press box. He estimated the distance at less than five hundred yards. It was on the high end of the optimal distance for the RPG, but he thought anything close would get the job done.

His eyes searched the roof of the Hilton and spotted two sharpshooters prepping their weapons. Two of their compatriots scanned the area beneath them with high-powered binoculars. Mularah opened the truck bed and with as little movement as possible got in. From there he continued his surveillance. He saw four more Secret Service agents on the roof of the west parking garage across the way. He figured there was a team on the top floor above him. He began to realize that he would have to be quick.

Steady but quick.

Hassani was weaving his way through traffic at eight-five miles per hour on Interstate 70 on his way downtown. He didn't worry about getting stopped by the police since most of the law enforcement in the greater St. Louis area was in and around the ballpark. When he finally got off the interstate at the north end of downtown, the traffic slowed to a crawl. He knew he would have little chance of getting in position to offer a second strike once Mularah pulled the trigger so he pulled into a lot where a man was still flagging takers for ten bucks.

With his surveillance complete, Mularah crawled up the truck bed and fiddled with those ostentatious looking exhaust pipes. Each chrome pipe had a secret door that hid separate pieces of the RPG. It was the perfect hiding place, and Mularah had even rigged the pipes so the outsides were hot to the touch. No cop, and no police canine, would dare spend much time checking them out lest they lose sensation in the tips of the fingers or noses. With a pair of insulated gloves, Mularah opened the left door and slowly brought out the pistol-grip butt of the launcher. From behind the door of the right pipe came the rocket-propelled grenade. Put them together and Mularah had himself a fully functional Soviet RPG-7, the same type used by Carlos the Jackal to attack an Israeli airliner in 1975.

Mularah placed the RPG on the floor of the bed and covered it with one-half of a large PVC pipe. He looked around and he could still see the sharpshooters on the roof. He could also hear the wail of sirens coming over the bridge from Illinois. Peering over the bed, Mularah saw the motorcade for a split second to the south of the parking garage as it made its way behind the stadium. It was about time for Mularah to throw out his first pitch.

President Schumacher quickly made his way into the clubhouses of both teams to shake hands and take pictures. He didn't want to delay the start of the game so he hustled in and out as quickly as he could. Plus, he still needed to warm up. He wasn't going to go out and make a fool of himself. In the batting cage beneath the stands, the President borrowed a glove and started firing strikes to the Cardinals backup catcher.

"Just go with the four-seamer," Wiley said, pacing back and forth like a very nervous pitching coach instructing his rookie before the seventh game of the World Series. He prayed everything would go right.

The President tried to shake his arm loose. "We should have started practicing a couple weeks ago."

After a handful of warmup pitches, Agent Craig walked up with a Cardinals jacket and one other unfortunate necessity. From behind the safety of the cage, he held both of them up for the President to see.

"I'm not wearing that," the President said, pointing at the bulletproof vest. "And I'm not wearing the jacket either. It's eighty-five degrees outside."

Agent Craig lifted the netting and made his way to the pitching mound. "Sir, if you don't wear it then it's going to be really difficult for you to throw with eight large men circling you."

The President rubbed up the ball in his hands and looked at Wiley. No one said another word. Agent Craig wouldn't make him do it without a good reason. On went the vest and then the Cardinals jacket.

"Couldn't you have asked for a windbreaker?"

"Sorry, sir."

"I'm going to be hotter than hell wearing all this."

With the full protective regalia on, the President fired one high and wide into the netting out of the catcher's reach. He cursed under his breath. Wiley started sweating the stories that would undoubtedly be written about the President's wild pitch in front of 45,000 fans. The late-night comedians would have a field day. The YouTube viral would make the rounds of office computers around the world and the President would be laughed at for weeks on end.

"Maybe you ought to stay off the mound," Wiley suggested. "Nobody will care if you throw it from fifty feet instead of from the pitching rubber."

The President nodded his head and wiped the perspiration beginning to form on his forehead. He then turned to Agent Craig, "Let me go to the bathroom before we head out." He made eye contact with Wiley to join him.

Once inside, the President whipped off his jacket. "Hurry up and take your suit coat and shirt off." He then ripped open the velcro straps of the Kevlar vest and pulled it over his head. He handed it over to a now shirtless Wiley.

"I don't think you should do this."

"I'm only going to be out there in the open for at most ninety seconds," the President said as he put his Cardinals jacket back on. "Maybe two minutes tops." The jacket would still be hot but he would sacrifice some sweat for some freedom of movement. "Besides, nobody's going to take a shot at me on the mound at Busch Stadium. Everyone has been screened. The Secret Service has eyes all over the place. Plus, don't forget, these people love me."

The worry on Wiley's face was clearly evident. Something didn't feel right.

With both men fully buttoned up, the President and Wiley exited the bathroom and the Secret Service led the way through the tunnel and stopped just outside the dugout.

"Remember, four-seam fastball," Wiley reminded. With his new bulletproof vest on, not to mention his new reason to worry, the sweat began pouring off his bald head. "Nothing fancy."

With the crowd already roaring its approval, the PA announcer had to shout into the microphone. "Ladies and Gentlemen, please welcome 'The First Cardinal Fan,' the President of the United States!"

The "First Cardinal Fan" line wasn't an ad-lib. Wiley had it inserted into the introduction after the President gave his OK. The Cub fans would most likely take offense to it, but Wiley would just tell them to wait 'til next year and maybe it would happen for them.

The applause from the fans was so loud the stadium seemed to be shaking. Mularah could hear the response from the fifth floor of the parking garage. His back was wedged tightly against a cement girder, shielding him from the prying eyes of those on the rooftop to the north. Those peering in from the west could probably see him so he would need to be quick.

He had placed the RPG on the garage floor underneath the front bumper of his truck. He had the broadcast playing on his radio to cue him in on when the President took the field. On his phone clipped to his hip, he could hear the voice of Abdullah Hassani telling him to wait for the right moment. Hassani knew he could not make it down to the stadium in time so he stopped outside of an Italian eatery downtown. The restaurant had a TV over the bar that Hassani could see from the sidewalk.

"Not yet," he instructed.

The President strode to the mound waving his right hand to those down the right and left field lines. His left hand was covered by the borrowed Rawlings baseball glove. For a split second, he thought about taking Wiley's advice to stop short of the mound.

No way, he thought. He had been throwing a baseball for fifty odd years and if he couldn't make it sixty feet six inches he deserved to get booed. He walked up the mound and stood on the rubber. He doffed his red Cardinals cap and waved it to the fans in the left and right field bleachers. He held the pose long enough for the photographers to get their money shot for the next day's *Post-Dispatch*. Then a deep breath.

"Now!"

The voice was Hassani's yelling at Mularah to pull the trigger. Mularah bent down on one knee and reached for the RPG.

"Now! Do it now!"

Mularah slid the RPG halfway out from underneath the truck when he stopped cold from a commotion behind him.

"Fire! Damn it! Fire! I can see him on the mound!" Hassani was expecting to see a trail of white smoke streaking past the centerfield camera.

Mularah looked over his left shoulder. His eyes had never been so wide.

"Hey," the drunk man slurred, pointing at Mularah, "it's Cactus Jack!"

Hassani was screaming into his phone, "Shoot him! Shoot him right now or you're a dead man!"

Some of the patrons at the restaurant bar looked out the window and the crazed man yelling something into his phone. What an idiot, they thought. Doesn't he know he's making a fool of himself in public? A quick glance back to the TV let them see the President firing a fastball right down the middle of the plate for a strike.

"You son of a bitch!" Hassani yelled. The fury in his voice radiated through the phone line.

Mularah grabbed the phone off his hip and pushed the walkie-talkie button. "Quiet!" he whispered angrily. "I've been spotted."

"Cactus Jack! How the hell are ya!?"

Mularah kicked the RPG back under the truck with his right foot as best he could. He couldn't believe what he was seeing. He blinked his eyes to make sure it wasn't some strange vision brought on by the excitement of the moment.

"Son of a buck," he mumbled to himself in utter disbelief.

No, it wasn't a son of a buck. But it was the son of a Buckshot. It was none other than Muddy Rock, Kansas' own Buckshot Barnes, Jr., himself. And there was Butch, and Bump, and Bubba, and Joe Billy, too. The Muddy Rock crew had come to St. Louis the day before for yet another Border Brigade rally underneath the Gateway Arch. After the rally, they spread the last of Bo Duncan's ashes into the Mighty Mississippi.

Since the Royals were in town for interleague play, the Brigade boys' plan was to go to the game on Saturday afternoon. Being from Kansas, they were all die-hard Royals fans. Although their enthusiasm for the team had dwindled ever since the great George Brett retired. Their plan went awry after they decided to make a quick stop at the riverboat casino to imbibe in the cheap drinks and try their hands at the loose slots. What started out as an early Friday evening of craps and blackjack turned into an all-night gambling fest where their decrease in cash was offset by the increase in their blood-alcohol levels.

They stumbled out of the casino at midday and shielded their eyes from the blazing hot sun searing their inebriated brains. Wearing the same bib overalls on from the day before, they walked back to the parking garage to get their trucks. Who was going to drive them back to Kansas hadn't crossed their minds. On the fifth floor, Buckshot, who was the drunkest of them all, noticed someone familiar kneeling next to a truck in front of them.

"Hey, everybody, it's the guy from Arizona with the giant cactuses!" Buckshot bellowed, pointing a wobbly finger at Mularah. Even though he was plastered, Buckshot had one hell of a memory. Perhaps the alcohol had the opposite effect on his brain cells. He could remember the face of a stranger he met a decade before. Sometimes he couldn't remember where he left his truck or his keys, but he could recall the exact time and place of a prior meeting.

The others in the group looked through their bloodshot eyes at the man.

"It *is* Cactus Jack!" Butch exclaimed with a great gregarious laugh. "Son of a gun!"

The Brigade boys crowded around Mularah and treated him like a long lost brother. None of them knew his name but today he would be called Jack. They all shook his hand, and Bubba even gave him a bear hug. They asked about the saguaros, and Mularah said they had been delivered safely to their final destination.

"What are you doing here, you ol' cactus farmer?" Butch asked.

Mularah had never been so tongue tied. He was almost overcome by the smell of alcohol coming from their breath. "I'm on my way back to Kansas."

"Hey, so are we!" Buckshot stammered. He jingled his keys in front of his face like he was ringing a bell.

"But we're in no condition to drive," Joe Billy said, that conclusion finally hitting someone in the group.

"No, sir, we are not," Buckshot said, laughing almost to the point of vomiting. "Let's go back down to the riverfront and show Cactus Jack a good time!"

"No, that's all right," Mularah protested slightly, trying to back his way out of the circle. Out of the corner of his eye, he could still see the butt end of the RPG protruding out from underneath the front bumper of his truck.

"We're not taking no for an answer," Butch said.

Bump and Bubba grabbed Mularah by the arms and escorted him out of the parking garage all the while singing some incomprehensible tune. Their intention was to get their new friend drunk and enjoy the rest of the day in St. Louis. Maybe they'd head back to the casino and help Mularah lose some of his money. They weren't going anywhere today anyway, at least not until their stupor wore off.

Mularah could do little more than go along with them. The plan had failed, and Hassani would be on the warpath once he found him. He might end up killing him for cowardice. That was one of a million thoughts racing through Mularah's mind at the moment.

The Brigade brothers, however, were having a grand time. They may not have uncovered the mystery of the man in their midst who just happened to take the life of their friend Bo Duncan, but America did owe them a debt of gratitude for saving the life of the President of the United States.

CHAPTER 17

The Supreme Court of the United States – Washington, D.C.

The Supreme Court's term usually ends in late June, and oral arguments are typically completed by the end of April. But all nine justices voted to hear the case of *Abullah v. Schumacher* in an expedited appeal. It was too big a deal and too important to kick over to the next term. Thus, their summer vacations and lectures were pushed back into late July or early August. This case would require all hands on deck, and each justice told their law clerks to expect long nights in the coming weeks.

The briefs filed with the Clerk of the Supreme Court had come with lightning speed but that really wasn't much of a surprise. The same or similar arguments had been made since the Civil War. Following the aftermath of the attacks on 9/11, the arguments intensified and played out on twenty-four hour cable news shows.

Brennan's brief for the Civil Liberties Alliance ran for eighty-one pages. The last page indicated five different attorneys had worked on the case. The seventy-one page brief of the United States of America was signed by the Solicitor General, an Assistant Attorney General, a Deputy Solicitor General, an Assistant to the Solicitor General, and two other attorneys. Brennan and his team fired back with a thirty-two page reply brief hoping to debunk the Government's argument. A flood of twenty-seven "friend of the court" briefs were also filed just in case the justices had a hard time making up their minds.

The oral argument was set for Tuesday at 10 a.m. sharp. A line of those hoping to view the arguments had begun at 3 a.m. the night before in the front plaza on the west side of the Supreme Court Building. Family, friends, and acquaintances of the justices had been calling their offices in hopes of snagging a reserved seat, thereby saving them the indignity of standing in line with the "riffraff" and "peons of society" who weren't connected enough to bypass the public line.

The Courtroom began filling up at 9:30 a.m. The press corps came armed with their pens and note pads and immediately went to work noting the dignitaries in the room. Two syndicated conservative columnists sat three rows back whispering quietly to themselves. A former Attorney General was seen admiring the Spanish and Italian marble of the friezes and columns bordering the Courtroom. Two retired Supreme Court justices made rare appearances and took seats in the reserved section to the right of the raised winged-shaped Bench.

Jodi A. Black, Esq., the second female Solicitor General of the United States, took her seat at the table before the Bench. The Office of the Solicitor General represents the United States in the Supreme Court. As part of the Department of Justice, the Office has been in existence since 1870 and the statutory act authorizing the position requires its occupant to be "learned in the law." With her offices in the Justice Department and at the Supreme Court, General Black was one of only two federal officials with offices in two different branches of government – the other being the Vice President.

Seated next to her was Deputy Solicitor General Carlton O'Bannon. Both were "learned" Harvard law graduates and former U.S. Attorneys. Some attorneys are good at trial work – cross-examining witnesses and making emotional arguments to gullible juries. Others work their magic behind the scenes – drafting wills, executing contracts, and handling divorce cases. It is a rare breed though that perfects the art of appellate advocacy – especially in the Supreme Court of the United States. Some appellate courts sit in three judge panels, others might use seven. But the stakes are never higher when the nine robed justices walk out from behind the curtains to take their seats in the Supreme Court.

Black had gained the reputation as a cool head with a mind like a steel trap. She had personally argued twenty-five cases before the High Court, winning twenty with the last ten being in a row. She handled the rapid fire questions from both liberal and conservative justices with ease, and court watchers were always amazed at her ability to recall the facts and law of almost every case the justices happened to bring up during oral argument. She was once married, but found the law more interesting and more rewarding. She was a fierce competitor, and no one could outwork her.

On the other side of the lectern sat the petitioners' attorneys – Art Brennan and Christopher Gache. Brennan would not be making the argument today, and it wasn't out of fear of arguing with intellectuals because he loved doing that. He had made one argument before the Supreme Court in his career, and it was a complete unmitigated disaster.

In an emotional and highly charged case on prayer in the public classroom, Brennan started arguing with one of the conservatives on the Court and wouldn't let it go, repeatedly telling the old Justice that his best legal years had passed him by and that he needed to come to grips with the idea of a "Living Constitution." The silver-haired Justice would have none of it and told Brennan he should stick to reading the lines of the Constitution and not in between them. Unable to control his temper, Brennan blurted out a string of profanities that drew a rare but stern rebuke from the Chief Justice. One of the liberal justices even lectured him from the Bench about the decorum the Courtroom demanded of its participants. Thereafter, word made the rounds of the Supreme Court Bar that Brennan would be well-advised to let someone else do the arguing next time.

Several law clerks to the justices decided the high-profile nature of the case was too important to miss so they took seats on the right side of the Courtroom. Sharif al-Rashad, clad in a dark blue suit and matching tie, sat next to Katherine Mais, one of the law clerks to Chief Justice Shannon. After a quick glance around the room, Sharif found who he was looking for in the back row of the reserved seating section on the far left. He gave the man a quick nod. The man reciprocated and smiled.

It was his old friend from Chicago – Abdullah Hassani.

The White House – Washington, D.C.

Contrary to a widespread rumor circulating around the Beltway, President Schumacher would not be attending the oral argument at the Supreme Court. Wiley thought it might make for grand theater to have the President of the United States sitting at the Solicitor General's table as the Supreme Court listened to arguments on how he should conduct his role as Commander-in-Chief in the time of war. The President thought about it, long enough to envision a sketch artist's rendering of the nine justices and the President of the United States facing off in the historic Courtroom, but decided against it. He would let the legal experts handle it. Plus, he didn't want a circus atmosphere to descend upon the dignified aura of the Court.

He also had important work to do.

"Mr. Daniels, thanks for meeting with me."

"Mr. President, it is always a pleasure. I haven't seen you around for some time. You should stop by."

Barry Daniels was the Archivist of the United States. After his unanimous confirmation by the U.S. Senate, Daniels had been on the job for twenty years leading the National Archives and Records Administration. The National Archives is in charge of preserving documents created by the federal government for future generations. Although the Archives has regional sites across the country and oversees presidential libraries, its most famous location sits between Pennsylvania and Constitution Avenues in the District of Columbia. There in the Rotunda are housed the Charters of Freedom – the Declaration of Independence, the Constitution of the United States, and the Bill of Rights. And Daniels took his charge to protect the Founding Documents with great energy and devotion.

"I would like to do that," the President said as he took his seat behind the Resolute Desk in the Oval Office. "I don't want to take up much of your time. I think you know why I called you in."

"This is about your daughter."

"Yes, sir. Do you think you could find work for her at the National Archives this summer?"

"As an intern?"

"Yes. She's willing to shuffle papers or whatever. But she has developed a great love of American history, which I know you cherish a great deal."

"Yes, sir, absolutely."

"And, of course, it would be free labor for you."

"That never hurts."

"But I don't want her to take the spot of someone you already had plans for."

"That's not a problem." Daniels responded as he glanced off to the wall of the room and looked at the portrait of Ronald Reagan, one of his favorite Presidents. He did have something else on his mind though. "I'm all for it, Mr. President. Although there is the matter of the Secret Service."

"I understand. I don't expect you to put Anna on full display if that is going to disrupt the tourists in the Rotunda. I won't tell you how to run the National Archives. And I would instruct the Secret Service and Anna to follow the boundaries you feel the need to set."

Daniels smiled and nodded in agreement. "Mr. President, I think we can make this work for you and the First Daughter."

"Thank you, sir."

As Daniels left, the President promised to make an appearance at the National Archives whenever the Archivist wanted. It was the least he could do, he said.

With that order of business quickly finished, the President could now break the good news to his youngest daughter. He phoned his secretary and asked that she call the Residence and have Anna stop by the Oval Office before she left for her summer classes at Georgetown. Within ten minutes, she bounded in the open door after seeing her dad sitting at his desk.

"Hi, Daddy."

The President looked up from his briefing materials to find his youngest daughter taking a seat in the chair the Archivist just left. "My lovely Anna Julia, how are you today?"

Twenty-two-year-old Anna Schumacher wore a tight pair of blue jeans and a red pullover. Her golden brown tan indicated her down time was spent sunning herself out near the pool. Her long blonde hair rested gently at her shoulders and one diamond studded earring could be seen in her right ear. She had obviously obtained her beauty from her mother, but her father did try to take some credit for her intelligence.

"What classes do you have on the schedule for today?"

"American Judicial Process and Sociology."

She was majoring in Politics & Government and was contemplating attending law school like her dad and her older brother. She had the looks of a cover girl or a Hollywood actress, and she would cut a stunning figure on the red carpet, in the courtroom, or on any political stage. The Republican Party definitely had a superstar in the making.

"Well your judicial process class ought to be interesting. What with the media circus down the street at the Supreme Court."

"Yeah," she said, twirling her hair with the fingers of her right hand. Her mother used to do the same thing. She could not restrain the roll of her brown eyes. "But my professor is too liberal. All he wants to talk about are these constitutional rights that somehow don't even show up in the Constitution."

Ah, the President smiled with great contentment at one of the great joys of fatherhood – when your young offspring has shown that they were actually listening to the lectures you gave them during their formative years. He had taught her well.

"Surprise, surprise," the President said.

"And, of course, he always looks at me when he's trying to make his stupid, liberal-fascist points. He's an idiot."

The President laughed with delight. "You are going to make a great politician someday, young lady."

Anna smiled her sweet smile, the dimple forming on her cheek another trait from mom.

Changing subjects, the President asked, "How is everything working out with your new Secret Service detail?"

Anna's eyes lit up with great excitement. "Oh, Dad, Jason is smokin' hot!"

The President was slightly taken aback at the sheer joy in his daughter's voice. This was news to him. "Excuse me? He's what?"

"He is a hottie."

She said "hottie" slow enough to emphasize both syllables, like a fawning teenager confronted with a poster of the good looking young member of this week's hottest boy band. Special Agent Walter Wilson, the old fogey that had been following Anna around, was transferred to Palm Springs so he could watch over one of the country's aging ex-Presidents on his daily trips to the country club and his office. It suited Walter just fine, he loved the endless sunshine and golfing on his off days.

Special Agent Jason Sessions was thirty years old but barely looked a day over twenty. Dressed in the college garb he still had in his closet from his undergraduate days, he shadowed Anna to all of her classes while the rest of her detail in their suits and sunglasses kept watch nearby. Everyone in the class knew he worked for the Secret Service because of that squiggly piece in his ear, but if someone didn't know it, it would be one hell of a surprise if they tried something on the President's daughter. Agent Sessions had played linebacker for the University of Illinois with such animalistic ferocity that he garnered comparisons to the great Dick Butkus. With his natural athletic ability being very noticeable and even more formidable, guys looking to score with Anna thought twice about even approaching her. He was a three-year veteran of the Secret Service and was personally recruited by the higher-ups because of his youthful look to keep a close eye on Anna

Schumacher.

"You do remember he's your bodyguard, don't you?"

She pursed her lips and took a deep breath at the thought of her square-jawed security stud. "Ooh, baby, he can guard my body all he wants."

"Anna Julia!" the President said sternly. Perhaps he still had some fatherly wisdom to impart on his youngest daughter.

"He's got nice big muscles under that shirt of his," she said, her left hand covering the flexed biceps of her right arm. "A nice firm set of pecs, too."

"Anna, you're not allowed to touch the agents. I'm pretty sure it's written down in the Secret Service rules somewhere."

"Oh, Daddy."

"I can get Walter back from Palm Springs if you want me to." He picked up the phone like he had Walter's number on speed dial.

Anna shook her head vigorously. Don't even think about it said the look in her eyes. She promised him she'd be good. Her girlfriends would never speak to her again if someone took their handsome secret agent friend away. They all thought he was a hottie too.

Slightly flustered at the emotional ups-and-downs of fatherhood, the President got down to the business of the day.

"I talked to Barry Daniels this morning, and he said he's going to find something for you to do at the National Archives this summer."

"Sweet."

"I'm not sure exactly what he has in store for you, but I told him you were open to anything."

"Absolutely."

"I also invited him over for dinner on Thursday night. That way we can get you and the Secret Service on the same page."

"Fine by me."

The President saw some stirring outside the windows on the Colonnade – a couple of suits and some frat-boy looking young man wearing a well-worn Georgetown hat and loose fitting jeans. The President actually craned his neck to see if the Secret Service might have arrested the young man, maybe he had jumped the fence and they were escorting him away. One of the men in the suits saw the President looking at the window, knocked softly on the bulletproof glass, and then pointed at the young blonde sitting to the side of the desk.

Anna swung her head around. “Ooh, my boyfriend’s here! My boyfriend’s here!” she exclaimed, squealing like a ten-year-old girl and fumbling for the backpack at her feet.

It used to be so much easier for Dad. Now he couldn’t tell if she was serious or pulling his leg. “Agent, Anna. Remember, he’s your Secret Service agent. Try to keep your hands off of him.”

“Bye, Dad,” she said, planting a kiss on his cheek. “Love ya.”

She was out the door before he knew it and the frat boy said something into the microphone protruding out of the sleeve of his shirt. It was time for Anna’s detail to whisk her off to school.

Anthony J. Schumacher, simple father of a twenty-two-year-old daughter, sat alone at his desk in his oval-shaped office and sighed. “Oh for the good ol’ days.” Those were the less stressful days when it was only the big yellow bus taking his little Anna Julia away to school.

CHAPTER 18

The Supreme Court of the United States – Washington, D.C.

"Oyez! Oyez! Oyez!" the Marshal cried. "All persons having business before the Honorable, the Supreme Court of the United States, are admonished to draw near and give their attention, for the Court is now sitting. God save the United States and this Honorable Court!"

All persons seated inside the Courtroom rose at the sound of the pounding Marshal's gavel. Art Brennan had to bite his tongue at the pomp and circumstance, especially considering that the Marshal actually used the word "God" in a federal building. And there was Moses right there in the frieze in that very Courtroom! He made a note to add them to his list of phrases and images to sandblast from the historical traditions of the Nation.

The justices entered the silent Courtroom from behind three curtains – the Chief Justice and the two longest serving associate justices from the curtain in the middle and two sets of three associate justices behind the other two curtains. Each took their respective seat, the Chief Justice in the middle and the other justices to his right and left in order of seniority.

They had already huddled in the oak-paneled Robing Room – where the vaunted black robes hung like jerseys in the lockers of great ballplayers. They then made the rounds of shaking each other's hand – a common practice of collegiality, which did not always last through the entire hour-long arguments.

Chief Justice Shannon looked each direction to see that his legal compatriots had settled in their high-backed leather chairs and banged the gavel.

"We will hear arguments this morning in case 16-001, *Abullah, et al. v. Schumacher*."

He then looked at the petitioners' table.

"Mr. Gache, you may proceed."

Gache's lean six-foot-six frame rose out of his seat at counsel's table and he placed his notes on the lectern. He had graduated *summa cum laude* from Harvard with degrees in economics and English. He then marched on down to Harvard Law School, edited the Law Review, and graduated at the top of his class. He had been raised by elite Harvard professors and the blue-blood of liberalism had been infused into his body and mind at birth. Turning down six-figure salaries out of law school, he became Art Brennan's go-to guy at the Civil Liberties Alliance. With his slicked back dark hair and horn-rimmed glasses, he looked every bit the blue-blood East Coast intellectual.

"Mr. Chief Justice, and may it please the Court."

The customary phrase indicated to all present that the feeding frenzy could now begin in earnest.

"The petitioners in this case seek justice."

"Counsel, let me interrupt you for a second."

The early break in the action came from Associate Justice F. Lloyd Rickenbacker, the Court's most conservative member. No one was surprised by the intrusion. Sitting to the left of the Chief Justice, Rickenbacker was the darling of the strict-constructionist crowd and as right-wing as a judge could be. With shoulder-length gray hair that flowed proudly like a lion's mane, he was loud, bombastic, and completely full of himself. He was the son of a fire and brimstone Baptist minister from the Bootheel of Missouri and sometimes thought the Supreme Court Bench was his very own legal pulpit. Those lucky enough to witness an oral argument came away from it either loathing the man or thinking he had the greatest legal mind God had ever bestowed in a human being. He loved the law and his work on the Court. His fellow justices loved him too, he being the hell-fire legal conservative who they knew simply enjoyed playing to the crowd every now and then to add a little spice to oral arguments. He was always good with a quip to lighten the mood. He went by Lloyd to his colleagues because the "F" stood for "Festus." Although he claimed it stood for "Fun." Some on the Left claimed the "F" stood for something a little more derogatory.

"A perusal of your lengthy brief seems to say this case is about declaring your clients have rights that they are not entitled to."

Justice Rickenbacker left the end of the sentence hanging like it might be a question or it might not. It was more of a statement so everyone who could hear or would read about it later that day online or in tomorrow's paper would know his position on the matter.

Gache was unfazed. "Justice Rickenbacker, the petitioners have solid ground on which they base their claim. The Geneva Conventions provide a comprehensive set of rules for warring parties to abide by during times of conflict."

The Chief Justice felt the need to chime in. "Counsel, do the Geneva Conventions even apply to your clients?"

"Mr. Chief Justice, they absolutely apply."

"What uniforms were your clients wearing when they were captured?"

"They were not wearing any special type of uniforms or insignias, Mr. Chief Justice."

"Did al-Qaeda ratify the Geneva Conventions?"

"No, Mr. Chief Justice."

Associate Justice Pamela Anders, the Court's only conservative female, beat Justice Rickenbacker to the punch. "So the United States is supposed to give them the rights under the law of war when they refuse to abide by those rules themselves?"

"Justice Anders, we as a Nation should strive to protect the rights of all humans, no matter their name, their rank, or whether they even have a serial number. In the armed conflict that the United States finds itself in, certain rules of war should apply."

"Counsel," Justice Hussein interrupted, "has Congress provided adequate protections for the rights of the petitioners in these military tribunals?"

The nod of approval from Sharif al-Rashad was noticed only by Hassani in the back of the seating section. Sharif was itching to get out of oral arguments so he could start writing up whatever Justice Hussein asked him to write. He was begging for the chance to write the majority opinion – that is, if Justice Hussein was in the majority.

"Justice Hussein, we believe the rules set forth by Congress are deficient." Gache then ran through the reasons why and peppered the justices with the rules of procedure from military tribunals in far off countries in support.

The rest of Gache's arguments went with multiple questions from each of the nine justices, but mostly from the conservative bloc of the Court. The more liberal wing – Justices Mario Alonso, Marco Pentano, and Wilma Bonderman – held their fire for the Solicitor General's argument. When the red light blinked on on top of the lectern, Gache stopped immediately and nodded in respect.

"Thank you, counsel," the Chief Justice said before turning his eyes to opposing counsel. "General Black."

The Solicitor General proceeded to the podium on which she placed two pages of notes. The notes were simply a backup as the argument was all neatly arranged in her mind.

"Thank you, Mr. Chief Justice, and may it please the Court."

Justice Rickenbacker didn't even wait for General Black to begin her argument. He wanted to make the first point – like an eager second-grader, hand reaching for the sky, begging to give the answer to the teacher so everyone would know he was the smartest kid in the class.

"General, is this case governed by the *Quirin* decision?"

"Justice Rickenbacker, I do believe it is."

In June 1942, the FBI captured eight German saboteurs who had landed via submarines on American soil in New York and Florida. President Franklin Roosevelt appointed a military commission to try the men under the international law of war and the Articles of War enacted by Congress. During the trial, seven of the alleged saboteurs filed a petition for *habeas corpus* claiming their detention was unlawful and the President had no authority to order their trial before the military commission.

In a unanimous opinion, the Supreme Court in *Ex Parte Quirin* held the men had a right to judicial review of their detention. However, the Court upheld the use of the military tribunals based on the President's authority as Commander-in-Chief and congressional legislation allowing for the trials. Following the trial, the Nazi saboteurs were sentenced to death and six were electrocuted.

"The facts here are sufficiently similar to uphold the use of the commission under a fair reading of *Quirin* as well as other cases."

"Counsel," Justice Hussein interjected, "the defendants here have not been afforded the right of their case being presented to a grand jury or the right to a trial by jury, have they not?"

Justice Rickenbacker decided to answer the question put to the General with one of his own. "The courts are to afford the Executive Branch great deference in the prosecution of a war, correct?"

"I don't think the General had a chance to answer my question," Hussein shot back into his microphone.

Justice Rickenbacker ignored him, as he was wont to do of liberals when he was on the Bench. General Black's head was oscillating back and forth like she was center court at a tennis match. For the good part of Black's thirty-minute argument, the justices argued amongst themselves and she felt it best to stay silent.

"These black robes," Rickenbacker said tugging at his sleeves, "do not come with shiny silver stars or battle ribbons. Am I to consider myself like a four-star general," he stopped ever so briefly to further preen his magnificent legal plumage, "or in my case, a five-star judge, and tell the President and the Pentagon how to win the war on terror?"

"No, Justice Rickenbacker, I believe Congress has properly provided for the military tribunal and the President can now implement it."

"Thank you, counsel," the Chief Justice said at the appearance of the red light. "Your time has expired. Mr. Gache, you have five minutes of rebuttal time remaining."

Gache decided he would make his rebuttal quick. Try to have the last word and then sit down, he told himself.

"Thank you, Mr. Chief Justice. I would like to address Justice Hussein's concerns. The law passed by Congress is clearly deficient under a reading of *Quirin* and even going back to cases during the Civil War. The petitioners' rights are not protected to the fullest extent required by the Constitution. Respectfully, this Court should reverse the decision of the District Court and tell Congress and the President to try again. Thank you."

"Thank you, Mr. Gache. The case is submitted."

With a bang of the gavel signaling the end of the proceedings, the Marshal cried for all to rise as the justices filed out of the Courtroom and disappeared behind the curtains. The justices paraded back into the Robing Room where they shed the robes and, for those that were wearing them, loosened their ties. Since there were no other cases on the docket in this special summer session, they proceeded into the Conference Room to discuss the case they had just heard.

The Chief Justice took his spot at the head of the long oak table under the portrait of "the Great Chief Justice" John Marshall. Justice O'Malley, as the next most senior member, took the chair at the opposite end. The other justices took their seats with Justice Alonso, the Court's newest member and an appointee of the disgraced and now deceased President Fisher, taking the seat closest to the door. As this was as closed a meeting as one could get, anyone wanting inside had to knock and wait for Justice Alonso to do his chore of answering the door.

Surrounding them all, the recessed shelving of the room beckoned their legal minds with volume upon volume of case reporters containing the written opinions of Justices' past – Chief Justice Taney in *Dred Scott*, the seven member majority in *Plessy*, Justice Blackmun in *Roe*. What were they thinking when they penned the opinions that are still talked about generations later? If only the opinions could give the insight of their hearts and minds.

"All right," the Chief Justice started. He usually allowed for a free-for-all before calling for order after everyone had their say.

Justice Rickenbacker's thoughts shot out like a cannon. "I think we should affirm the District Court's ruling. The law gives the President the right to utilize a military tribunal in a time of war."

"Now just hold on, Lloyd," came the quick retort from Justice Wilma Bonderman.

Justice Bonderman was a diminutive woman from San Francisco. Needless to say, she was a Liberal. She had once headed the California office of the CLA in her early legal career, a tidbit that some said required her to recuse herself from the case. She flat out said no, stating her affiliation with the CLA had ended twenty years ago and had no bearing on the case at bar. She had been the most liberal jurist during her tenure on the Ninth Circuit Court of Appeals and brought her left-wing ideology with her to Washington. Conservative pundits called her a feisty old bag behind her back, and others said she was the ideological counterweight to Justice Rickenbacker.

"We need to treat these people with respect," she said.

"Who are *these people* you're talking about?"

"The petitioners."

"Their terrorists! And they should be treated like terrorists!"

"They should be treated fairly in a court of law. The military tribunal is nothing but a sham trial!"

The two raged on in their verbal warfare across the oak table. They could go at it like an umpire and an irate manager going nose to nose trading bawdy insults and tobacco spit. Both of them loved to argue and would later resume their bickering behind the closed doors of their chambers. The rest of the group was not for loud rants but preferred arguing legal principles through e-mail and personal messages to their colleagues.

The tapping on the table came from Justice Richard Somerton from Mississippi. A man of genteel Southern qualities, whose voice sounded like a cross between Foghorn Leghorn and Colonel Sanders, his white hair stood out strong when he was adorned with his black robe. He hailed from Vicksburg, Mississippi, and would oftentimes stroll the grounds of the Supreme Court in his white suit and black necktie and visit with unsuspecting tourists – some of whom had no clue who he was and others who thought he was obviously suffering from Alzheimer's or dementia based on his outlandish claim of being an associate justice of the United States Supreme Court. He was affectionately known as "Whistling Dick," a nickname from his childhood days in Vicksburg, but he wasn't known to whistle. "Whistling Dick" was the name of an eighteen-pound Confederate cannon in use during the Civil War at the Battle of Vicksburg. Given his white hair, he playfully reminded those who were told the story that he didn't actually hear the whistling of the cannon's projectiles during the War Between the States.

The tapping of Justice Somerton's pen stopped. "I do declare we have a bit of an impasse here, Mr. Chief Justice."

"Well, why don't we take a preliminary vote," the Chief Justice offered. "That way we can see where everybody stands and get a draft written."

Justices Hussein, Alonso, Pentano, and Bonderman were all firmly in the camp to reverse the trial court order and declare the military tribunal law unconstitutional. On the other side, the Chief Justice along with Justices Rickenbacker, Somerton, and Anders wanted to affirm and let the tribunals go forward.

That only left Justice O'Malley.

"Tom," the Chief Justice said, "where do you stand as of now?"

Justice O'Malley laid his pen down on his notepad in front of him. In the back of his mind, he now knew he had the most powerful position in all of the United States Government. It was his decision on who would win the case – the petitioners or the President. The power was in his hands. None of the other justices tried to sway him one way or the other. They just waited with bated breath.

With a quick tug on his red bow tie, he cleared his throat. "I believe I come down on the side of the petitioners."

Justice Rickenbacker's chair started rocking back and forth with increasing intensity. His face looked like a volcano ready to explode and unleash a torrent of red-hot conservative lava toward the end of the table. But he didn't because it was not proper decorum when a justice was announcing his or her vote. He would save his fire for the dissent.

"For now," Justice O'Malley clarified. "Maybe something might change my mind in the future."

"Okay, we have five to four to reverse," the Chief Justice said as he jotted down a note on his yellow legal pad. "Tom, since you're the most senior member of this majority, you get to pick who writes the opinion."

Justice O'Malley looked around the table. Any other justice given the choice of authorship on such a high profile case would have snatched it for himself or herself in a heartbeat. The opportunity to have your name as the author of such a landmark Court decision that would find its rightful way into every history and legal textbook from here to eternity was too good to pass up. But Justice O'Malley was eighty-eight years old and his eyesight was beginning to fade (although he never told anybody). Sure his clerks would do all the heavy-duty lifting in researching the law and drafting a coherent opinion, but he wanted someone with a sharp analytical mind and a passionate voice for the Left. Someone who could use it as a springboard to the upper echelon of legal jurists.

"I think this case is for you, Justice Hussein. If you feel up to it."

Justice Hussein's eyes widened and his chair rocked slowly backward. He hadn't expected to be the author of the majority opinion but had already been making mental notes for a concurring opinion.

"I'd be happy to take it, Justice. Thank you."

"I could still change my mind," Justice O'Malley interjected. Just to let you know, he insinuated. It was his way of keeping the power. Both sides had better fashion their arguments in a way that he could agree to or he would jump ship to the other group and make someone else the authoring king or queen.

The justices closed up their notes and headed back to their chambers. Once Justice Hussein got back into his office, he pumped his fist in front of his clerks. "We're authoring this one, folks!"

CHAPTER 19

The National Archives – Washington, D.C.

Anna spent her first week in the research rooms at the National Archives helping the deputy archivists chronicle everything that came through that might be of historical value. She saw her dad's signature on two pieces of legislation and the written statement of condolence on behalf of the American people that he made at the funeral for a former First Lady.

After some playful begging, the Archivist finally relented and allowed her to lead a private tour group through the Rotunda.

"Okay, if you would follow me."

Twenty seventh graders had been bused in from Baltimore to tour the Archives before they headed down to the Capitol. Anna had dutifully done her homework and pointed out the Faulkner murals depicting the presentation of the Declaration of Independence and the Constitution.

"Who authored the Declaration of Independence?"

Every hand shot up, the kids eager to show the knowledge they had learned in their History class during the last school year. "Thomas Jefferson" came the response.

"Very good."

She then pointed out the fading signatures of the brave men who risked their reputations, their property, and their lives by putting their names in the crosshairs of King George III – autographs of Jefferson, Benjamin Franklin, John Adams, and even the bold and defiant John Hancock of the very man himself.

After the tour had ended, she walked the group outside and posed for a picture. She also handed out pocket-sized copies of the Constitution. Her dad had given her a hundred dollars to buy them so she could pass them out if the situation presented itself. It was something he used to do when he was campaigning for Congress.

"These are gifts to you from the President of the United States."

Some of the kids looked at them like they had been given a bar of gold. Others rushed back to her in hopes of snagging her autograph. They couldn't wait to get back home to tell their parents they met the President's daughter.

The Supreme Court of the United States – Washington, D.C.

While the Baltimore school kids were making their way down Pennsylvania Avenue to tour the Capitol, the justices of the Supreme Court and their law clerks were locked away in their chambers. Reporters had been camped outside on the front plaza for a week now in anticipation of the Court handing down its opinion on the military tribunals.

Sharif al-Rashad had taken the lead as *the* law clerk to Justice Hussein, elbowing the other three out of the way to worry about the more menial certiorari petitions that usually get denied and the death penalty motions that usually meet the same fate. Sharif was constantly in and out of Justice Hussein's office, showing him the latest draft and reworking entire sections. If the Justice was working, Sharif was working. If the Justice went home for the evening, Sharif went home to continue the work at his condominium in Georgetown. The two kept in close contact with texts and e-mails. The Justice even obtained a second government-issued encrypted cell phone for Sharif so they could speak freely about the case without fear of the media or whoever from listening in on their conversations.

Other than eating and a few hours of sleep, Sharif thought about nothing other than this case. His only distraction was Hassani calling every day, sometimes three times a day even while Sharif was in the office.

When the cell phone buzzed at his desk, he looked at the number and contemplated letting it go to voice mail.

"Hello."

"Sharif," Hassani said. "How's it going?"

Sharif rolled his eyes. Again, he thought. "I'm real busy," he said, hoping the man would get the hint.

"How's that opinion coming?"

"It's coming along. A preliminary draft has been circulated among the other justices to see what they think. But like I've said before, I can't really discuss it until the decision is finally handed down."

"I know, I know," Hassani said. He couldn't help himself. He had to know. He felt he had the weight of the movement on his shoulders and he was tired of the American infidels imposing their will on his brothers throughout the world. This would be the statement that would start changing people's minds and see how America's power had tarnished its image with other world leaders.

"I should get back to work."

Hassani relented. He told him he'd call some other time. "We're going to win, right?" He was just checking. It helped ease his anxiety and made the long agonizing wait somewhat bearable. He was not a patient man.

Sharif was confident, but he was not ready to sing it from the rooftops. "Yes, we are going to win," he whispered.

Across the building's courtyard sat Justice Rickenbacker's chambers and the discussion inside was as lively as any other. Leading the law clerk quartet was Bryan Lockhart, a straight-laced, dyed-in-the-wool Goldwater/Reagan/Limbaugh conservative from Houston, Texas. Known as "The Machine" to those around the office for his late nights and early mornings fully engrossed in his work, he had served on Justice Rickenbacker's staff for two years. The two would often get into heated arguments of who was the most conservative. At the end of the argument, both would think they had laid claim to the title of supreme right winger. Although disappointed that his boss would not be writing the majority opinion, Lockhart's spirits were buoyed by the thought of helping draft a blistering dissent. One that commentators would describe as "biting," "hard-hitting," and "powerful." At times, clerks thought the dissents were more fun to write than the majority opinion because you can fire both barrels and not have to worry about placating another justice or toeing the line of political correctness.

Justice Rickenbacker had been hurling expletives all morning upon receipt of Justice Hussein's preliminary draft.

"Can you believe the line he put in there that *Quirin* involved a 'legitimate war?'" he huffed. "What the hell kind of war are we in now?"

"I guess he thinks we're fighting an illegitimate war," Lockhart mused, knowing Rickenbacker's fuse had been lit.

"That son of a . . ." Rickenbacker slammed the draft on his desk and spun around in his chair to look out the window in hopes of calming down. "I don't understand why people would want to rule in favor of terrorists when the law clearly does not require them to do so.

Sometimes I wonder whose side those liberals are on."

"Maybe you ought to write that in your dissent."

Justice Rickenbacker spun back around with a shit-eating grin on his face. He was ready to write the mother of all dissents. He had glanced over the proposal that Lockhart had given him earlier that morning – one that the Machine had crafted in the wee hours of the morning. It was a good start. But he did have one question.

"'The majority hangs its hat on the belief that (1) because we are at war and (2) because the Geneva Conventions apply during wartime, then irrespective of the powers of Congress and the President, (3) the Geneva Conventions must be applied to these terrorist detainees. QED.'"

Lockhart sat back in a chair in front of the Justice's desk, his hands clasped behind his head. He was grinning from ear to ear.

"QED?"

"Yeah."

"I don't even know what that means."

"It's Latin for *quod erat demonstrandum*, which translates to 'That which was to be demonstrated or proved.' The majority is saying that because there's a "one" here and a "two" there, then it must be right to have a "three" here too. And the three is whatever answer they had sought to find."

"Has it ever been used before?"

"Yes."

"In an opinion of this Court?"

"Yes, and other courts too. Federal and State."

Justice Rickenbacker liked it. It brought a certain flare to the dissent. And one that would send the reporters to their legal dictionaries to help them decipher what nugget of legal wisdom he was trying to impart.

The White House – Washington, D.C.

For the past two days, the President was huddling with his advisors on his plan of attack if the Supreme Court ruled against him. Attorney General Claire Donovan had her lawyers at the Justice Department researching the legal and constitutional issues and weighing the President's options. Wiley had his political hat on, and his ideas might not be in line with what the DOJ lawyers were telling the President.

"I think that if the Supreme Court rules in favor of the terrorists that you should just ignore it," Wiley said, as he and Attorney General

Donovan sat in front of the President's desk in the Oval Office.

"Defy the Supreme Court?" the President asked.

"You're the Commander-in-Chief and we're at war. What are the justices going to do? Come down here with their gavels and stop you?"

"He does have a point, Mr. President," Attorney General Donovan said. Her tone indicated she couldn't believe she was actually agreeing with Wiley.

"How so?"

"Lincoln suspended the writ of *habeas corpus* in the Civil War. He had newspapers shut down. He imprisoned Southern sympathizers. Courts may have found what he was doing unlawful, but he was in the midst of a war threatening the very survival of the Union."

The President, a student of history and of Lincoln added, "And he said something to the effect that 'are all the laws, but one, to go unexecuted, and the government itself to go to pieces,' lest that one be violated?'"

"That's right. In the *Quirin* case, FDR told the Supreme Court he didn't care how they came down on the case because, as Commander-in-Chief, he was not going to release the German saboteurs as the war was very much still raging on."

"So we just continue on with the military tribunals?"

"Yes."

Wiley had to jump in. "Just remember, Mr. President. The Executive Branch is the one with the guns. And the agents of the government with the guns are going to rule over those without any."

"I can just see liberals protesting in the street led by that idiot Brennan and his Constitution-shredding antics."

"Mr. President," the Attorney General said, "the American public know we are at war. And they know you are going to do everything within your power to keep them safe and preserve, protect, and defend the Constitution. Some worthless protests will not sway public opinion."

"Well, I'll have to think about it. From what I've heard, the chances of the Supreme Court ruling against us are pretty good. Maybe Justice O'Malley will come down on our side. But unless he does, I'm going to have to make the decision." He took a deep breath and closed the meeting. "Start drafting a statement on how we will proceed. We'll talk again tomorrow."

CHAPTER 20

The Supreme Court of the United States – Washington, D.C.

Justice O'Malley called Justice Hussein the night before and told him he could go along with his proposed draft. That would give Hussein his five-to-four majority. O'Malley did have a few suggestions that he asked Hussein to look at and consider as possible changes. For one, he wanted the language regarding the "legitimate war" to be reworded or taken out altogether. He didn't think it was appropriate or necessary for the proper disposition of the appeal. Also, if Hussein could move the citations of international case law to the footnotes it would make it easier to read and more concisely focused on the law of the United States.

Other than that, he had only one other request – that Hussein give him the evening to read over the whole draft one more time. Then he would write his formal note to the rest of the justices in the morning so they could make their final preparations.

Kirsten McGrath was one of three female law clerks on Justice O'Malley's staff. O'Malley was the only justice with three women law clerks, and the only reason why he didn't have four was he didn't want to raise suspicions amongst the rest of the Court. Some might whisper or raise an eyebrow. Even though he was eighty-eight years old, he was a still a red-blooded American male who liked to look at the pretty ladies.

He especially liked the cheerleader types, and McGrath, at the ripe old age of twenty-seven, would not look out of place in a short skirt jumping up and down on the sidelines cheering on her favorite team. She, like her female cohorts, was roughly five-five and a buck ten. Also like the others, she had a perky bust line which, when the top two buttons of her blouse were undone, could be quite revealing even to an old codger like O'Malley. The Justice's eyesight was never better than on those days. The male justices on the Court couldn't help but notice O'Malley's hires, and if Rickenbacker's Lockhart said he was heading down to Hooters during the middle of the afternoon, it meant he was going to drop off a draft or a memo at Justice O'Malley's office.

O'Malley took his time choosing his law clerks and pored over resumes like it was a matter of great constitutional importance. Why don't those prospective clerks put their pictures on their resumes? he would mumble to himself. He liked young white women with blonde or brown hair and those from California shot straight to the front of the line. He had three Stanford law grads on his staff. All of them tanned very easily. The sole male law clerk, who O'Malley oftentimes forgot what his name was, had come from Northwestern. Or maybe it was the University of Chicago. Somewhere in Illinois, he couldn't remember. The man might have been gay. O'Malley wasn't sure of that either. It wasn't on his resume. He hoped he was though. O'Malley didn't want some other heterosexual guy in the office distracting his young "girlfriends."

Contrary to many males, O'Malley was not a leg man. The legs, he lamented, were most often hidden under the desk anyway. Plus, those pesky pantsuits were none too revealing. Although he did like casual Fridays when the women wore their tight jeans along with their revealing T-shirts.

During the interview process, O'Malley had perfected the trick of sliding his glasses down his nose so that his eyes would be hidden behind the top rim. The unsuspecting female had no idea he was sizing her up. Scribbled notations on the top of resumes would most likely include 36B, 36C, or 39D. He actually had a 40DD on his staff once, but she left the legal profession after finding more lucrative work out in Hollywood where she was born and raised. He was surely violating some federal hiring law, but who was going to file a discrimination lawsuit against some sweet, old Supreme Court justice.

McGrath, the 36C of the current group, was a favorite of O'Malley. She liked to hover around his desk and bend over to point out words in a draft. She would also playfully flirt with the Justice and wink at him when he said complimentary things about her. Plus, she smelled nice too. Like a Hawaiian beach with its sun, sand, and trade winds. She was the real reason he had remained on the Bench these last two years.

McGrath was an early riser and on several occasions even beat Rickenbacker's Lockhart into the empty Supreme Court Building. Today, being Friday, she had on her blue jeans and her favorite Stanford sweatshirt. Underneath, she wore a form-fitting black T-shirt. The office could be chilly on some days even in the swamp-like summer months of Washington, D.C. Although sometimes she had to take off the sweatshirt because it felt like someone had turned up the thermostat.

Carrying her large Starbucks latte, with what she claimed was filled with extra caffeine, and her laptop computer, she entered her office and shuffled the mess of papers she had left last night. She could see Justice O'Malley's office door from her desk and it was slightly ajar. O'Malley told the Court security officers that he was not going home the previous evening as he wanted to do some late-night reading. He slept in his chair at home anyway, so he could do the same as he often did at the office. Plus, the widower didn't like the loneliness of his condominium.

After a sip of caffeine, the perky McGrath headed for the door before stopping. Either the furnace had been turned on or she was working up a sweat. She whipped off the sweatshirt and hung it on the hook behind the door. She walked across the hall and peeked into Justice O'Malley's office. The back of his chair was to the door but she could see his loafers on the footstool behind his desk. She gave a firm knock.

"Justice O'Malley, can I get you anything?"

It was not unusual for the Justice to nod off during all hours of the day. His head was even seen bouncing up and down on the Bench one day as he tried to stay awake during an argument about federal water rights law. Truth be told, even the younger justices had trouble keeping their eyes open for that one. She knocked harder this time.

"Justice O'Malley?"

She pushed open the door and walked to the side of his desk. O'Malley had Hussein's draft in his lap and a yellow legal pad on his desk. The pen was on the floor.

"Good morning, Justice."

McGrath was almost afraid to touch him. Startling an eighty-eight-year-old man could do bad things to his heart. She decided a light tap on his shoulder would do no harm.

"Justice O'Malley?"

She leaned in a little closer just the way he liked. Maybe a whiff of her coconut-scented shampoo would snap him right out of his slumber. She noticed the old man's chest did not seem to be moving under his sweater vest. She then looked at the carotid artery in his neck. It didn't seem to be pulsating. Maybe this was his way of joking around with her.

Any time now he was going to jump out of his chair and scare the wits out of her, maybe causing her buxom breasts to bounce up and down in sheer terror much to his delight.

This time she shook him harder. "Justice O'Malley, are you okay?"

No, he was not okay. He was dead.

"Oh my God! Oh my God! Oh my God!"

She could not believe this was happening. She didn't know what to do. She didn't know who to call. Her mind went completely blank. To her surprise, O'Malley's male law clerk had just walked in early and was on his way to the rest room.

"Hey!" She was so flustered she couldn't think of the man's name. It must have been contagious in the office. "I need some help in here."

The clerk with no name peeked into O'Malley's office to see if McGrath was talking to him.

"I think Justice O'Malley is dead!"

The male clerk walked around the desk and gave O'Malley a good shake, causing the Justice's copy of the draft opinion to fall to the floor.

"Oh my God," he said. A thought entered his mind that he had just become unemployed.

"What are we going to do?"

The issue had come up before. During the office Christmas party, actually this year it had been called the Holiday Party so no one would get offended, O'Malley's law clerks sat around the office to finish their beers after the Justice had bid them adieu for the evening. When the question was asked by one of the quartet of what they would do if O'Malley kicked the bucket, the male clerk suggested they just prop up the Justice in his chair and tell the other justices that he was sleeping and couldn't be disturbed. The clerks could then run the show and file as many orders and opinions as they could before the stench became too much to bear.

"He was going to make his decision today on *Abullah*," McGrath whispered to remind her fellow clerk.

"I know."

He looked at her. He knew what she was thinking. She knew what he was thinking. If O'Malley's concurrence was officially transmitted today, the opinion could be handed down immediately. It would stand as O'Malley's last judicial act on the Court. And what a hell of a way to go out. He looked in her eyes again and bit his lip. He then glanced toward the hall.

"Go lock the door."

Union Station – Washington, D.C.

Less than a mile away from the Supreme Court Building, Sharif al-Rashad and Abdullah Hassani were having a breakfast of coffee and donuts. Sharif had called his old friend the night before and told him today was the day. If all went as planned, the announcement would probably be made at 11 a.m. If something came up, the Court might wait and hand the opinion down at 4 p.m., just in time for the evening news anchors to get their stories together for their nightly shows.

Sharif was a proud young man. He sat back in his seat as he and Hassani watched tourists and travelers walk by. Sharif had never felt so powerful. Most pedestrians walking down the sidewalks of D.C. can smell the power the city exudes. The marble monuments, the massive edifices of government largesse, the stately Capitol Dome – this is where it all happened, where the movers and shakers made the deals that ran the country. Sure, those pin-striped suit wearing bankers on Wall Street had a say in it, but those in Washington could always tax and regulate those who got too big or arrest and prosecute those who got out of line. But the pedestrians rarely had a say in how the governmental machine turned. That was reserved for the President and his team of Cabinet secretaries, the congressional leaders, and the justices of the Supreme Court. Of course, the guys with the stars on their shoulders had their say over at the Pentagon.

But Sharif will have had his hand in the cauldron of power on this day. Although Justice Hussein's name would be on the opinion, Sharif's resume would no doubt accentuate his work for the man and just happen to list cases he was involved in. This case would be his calling card to left-wing social functions and top law firms. Some day in the future, cable news shows would request his presence to expound on the inner workings of the Supreme Court and pick his brain as "The One" who once clerked for Justice Ali Hussein. As many law clerks often do, Sharif believed he was well on his way to becoming a Supreme Court justice in the future.

"Does your office have anything planned for tonight?" Hassani asked. He envisioned a great soiree where the Justice and his clerks would be jubilantly hoisted in the air for all to praise.

"I doubt it. We never have in the past."

"But today is extra special."

"Maybe Justice Hussein will treat us to dinner for all our hard work."

"Can I come?"

"You want to come out to dinner with our office?"

"I would like to congratulate Justice Hussein," Hassani gushed. "He is a great man. And we could use more like him."

"I'll agree to that."

"And more people like you too."

"Thank you, my friend." Sharif glanced at his watch and thought he had better head to work. He wanted to walk around the building and take in the atmosphere. A reporter had recognized him the other day and asked if he would be available for questions. He demurred, but gave him his card. "Soon we can talk," he told the man.

"How about I call you tonight?"

"Yes," Sharif said, pushing back his chair. "And if Justice Hussein treats us to dinner I will give you a heads up so you can drop by."

"Thank you, my son."

The two hugged and went their separate ways. Sharif blended in with the tourists and bureaucrats as he walked down the sidewalk on his way to the Supreme Court. Hassani was in no particular hurry. He strolled down Pennsylvania Avenue, thinking he might do some sightseeing. He made a stop at the National Archives and eyed the Constitution and the Declaration of Independence. It brought no chills to his skin. He felt like spitting on the protective glass. On his way out he noticed a strikingly beautiful blonde leading a tour group. She looked familiar, like he had seen her recently. Maybe she had been on television, he thought. Thinking of TV, Hassani reminded himself to find a place with one so he could watch the news when the Court handed down its decision. It would be a moment of celebration he didn't want to miss.

Sharif hit First Street and saw a mass of satellite trucks and fixed camera positions. Reporters were checking their hair and dusting off their suits. Word had leaked that today was the day, and the cable news shows went live at 8 a.m. The banner across the bottom of one network read "Showdown at the Supreme Court" and the anchors billed it as the great heavyweight match of the century – the Supreme Court versus the President of the United States.

Sharif decided to take a seat on the ledge of the fountain in the front plaza and take in the scene while reading the news stories on his BlackBerry. He took a picture and e-mailed it to Hassani. Someday the picture would go in his legal scrapbook. Maybe it would even be included in the legal papers he would donate upon his death to some institution of higher learning wanting the writings of a great legal jurist.

He just knew his day would only get better.

CHAPTER 21

The Supreme Court of the United States – Washington, D.C.

McGrath and the nameless clerk were pacing back and forth in O'Malley's office while the old man rested in peace still slumped in his chair. They had searched the papers on the Justice's desk to see if he had written down something on the *Abullah* case – a memo of concurrence, a written concurring opinion to be filed with the majority opinion, anything. The ringing telephone caused McGrath to screech in fright, her shaking hand quickly covering her mouth.

The male clerk held out his hands, a motion telling her to control herself and calm down. Relax, nothing out of the ordinary here. "Hello, Justice O'Malley's office." The clerk looked at the ceiling with the phone to his ear. His voice was calm, almost soothing. "This is Paul speaking."

"Paul," McGrath mouthed to herself. Yes, she now remembered. His name was Paul. His last name still escaped her.

"He's unavailable at the moment. Can I take a message?" He grabbed a pen from Justice O'Malley's desk and then threw it back down. What was he thinking? He picked it up again by the tip and wiped the barrel on the leg of his jeans. He was a lawyer by training, and even in the hubbub of the last twenty minutes, he knew fingerprints always seemed to come back and bite a person in the ass. He decided against writing the message down. It's not like the Justice was going to get back to the caller. He dropped the phone in the cradle, wiped it with his sleeve, and took a breath.

"Who was it?"

"The Justice has a couple of shirts at the cleaners that need to be picked up."

Wanting to get back to the more pressing business of the day, McGrath blurted out. "Paul, what are we going to do?"

Paul racked his brain trying to think of everything Justice O'Malley had said the day before about the case. He thought he overheard the

Justice say he might just simply sign on to the majority opinion. If that was the case, Paul could get on the computer, type up a concurrence memo, and send it out. No forged signature would even be required. He started opening the drawers carefully but nothing in the old memos jumped out at him. The desk's lap tray was full of number two pencils, red pens, and paper clips. Paul then bent over and saw a mess of papers scattered under the desk. He gently maneuvered the Justice's chair and tried to reach underneath the desk. He then recoiled in fright.

"Oh shit."

"What?" McGrath asking, shooting a look at him with her brown eyes. Did you find what you were looking for? the eyes wondered. The look on Paul's shocked face indicated no. He was whiter than the corpse of Justice O'Malley sitting right in front of them.

"I pushed the button."

"What button?"

"The panic button."

Every justice had a panic button on the underside of his or her desk. If a justice was confronted with someone who either was uninvited or had worn out their welcome, a push of the button would bring court security officers running – guns drawn if they felt like it. The now blinking light on the button indicated it had been pushed and the cavalry would soon be on its way.

"Oh shit," McGrath responded in agreement. The button must have worked because they were both in a full blown panic. McGrath had walked into the building carrying a cup of coffee and her laptop. She now envisioned leaving it in a pair of handcuffs.

"Go unlock the door!" Paul yelled. "Now! Hurry!"

McGrath ran to the door and lunged for the lock. She then opened it slightly and peeked around. She could hear footsteps pounding down the marble hallway.

"Hey! We need some help in here!" Paul yelled to anyone within earshot. He grabbed the phone and dialed 9-1-1.

McGrath caught on quickly. "Help!" she yelled, sticking her head fully out the door and waving the security guards in. "It's Justice O'Malley!"

The guards holstered their weapons as they entered and saw Paul on the phone and Justice O'Malley in his chair with his chin resting against his chest.

"Yes, we need an ambulance at the Supreme Court!"

The guards took over and took the Justice to the ground. Finding no pulse, they proceeded to give him CPR. Paul moved the Justice's chair to give them room and stood with his arm on McGrath's shoulders. She began to cry.

Their boss for the last two years had died.

The White House – Washington, D.C.

The President was in his private office just outside the Oval. Wiley and the Attorney General had been there for five minutes and they all whispered amongst themselves. All of them felt a little uncomfortable at the discussion. Lawyers at the Department of Justice had come up with a plan that might help the President's situation. Or make it worse, nobody was real sure.

"So the terrorist detainees are still in West Bend?" the President asked.

"Yes," the Attorney General responded. "They've been in a holding pattern ever since the lawsuit was filed."

"And you think if we put them on a plane to Guantanamo Bay that might change the complexion of the game?"

"Guantanamo Bay is not American soil. The federal court has no jurisdiction over them down there."

"Hasn't the court already obtained jurisdiction over them here?"

The Attorney General shrugged her shoulders. "Well, the Government's position is the federal courts have no jurisdiction and any precedent to the contrary should be overruled. And remember, Mr. President, you're the Commander-in-Chief and if you tell the military to move the prisoners, they'll move the prisoners."

"It's not actually the battlefield though," the President responded.

"Well, then ship 'em back to Afghanistan," Wiley snapped. "They shouldn't have been brought to the U.S. in the first place. They're not even U.S. citizens."

The President slammed his fist in his palm. He prided himself on being decisive. But this decision just felt problematic, like he would be opening up a legal and political can of worms. And he wasn't sure he could explain his actions when the liberal media lions pounced on their Republican prey. He sat down in his desk chair, folded his hands, and rested his elbows on his knees.

"Mr. President," the Attorney General said softly. "It might help if the detainees were in the air before the decision was handed down."

With his hands still folded, he looked at his left wrist and then up at the Attorney General.

"Move 'em to Gitmo now."

Outside the gates on the north side of the White House a group of protesters had taken up residence near Lafayette Park. It was the usual crew with their cow bells and bass drums hoping to force the President out of the Executive Mansion with hours and hours of bad music. The signs called him a "warmonger" and "Herr Schumacher," and one even had a picture of the President with a Hitler mustache and a swastika on his forehead. Most of the protesters were unkempt with long hair and wore Vietnam era clothing that smelled like it hadn't been washed since the Nixon Administration. The media photographers loved them and goaded the most radical ones into saying the most vile thing they could muster against "that damn Schumacher in the White House."

Hassani had made his way up Pennsylvania Avenue. He hadn't been in this good a mood for quite some time. The thought of the St. Louis assassination debacle hadn't even crossed his mind in days. He stopped at the White House gates and took a picture. He smiled knowing the President was going to get his beat down today. He then turned his attention to the protesters and held out his cell phone again. He thought he'd take a picture and send it to al-Rashad. Maybe later he would join the group of dirty anarchists in celebration.

The Supreme Court of the United States – Washington, D.C.

Chaos was breaking out inside the justices' chambers. The Marshal had notified the Chief Justice that the Court suddenly had only eight members. The Chief Justice ordered that no one on any staff leave the building. No one was to make any calls, e-mails, texts, or even update their Facebook page; nothing until the emergency meeting of the Court had concluded. Any staff members not in the building were ordered to be denied entry for the time being.

The eight remaining justices filed into the Conference Room and took their usual seats. A bouquet of fresh flowers sat on the table in front of Justice O'Malley's empty chair. The female justices both had red eyes and clutched moist tissues. Justice O'Malley had welcomed the women onto the Court and a close friendship grew between all of them over the years. The Chief Justice, along with Justices Rickenbacker, Pentano, Somerton, and Alonso wore long faces knowing they would never see their colleague again. Justice Hussein's face was not one of somber reflection though. It was full of anger. He knew his case of destiny was most likely gone for good.

"All right," the Chief Justice started. "As you all know, Justice O'Malley did not have any family. Outside of us, I guess. I have instructed the Clerk to begin preparations for a public viewing in the Great Hall within the next few days. I believe the Clerk also has Justice O'Malley's burial wishes so I will oversee those preparations. I believe he will be buried at Arlington."

The Chief Justice asked those in attendance if they had anything to add. Justice Anders asked about a statement from the Court, and the Chief Justice said a formal statement by the Clerk of the Court would be made within the hour. Thereafter, the individual justices were free to offer their own thoughts of condolence.

The Chief Justice then moved on to Court business – the real reason they had showed up on this summer day.

"We also need to discuss the status of the *Abullah* case."

Justice Hussein could be seen glaring at the table in front of him.

"As it stands now, each side has four votes and no one has indicated any desire to switch sides. Obviously, we don't have a majority. We can do one of two things – we can announce the decision as affirmed by an equally divided court, which means the lower court ruling will stand and our decision will have no precedential value. Or we can hold off and wait for a new justice to be nominated and confirmed and maybe hear the case again."

The Chief Justice then asked the other justices for their thoughts. The conservative justices wanted the decision to be filed, thereby letting the District Court decision stand and allowing all parties to move on. The liberals on the Court didn't like the idea of proceeding without a majority on such an important issue. They were willing to wait for a new justice even if it meant they would be in the dissenting party. Justice Rickenbacker, his head shaking back and forth, responded that waiting would result in a political and media circus that would make a mockery of the confirmation process.

The Chief Justice nodded his head and jotted down a few notes. "Ali, what about you?"

Justice Hussein slowly turned his head toward the Chief Justice. His smoldering eyes could have bored a hole in the oak paneling.

"What the hell difference does it make?" he lashed out. "I don't give a damn what you do." He then pushed back his chair and stomped out of the room.

The Chief Justice waited for the Conference Room door to close before speaking. He told the remaining six justices that the decision would be announced following Justice O'Malley's funeral. That way they could properly honor him without having the media distractions. The justices said nothing else and left for their chambers.

CHAPTER 22

The White House – Washington, D.C.

Constructed during the Theodore Roosevelt Administration, the West Wing of the White House contains some of the most prized real estate in all of the United States. Staff members beg for the prestigious honor of saying they work in the West Wing. Some would even be okay with working in a storage closet, on a chair in the hall, or even in a bathroom stall. Whatever it took to say they worked down the hall from the President.

President Schumacher's staff was hard at work wondering when the Supreme Court's decision would be handed down. Some were preparing the counterassault, others trying to find a way around it. Those in the West Wing with offices had their doors open just in case someone they had to know about walked by. The deputy chiefs and secretarial pools buzzed with energy, answering phones and peering at computer screens. Close-captioned TVs ran along all four walls, giving every occupant the ability to know what was going on anywhere in the world twenty-four hours a day.

The busy bees at their desks were startled by the wild man screaming at the top of his lungs running through the cubicles.

"Schu! Schu! Turn on the TV! Get to a TV!"

It had to be Wiley. He was the only one who would call the President that. In a blur, the President's bald chief of staff was seen hurtling over chairs and boxes on his way to the Oval Office and announcing his reasons to the greater bi-state area. The Oval Office was down the hall to the right then down another hall but Wiley had important news to tell. He'd probably head to the rooftop next. The startled staff members gathered their wits then reached for their remote controls and hit the mute button.

The President was in the Oval Office reading his briefing papers when Wiley barged in and told him to get to a TV. He had been tipped off by the Supreme Court that an unexpected announcement was going to be made. Both of them hustled into the President's private study and stared wide-eyed at the TV.

The media throng had crowded around the Clerk of the Supreme Court who was preparing to read off a statement from the steps of the west front. On some occasions, the justices read portions of their opinions from the Bench. Perhaps they just wanted to get out of town for the summer and left the Clerk to make the announcement of the vote.

The plaza below was a packed frenzy of protesters on both sides and a horde of police officers keeping them a safe distance apart from each other. The news anchors were chomping at the bit readying for the announcement of the Court's landmark decision and the rest of the day's schedule centered on deconstructing the opinion with expert legal analysis and discussing its political ramifications with the bevy of pundits ready to show how smart they were. The Clerk looked over the microphones and tape recorders to see if the reporters were ready. All indicated they were and some had thought ahead by preparing two e-mails containing stories on how they thought the decision would turn out. That way they could be the first to get the story out.

The Clerk cleared his throat and read from his prepared statement.

"Thomas P. O'Malley, Associate Justice of the Supreme Court of the United States, died this morning in his chambers of what are believed to be natural causes. He was eighty-eight years old. Justice O'Malley's wife, Constance Rutledge O'Malley, died in 2000. They had no children. Justice O'Malley had served on the Supreme Court for twenty-five years. Funeral arrangements will be forthcoming."

Some of the reporters almost tumbled down the steps of the Court in disbelief. The banner on CNN incorrectly showed that the Supreme Court had ruled against the President, someone in the control room obviously jumping the gun. A bombshell had just landed on One First Street Northeast in D.C. Two flashing red and blue lights suddenly greeted web visitors to the *Drudge Report*. Reporters were yelling into their cell phones, their preplanned e-mails now worthless. Some, who had run down the steps like madmen, were seen huffing and puffing back up them two at a time to hurl questions at the Clerk. The questions regarding Justice O'Malley's long tenure on the Court or his place in legal history were about as front and center as who would be the next Surgeon General or drug czar. Who cares about such trivial things! they cried.

"What about the *Abullah* case!" came the shouts.

"The Court will have no comment on the case until after Justice O'Malley's funeral." The Clerk then turned around and walked back inside.

The President and Wiley had to take a seat at the breaking news. The announcement of the decision had been postponed but most knew how it would turn out now. With four hard-core conservatives, the case would either be won with a liberal swing vote or simply result in a tie. Attorney General Donovan raced into the study, her heels in her hands as she had removed them to run through the West Wing.

"Mr. President," she huffed. "Unbelievable news, isn't it?"

"Indeed it is."

The President told Wiley to start working on a statement regarding Justice O'Malley's death that he could deliver in the Rose Garden sometime that afternoon. The President and the Attorney General then had a discussion that most Presidents have on the rare days when a Supreme Court justice dies while still a member of the Court. With a vacant seat on the Bench, the President had the responsibility to nominate a replacement.

"I can get you a handful of names by the end of the day, Mr. President," the Attorney General promised.

The President started pacing the floor of his private study. As most Presidents do, he had thought about filling a vacancy on the Supreme Court long before one opened up. It was one way that Presidents could impart their legacy well after their one or two terms had ended. With a lifetime appointment, a justice could serve twenty to thirty years after their nominating President was long gone.

"I'm fine with you getting a list ready. But just make sure Judge John Lincoln's name is on it."

The Supreme Court of the United States – Washington, D.C.

The door to the chambers of Justice Hussein was closed tightly and the yelling that could be heard behind it kept anyone from entering. Hussein's secretary would whisper into the phone that the Justice was busy and would have to call back at a more convenient time. Three of his law clerks had been sent home because there would be no work to do anyway. Only Sharif al-Rashad remained. And now both of them vented in private.

"That bastard President!" Hussein screamed over and over again. "He's going to nominate a conservative and we'll be in the minority for the next twenty years."

With the *Abullah* opinion, Hussein believed he would solidify his place as the liberal lion of the Supreme Court. One who future Democrat Presidents would point to in response to the question of what type of jurists that President would nominate to the federal courts at all levels, not just the Supreme Court. So too did Hussein dream of becoming Chief Justice and it was a possibility given the current Chief Justice's age. But it would only happen if a Dem occupied the White House. If President Schumacher was elected in the fall, Chief Justice Shannon might retire to let the President choose the Chief Justice for the next generation. Now Justice Hussein's dreams would become his nightmares.

"He wasn't even elected President and now he gets to nominate a replacement!" Hussein ranted.

"He wasn't even elected Vice President!" Sharif reminded him.

"I hate that son of a bitch!"

Sharif was equally upset, not only about the loss of his moment in the sun, but also for his Muslim brethren that, he believed, would be harmed by the President's decisions. "He's going to try those innocent detainees in the tribunal! Think of the laughingstock America will be in the eyes of the rest of world when they're found guilty!"

"He is dangerous, Sharif!"

"He is at war with Islam!" Sharif yelled in response, pounding the desk in frustration.

"Then it is up to us to stop him," Hussein said calmly, his pulse lowering to a more reasonable level.

"How?" Sharif's tone indicated he thought stopping the President would be an impossible task.

After lifting his eyes to the ceiling, Justice Hussein pulled out a copy of the Declaration of Independence and found the passage he was looking for. "'A Prince whose character is thus marked by every act which may define a Tyrant, is unfit to be the ruler of a free people.'"

He then looked at the case reporters lining his shelves. The power of the word had been a forceful sword in the past and it would have to do so again. "We will dissent at every opportunity, and we will not hold back. We will plunge the sword into the heart of that tyrant President's arguments at every turn. And we will let our Democrat friends twist and turn that sword in their political campaigns and TV ads."

"That is meaningless!" Sharif shot back. "The President must be removed from office! He is shredding the Constitution."

Hussein got up from his chair and walked over to Sharif. He put his arm around his shoulders. "He will be stopped. He will be thrown out of office and disgraced. Our time will come."

Sharif struggled to restrain the tears from running down his cheeks. "We were so close," he whispered, worn out from the screaming and yelling.

Union Station – Washington, D.C.

Hassani wandered around before he wound up where he started that morning. At Union Station, he found a restaurant and headed for the bar. Once situated, he glanced up to the TV on the wall. The waitress was transfixed with Oprah on the couch with Angelina. He shook his head at all those lazy Americans he imagined were watching such fluff. He was in a great mood though and decided to celebrate with a drink. He made eye contact with the male bartender and he approached.

"What can I get you?"

"Non-alcoholic beer," Hassani said. "A glass of ice water too."

The bartender grabbed a bottle from the ice bucket and set it and a glass on the bar. The talk with his other customers had only been about one thing on that afternoon, so as he filled the glass with water, he put the conversation starter right out there. "Heck of a story down there at the Supreme Court, huh?"

"It was a great day," Hassani said, smiling. Picking up his drink, he didn't notice the shocked look on the bartender's face. He hadn't watched the news. Of course, he didn't need to since he had the inside track on the decision being handed down.

The waitress snapped her attention away from the TV. She gave him a cold hard stare. "A great day?" How could you say that? was her tone.

"Yeah," Hassani said. What of it? he said with his body language.

"You must be a conservative, huh?" she huffed, loudly throwing her tray down on the counter in disgust. "Damn heartless Republican."

"What's your problem?"

"Just because someone's a liberal doesn't mean he's not a real person." Most likely she didn't even know Justice O'Malley personally.

She was probably a Democrat, or maybe just a concerned citizen with an ounce of respect for the dearly departed. Although it wasn't like the Republicans had paraded into the joint with balloons and a cake to celebrate the new Court vacancy.

"I don't know what you're talking about lady." Hassani was beginning to get hot under the collar. He didn't take dissent very well. Especially from a woman.

"Do you live in a cave? Justice O'Malley died today, you insensitive jerk!"

The bartender ushered her away in a bear hug as Hassani almost fell out of his chair. His head had been so high in the clouds that he had no clue. With his mind now spinning, he stumbled toward the door.

"He probably voted for Bush too!" the now-restrained waitress yelled out at Hassani before he made it outside.

The insult made her feel good so she hurled another one at the man.

"Both of them!"

CHAPTER 23

The Supreme Court of the United States – Washington, D.C.

The public viewing of Justice O'Malley's casket was a dignified affair. The black hearse pulled up to the front plaza of the Supreme Court and a collection of his former and current law clerks carried the casket to the steps. Although they did have to recruit Rickenbacker's Lockhart shortly after the start of the procession because the Hooters' girls were having trouble carrying the three-hundred pound mahogany coffin more than five feet without appearing to buckle at the knees. The clerks eventually gave way and let the military honor guard carry Justice O'Malley up the forty-four marble steps passing under the "Equal Justice Under Law" etched in the Western pediment, through the open bronze doors, and into the Great Hall.

Once inside, the justices had a moment alone with their former colleague. The Chief Justice remarked how wonderful the red-white-and-blue flag looked amongst the white marble of the Hall. Some of the justices came to the realization they might be in O'Malley's position in the near future. Some nearer than others.

The President and the First Lady arrived via motorcade and paid their respects. The President's public statement had emphasized O'Malley's long and dedicated service to the Court and to his country and noted his "unquenching desire for fairness" and "a determined belief in the rule of law."

While the President's words were kind, diplomatic, and appropriate, those on the leftist fringe were coming unglued. Some were saying Justice O'Malley's death was highly suspicious, what with it coming on the day of the suspected announcement of the *Abullah* decision. Left-wing bloggers spread the rumor that one of the other justices might have poisoned O'Malley or snuck up behind him and given him a heart attack. Word got out that the Supreme Court Building had been on lockdown after O'Malley's body was found. No doubt so the conservative justices, all of whom were suspects in the weirdo bloggers' minds, especially "that right-winger Rickenbacker," could destroy evidence and make it look like "natural causes." Some claimed the President or the CIA might have been involved. They called on all Democrats in Washington to demand an immediate investigation into the circumstances of O'Malley's death. They then hid in their basement bunkers fearing the President would send his black helicopter strike teams to silence them.

The White House – Washington, D.C.

The day after Justice O'Malley's funeral, the Supreme Court Clerk issued the decision of the equally divided court in the *Abullah* case. The President's military tribunals would go forward at Guantanamo Bay. Over the next few weeks, he interviewed candidates for the Court vacancy. The President's staff along with lawyers at the Department of Justice had whittled the list down to five qualified candidates. Four of them were federal appeals court judges and their long lists of opinions were scoured over for possible issues that might derail a nominee in the Senate confirmation process. The fifth candidate was the Governor of California and a former U.S. Attorney General.

FBI agents were quickly sent out across the country to conduct background checks of each one – asking the friend, colleague, or acquaintance of the candidate about any possible drug or alcohol use they might have witnessed over the years or anything that would indicate the candidate could not be trusted as a federal employee. What about their demeanor? How did others in their profession view them? Nothing had raised any red flags on these well-vetted candidates.

"Judge Lincoln, good to see you again," the President said, extending a hand.

"Mr. President, always a pleasure."

The two old friends sat in the chairs in front of the Oval Office fireplace. The weather was blistering hot outside and the fireplace was not in use. A firestorm, however, would surely erupt in the capital if Judge Lincoln was nominated to replace Justice O'Malley.

Fifty-two-year old John A. Lincoln hailed from rural Indiana, somewhere amongst the corn and bean fields between Chicago and Indianapolis he liked to say. He was known to still farm the land when he wasn't writing legal opinions. He had graduated from Purdue and then attended Wabash State School of Law at the same time a young student named Anthony Schumacher was on the rolls. While the two took different career paths, they kept in touch over the years talking baseball, racing, and politics. Lincoln sat as a federal trial judge for ten years before his appointment to the Seventh Circuit Court of Appeals in Chicago, where he made his name writing staunchly conservative opinions that took to task those who sought to legislate from the bench. He had a "well-qualified" rating from the ABA and received equally high marks from conservative judicial groups.

"We are a long way away from our days in law school in little old Silver Creek, Indiana, aren't we?"

"Yes, sir, we are," Judge Lincoln agreed. "Two rural boys from the heartland of America have somehow ended up sitting in the Oval Office."

"One is President and the other is going to be on the Supreme Court."

Judge Lincoln bashfully nodded his head, as if to say he deeply appreciated the sentiment. "It could be a close call for me in the Senate, Mr. President."

"You've been confirmed before."

"Yes, but I was just going to be a harmless judge in the federal court in Indianapolis and then still somewhat harmless when I sat on the appellate court in Chicago."

The President nodded in agreement. Lincoln's nomination would result in all-out warfare between the Democrats and Republicans. When word leaked out that Judge Lincoln was on the shortlist, Democrats were heard shouting "No!" and then "Hell no!" War rooms were being constructed and crisis management teams went on full alert. The thought of their liberal five-four majority being replaced by a solid five conservative bloc sent Democrats over the edge. The liberals couldn't get their pet issues implemented in Congress because their agenda did not have majority support. So they desperately needed their judicial legislators to carry the load and find rights wherever they could – foreign law, international courts, or just make up whatever they needed. The Constitution offered no hindrance to their results-oriented jurisprudence.

Green freaks now worried their hard fought corporate killing environmental regulations would be overturned. Gays and lesbians feared a conservative Court ruling would force them back into the closet, as if the President of the United States was going to invade the sanctity of their bedroom and proselytize to them with readings from the eighteenth chapter of Leviticus. The pro-abortion crowd was by far the most upset. Think of the babies that will be born if Judge Lincoln gets on the High Court! They hadn't been this horrified since the days of Ronaldus Magnus.

"I have two questions for you."

"Okay.

"Are you going to change who you are and the way you rule when you get confirmed?" It was a legitimate question. Republicans in the past had been promised that certain nominees were reliable conservatives only to find out after the justice was confirmed for life that he or she was actually a Liberal. Republicans now wanted to be sure.

Judge Lincoln thought for a second before a sly smile appeared on his face. "A wise man once said, 'I was born a conservative. I will live a conservative. And I shall die a conservative.'"

That line received a big grin from the President. Someone had been listening to his campaign kickoff speech.

"I'm the same guy you knew in law school and I'll be the same guy when you and I are retired at home in Indiana."

"Good. Second question. Are you willing to fight?"

"Fight?"

"Are you willing to endure the crap the Dems are going to throw at you and give it right back at them? They will stop at nothing. They will lie. They will spread rumors and innuendo. Your good name will be dragged through the mud with reckless abandon. And they will win unless you take a stand and fight back."

This got another smile from Judge Lincoln. "There was another wise man who once said, 'I have not yet begun to fight.'" That was John Paul Jones. "And I will fight until the very last day."

The President reached out his hand. "Good to hear. We'll announce it tomorrow and get the process started. I've already told the Senate leaders I want you confirmed in time for the start of the term in October."

"I'll be ready."

The Holiday Inn – Arlington, Virginia

Abdullah Hassani was staying in his third hotel since traveling out to the Nation's Capital to visit with Sharif. Something was so out of the ordinary that his credit card company called to make sure his card hadn't been stolen. No, he angrily told them. He was simply at another hotel. But the growing number of rooms had not been his intention. His angry tirades on the room phone and late-night cursing caused multiple complaints from the guests trying to get a good night's sleep. The hotel managers politely told him to leave or they'd call the police.

The rage that had led him to St. Louis had returned and his cell phone statement showed multiple calls to Mularah, who was still smarting from his failure to kill the President.

"Rasoul here."

"It's me."

"I will drive the garbage truck out to Washington tomorrow," Mularah said. "I loaded the RPGs into the back and threw a week's worth of trash on top. It's already starting to smell. No cop in his right mind would dare dive into that mess."

"Good. Don't forget about the AK-47s."

"I have them in the back too as well as a box of Tovex. I attached four construction barricades to the top of the truck."

"Excellent."

"What about men?" Mularah wanted to use the drive east to begin thinking about the plan and how best to implement it.

"I put in a call to my friend in Pakistan. He has three Americans who are ready. The fourth has a temporary visa and wants to come as well. Can we do the job with six total?"

Mularah hesitated slightly. The mention of six men meant Hassani wanted Mularah and himself in on carrying out the attack. "Yes, six men will be plenty. We could do it with five if you want."

"I will think about it. They will arrive in New York tomorrow night and take the train down to Washington the next morning."

"Do you want me to bring enough orange vests and hard hats for all of us?"

"Yes. Just to be safe."

"I will get everything ready and see you tomorrow night."

"Good. By the time you get to Virginia," Hassani said, "I'll have the plan ready to go." The beeping on his cell phone either meant his battery was going dead or he had another call. It was the latter. "Rasoul, it's Sharif. I need to take this. I will see you tomorrow. Be safe."

CHAPTER 24

Capitol Hill – Washington, D.C.

Prior to the start of Judge Lincoln's Senate confirmation hearings, the Democrats in both Houses conferred on how to pull out all the stops to derail the nomination. He had made the obligatory "courtesy calls" to the individual senators where the Democrats smiled warmly for the cameras and hailed Lincoln's experience and intellect before setting out to stab him in the back once the bright lights were turned off.

Lincoln had been a federal prosecutor and then a respected federal judge. His opinions were conservative but not so over the top that they could be used as kindling by flamethrowing Dems. The President had stated at the announcement that Judge Lincoln was a firm believer in judicial restraint and would fully and fairly interpret the law as written not legislate from the bench. In response, the liberals on the Senate Judiciary Committee decided they would just have to make their same old demagogic arguments they used in the past – like how all Republican judicial nominees are for forcing women into the back alleys for their abortions or requiring blacks to sit at segregated lunch counters. Since the Dems could not win on the merits, they had to resort to their old standby – character assassination.

On the other side of the Capitol, Art Brennan was meeting with Congresswoman Sanchez. Brennan had taken to the bottle after Justice O'Malley's death, not only because it meant he lost the *Abullah* case but also because it signaled the end of the liberal majority on the Court. His job had become infinitely harder.

"We were so close," Brennan said as he slumped in the chair of Sanchez's office. The early morning glass of bourbon was half full, although considering Brennan's sour mood, it was half empty.

"What's our next move?" Sanchez asked.

"I think I'm out of moves."

"So we just give up and let the President win?"

Brennan emptied the remaining bourbon into his scratchy throat.

"My only thought is impeachment."

"Impeachment?" Sanchez asked incredulously. "Did you forget the Republicans are in the majority in the House?"

With the buzz finally starting to kick in and soothe his weary soul, Brennan thought about it some more and decided he was right. "Yes, impeachment is the way to go."

"On what grounds? Where is the treason, the bribery, the high crimes and misdemeanors that would allow for impeachment and removal under the Constitution?" Even Sanchez was dubious about Brennan's plan.

"Conviction and removal should not be a concern for you. It is the nature of the charge that will bring down the President. You call for a committee to investigate the President's handling of the detainees while the Court was considering the case. You make it sound like he was subverting the Constitution and attempting to perpetrate a fraud on the Supreme Court."

"I don't think that will sway House Republicans."

Brennan slammed his fist on the table. "You're not trying to convince House Republicans! You're trying to convince the voters! You relentlessly smear this President from now until election day and the moderate voters will jump off the President's bandwagon. It has to be an all-out campaign to ruin the President's reputation in the eyes of the public."

Sanchez knew Brennan was right. She knew what the Democrats had to do. "I'll start making calls to the media so they'll be prepared to play up the story as much as possible." She then leaned back in her chair and smiled. "By November, President Schumacher won't know what hit him."

The National Archives – Washington, D.C.

Anna Schumacher wore a dark pantsuit with a white blouse as she guided a group of fifth graders who had traveled from Mount Vernon to view the Founding Documents. Archivist Daniels had allowed Anna to show groups through the Rotunda on a more frequent basis. She was wonderful with children and, most importantly, she was knowledgeable about the Documents. Several group leaders had e-mailed Daniels about how enjoyable the Archives experience was with the President's daughter wowing the kids. Daniels believed she might be the reason attendance was up and the cash registers in the gift shop were humming nicely.

During the summer months, the Rotunda and the Exhibit Hall are open until seven. Anna started work at three every Wednesday, Thursday, and Friday after her summer classes had completed for the day. She assisted Roberta Lopez, one of the Archives technicians. If Roberta needed a document pulled from the stacks, she'd send Anna on the hunt for the treasure. At times, Anna could not believe she was surrounded by so much history.

Wednesdays were busy days even during the summer months with tourists from all over the world filing past the Charters of Freedom in the Rotunda on one of their many stops around Washington. At 4 p.m., Daniels walked into Lopez's office to tell her he was taking Anna away from her for an hour or two. A tour group was outside and the chaperones begged the staff to ask if Anna Schumacher might be available to show the group around.

"Anna, you're wanted as a tour guide again," he said, poking his head in the conference room where she had set up shop.

"Another one?"

"You're very popular. Our most popular tour guide ever." His gushing praise was a bit over the top but it was true. "It's a Girl Scout troop from Annapolis."

"Girl Scouts, okay." She reached for her suit coat and straightened her collar in the mirror on the wall. She brushed back her long blonde hair and it rested nicely on her shoulders.

"Her boyfriend," a/k/a Agent Sessions, stood quietly just outside the room. He had no college garb on today. It was the standard dark suit and tie. His sunglasses were in his pocket. His earpiece and wrist mike were ready for duty. Three other agents were stationed at the end of the hall and one roamed the building. One more sat in the SUV outside.

"How do I look?" she asked as she entered the doorway.

Agent Sessions never liked it when she asked him that. She was drop-dead gorgeous and anything he said would never be enough. Plus, he was there to protect her, not scrutinize her looks or her attire. "Very professional."

She smiled and playfully locked arms with him as they moved down the hallway. "Just professional? Is that all you see?"

He managed to escape her delicate grasp and radioed the others that they were on the move to the Rotunda.

"Don't you like me?" she pouted.

He kept his eyes forward as they approached the other agents at the end of the hall. "Ma'am, I'm just trying to do my job."

"I told you not to call me Ma'am."

His quick glance out of the corner of his eye noticed her smile. He couldn't resist a grin himself, his chiseled cheeks blushing. She was just playing with him, a part of her bubbly personality. He held up a hand before they entered the public gallery.

"In position," he radioed.

"All clear," came the response.

"Miss Schumacher," he said with wink and a wave of his hand, "after you."

Anna's appearance from the back room brought bright smiles from the Girl Scouts who had their numerous merit badges on full display. Some jumped up and down with restrained glee, faithfully adhering to their chaperones' admonishment to treat the Archives as a library and thus keep the exuberance to a reasonable level. When they returned home that night, the topic at the dinner table would not be about viewing the Founding Documents or the grand monuments to great American leaders. No, it would be "we got to meet Anna Schumacher!" With a quick introduction, Anna led the girls around the Rotunda and stopped at the Constitution.

Figuring none of the Scouts were packing heat, Agent Sessions held back and scanned the entrance to the Rotunda. The security checkpoint with the magnetometers was fully manned. It had been in use long before the President's daughter became a volunteer, which made the Secret Service much more agreeable to the idea.

"Who was the first President of the United States?"

"George Washington," came the replies from the Scouts.

"Correct. As I am sure you are aware, he was known as the Father of the Country. Let's see if we can find George Washington's signature on the Constitution." Once their hunt was complete, they searched for James Madison, the Father of the Constitution. The history lesson then proceeded on to the Bill of Rights.

With her back to the Rotunda entrance, she didn't see what was going on behind her. There near the entrance was a young man holding up his cell phone toward the glass encasements. After dawdling around the Rotunda, he sprang to life once Anna made her way into public view.

A young perky female volunteer noticed the man and approached.

"Excuse me, sir," she said politely. "There's no photography allowed in the exhibition areas."

The man ignored her, the screen on his cell phone capturing a video of the Girl Scouts with their tour guide looking at the pages of the Constitution on display.

The female volunteer, who took her job seriously, was not going to back down. The ID hanging around her neck indicated her name was Britney Waterson. She had worked at the Archives for two summers now, and this was not her first time laying down the law. She raised her voice and stood in front of the camera, her blonde hair filling the screen. "Sir, there's no photography allowed in the Rotunda."

The man sidestepped the pesky volunteer and kept his camera on Anna.

"Sir, if you want a picture you can purchase one at the gift shop."

"I'm not using a flash," the man grunted.

Those in charge at the National Archives had been worried that flash exposure could damage the original documents on display so a rule was implemented prohibiting all filming, photographing, and videotaping – flash or not. Some people were unaware of the rule, notwithstanding the sign at the entrance to the Rotunda. When confronted by staff, however, most apologized and put the cameras away. One man refused to comply.

"Sir, please."

The man was growing impatient with her, like an annoying fly was buzzing around his head. "Shut up, bitch."

The next thing the man knew his right wrist was in a death grip and his phone was falling to the floor. "Hey pal, what part of 'no photographs' don't you understand?"

It was Agent Sessions and he was not in a good mood. The other equally angry Secret Service agents were hovering around the two. They didn't like it when people failed to follow directions causing them to make a scene.

"Get your hands off me!"

"There's no photography allowed in the Rotunda." Agent Sessions had the man's wrist behind his back now and the man tried to wrangle his way out of the grip. The commotion starting getting people's attention.

"I'm a lawyer! I know my rights! They're the rights protected by that

Constitution, you prick!" His free arm was pointing to the glass cases.

Anna turned around to see what was happening. She could see Agent Sessions reaching for his handcuffs as the other agents started pushing them toward the exit. She felt strangely unprotected at the moment, although she was surrounded by a group of hearty Girl Scouts. The female agent at the entrance to the Rotunda motioned to her that everything was under control and to continue on what she was doing.

Agent Sessions took the man straight out through the bronze doors and onto the steps of the building. He paraded the man to the side of the steps in hopes of figuring out who he was.

"What's your name?"

"I don't have to tell you shit. I'm a federal employee. I haven't done anything wrong."

"Sir, if you don't give us your name you're going to jail."

The sweat beaded on the man's forehead and he spat on the steps. He had just stepped out of the office to get some fresh air, he thought to himself. Maybe gain some inspiration by looking at the Founding Documents.

"My name's Sharif al-Rashad, and I work for Supreme Court Justice Ali Hussein."

Agent Sessions looked Sharif over. Nice suit. Polished wing tips. He could be telling the truth.

"Okay, Sharif, you got any identification on you?"

"I'd get it out of my wallet if you'd take these damn handcuffs off me."

Agent Sessions reached for his handcuff key. Some of the pedestrians were looking in their direction. "Sir, there's no reason to cause a scene. Have you been drinking this afternoon?" The smell was faint but enough to be noticeable.

"No, I have not," Sharif snapped. "It's none of your business anyway." He pulled out his wallet and found his government identification card. Sessions took it and handed it over to another agent who was on the phone with headquarters.

"Did you know there's a rule prohibiting the taking of any pictures or video inside the Rotunda?"

Sharif wasn't in the mood to discuss his knowledge of the law or to get lectured on federal regulations by some fancypants with a badge. "I wasn't using a flash. I wasn't going to do any damage to the documents."

"Listen, I understand what you're saying. But it's the rule and everyone has to abide by it." The agent on the phone handed back Sharif's ID and said he checked out. No arrest warrants for him either.

"All right, Sharif, we're going to let you go."

"I've got a good mind to file a civil rights lawsuit on you guys."

Agent Sessions was about two seconds away from bringing the cuffs out again. "Listen, you can either leave or you'll be arrested for interfering with a federal officer. I doubt Justice Hussein would like to read about one of his clerks in the police blotter in tomorrow's *Post*."

Sharif snatched his ID out of Sessions' hand, mumbling something about the man not knowing a thing about Justice Hussein. He then marched down the steps, cussing at the men in suits standing at the top. He angrily pounded the pavement on his way back to the Supreme Court.

CHAPTER 25

FBI Headquarters – Washington, D.C.

With the Fourth of July holiday fast approaching, Director Stubblefield was coordinating the security plan for the capital with the myriad of law-enforcement agencies in the District. Every agency had their own turf and felt confident enough in themselves to protect it. There was the U.S. Capitol Police, the U.S. Park Police, the U.S. Secret Service, the D.C. Metropolitan Police Department, not to mention the military. Every agency was on high alert given the thwarted attack on Washington last Independence Day. The terrorists would love nothing more than to strike against President Schumacher after he gave the order last year to shoot down the bomb-laden planes.

"Director Stubblefield, it's Mr. Carter on line one."

"Thank you. Hold my other calls unless it's the President."

Stubblefield took a breath before picking up the phone. Carter had been in Pakistan for almost two months. His weekly intelligence reports did not indicate the terrorist activity had abated. If anything, it was intensifying. A week ago, Carter overheard something about a plan to smuggle weapons into the United States via the Mexican border. His attempts to infiltrate the inner circle of the local terrorist leaders had been slow going. They imposed what could be called a good, old-fashioned American "waiting period" for all new arrivals – to watch their movements and make sure they really seek to wage jihad on America. It appeared to be a "need to know" kind of operation.

"Mac, how are you?"

"I am safe," he responded. He had journeyed to a hotel in Karachi, doubling back every so often to make sure he was not followed. He went to the third floor and entered the sixth room on the right. Inside sat two FBI agents with a secure telephone, along with an assortment of American snacks that Carter had been missing out on while attending terrorist camp. He claimed the food there was worse than that served in the federal penitentiary.

"What have you got for us?"

"Something is going down," he said.

"How do you know?"

"Three nights ago, four men were brought to the head of the camp and given some instructions. There were hugs and kisses all around. I overheard the leader, al-Lakwa, say these men were on their way to America."

"Who were they?"

"Three of them were the Americans I told you about previously. The other has a temporary visa."

"Where are they headed?"

"All I heard was New York. I don't know if that's where they are heading or if that's where the attack is going to take place. I don't even know who the leader is in the U.S."

Stubblefield had already been on the phone with the FBI in New York City as well as the New York City Police Commissioner. Those in the Big Apple never stopped being on guard to stop terrorism.

"Anything on a plan of attack? Dirty bomb? Suicide bombers?"

"No, I have nothing. I didn't see the men leave with anything other than their clothes and their paperwork."

"All right. They're probably in the country by now. How much more intelligence do you think you can get over there?"

"To be honest, the camp is about ready to break up. Al-Lakwa gets jumpy after a month or two in one spot. He'll probably disband the camp and start over again once the attack has taken place."

"All right, Mac," Stubblefield said. He then gave the order that Carter had been praying for all those days in the mosque. "I want you back in Washington."

Dirksen Senate Office Building – Washington, D.C.

Article II, Section 2 of the United States Constitution grants the President the power to appoint the justices of the Supreme Court "with the Advice and Consent of the Senate." Over one hundred men and women have received the "consent" of the Senate – some unanimously and others just squeaking by. Justice O'Connor was confirmed by a vote of 99 to 0 in 1981, while the margin for Justice Thomas Stanley Matthews a hundred years earlier was a single senator – the vote being 24 to 23.

In the past, the Senate showed great deference to the President's picks, figuring he had been elected by the people and should be able to select justices that share his legal philosophy. But *Roe* came along and then the conservatives seemed poised for a majority on the Court. Litmus tests were raised and claimed not to be used. Something called a filibuster entered the American lexicon and was considered. But the Democrats needed a more powerful weapon, something to stop the nomination before it ever got started. So they revolutionized the art of character assassination and "Borked" nominees right out of the process.

They needed it now more than ever because President Schumacher was threatening the last bastion for the implementation of unpopular liberal policies – the United States Supreme Court.

The six-foot-four inch Judge Lincoln raised his right hand and swore to tell the truth before the Senate Judiciary Committee. This was his second day in the hot seat, and the Democrats had been spreading their lies to their buddies in the media to pick him apart during the evening hours. Justice Hussein himself even took the unprecedented step of publicly saying Judge Lincoln was not qualified during a question-and-answer session at a university lecture. The lack of civility drew an immediate phone call from the Chief Justice and a stern rebuke.

Some Democrats went on the morning news shows complaining that the President sent a nominee who was too conservative. They wanted a more moderate justice, someone who would be closer in ideology to Justice O'Malley. Others wanted a woman, or a Hispanic, or a Jew. Of course, the Constitution doesn't require the President to replace one justice with someone of a similar judicial philosophy. Nor does it reserve certain seats on the Bench for a particular gender or a certain minority group. At any rate, Judge Lincoln was not half this or half that – as some are quick to point out in professing their Italian, Hispanic, or African heritage. No, he was all-American and proud of it.

"Judge Lincoln, I have a few questions for you."

The first interrogator of the day was Senator Wallace C. Vanderbilt of New York. The Democrat had served in the Senate for thirty-five years solely on the basis of his family's fortune (it was the oil Vanderbilts, not Cornelius and his railroads), and definitely not on his own merit. He wore hand-tailored three piece Italian suits, often carried a black and white cane, and was even seen wearing a monocle on occasion. Staffers sometimes referred to the eccentric New Yorker as

"Senator Peanut."

Vanderbilt's head was not just in the clouds but in the upper stratosphere, and the only thing he knew about the law was what his staff told him about it in a memo. The Republicans thought he was a dimwit but loved him anyway because he was always putting his foot in his big mouth. Over the years, he had raised millions for conservative campaign coffers as Republicans put his idiotic liberal quotes front and center in GOP fundraising letters. Plus, he had the annoying habit of repeating everything he said, as if saying it a second time would prove his point. But neither his foot-in-mouth disease nor his trust-fund education deterred him. He was a United States Senator.

"Judge, I want to talk about the *Boykin* case."

Vanderbilt's staff had given him a stack of papers on the case to read the previous evening. In it were a summary of the case, photographs, and possible questions he could ask of Judge Lincoln.

"Are you familiar with that case?"

"Vaguely, Senator. I believe that was fifteen years ago."

"It was a case involving child pornography, and you reversed the defendant's conviction. How could you do that?" The snarky tone oozed out of Vanderbilt's mouth and into the microphone. He glared down from his perch at the Judge sitting in front of him.

"I believe the facts of the case justified reversal?"

"But this case involved child pornography!" The Senator was determined to use the words "child pornography" as many times as he could. He knew the media would replay it over and over again later that evening thereby damning Judge Lincoln's chances at confirmation. Even the conservatives would be scared off from voting for him. Eventually, an irate public would no doubt call for the President to withdraw the nomination.

Judge Lincoln took a breath. He was tired of the high-brow, low-ball tactics of the Democrat senators. Most of them were not lawyers and none of them on the Committee had been judges. Few had to make the real difficult decisions that made a difference in someone's life – the next election always softening their spines, their fingers always checking the direction of the political winds. In Senator Vanderbilt's case, he was just an idiot.

"Senator, that case involved a parent who took some photos of his eight-year-old son and some friends while in the middle of rowdy horseplay. He forgot all about it until the cops showed up at a drug store when he picked up the pictures. He had no child pornography in his house or on his computer."

"But the man was found guilty."

"Incorrectly under the law," the Judge replied. "And the panel of three judges, of which I was one, determined the pictures were not lewd and lascivious as required to sustain a conviction under the law."

Judge Lincoln's responses were calm and rational. And most Americans would not hold it against him considering appellate courts across the country do find defendants have been wrongly convicted on some occasion even when the facts appear egregious. Lady Justice does not peek out from behind the blindfold or stick her finger in the air to decide which way would be the politically correct decision to make.

But Senator Vanderbilt couldn't care less about the law or fairness or blind justice. He knew what he saw.

"I find your comments amazing, Judge," the seventy-five-year-old Senator huffed. "I spent last night looking at child pornography."

The room fell so quiet you could hear the air conditioning system humming at seventy-two degrees. Some of the Republicans on the Committee were seen with hands over their mouths desperately trying not to laugh. They knew this could be good. The Democrats were looking on in horror.

"I spent last night looking at child pornography."

He had no idea how he sounded. Senator Vanderbilt's words would indeed be replayed on the nightly news, and then on the cable news shows, and then the late-night comedians would run with it until he became the laughingstock of the Democratic Party. He started flipping through some of the pictures.

"I looked at this child pornography and kept saying 'wow.'"

A Democrat two seats over lightly tapped his knuckles on the desk trying to get the Senator's attention. His other hand was shielding his eyes from the cameras that might catch his disbelief. The senior Democrat on the Committee leaned over to the Republican chairman and asked him to turn off Vanderbilt's microphone. The Chairman could barely contain his laughter and said he wanted to hear what Vanderbilt had to say.

"It looks like child pornography to me. Look at these half-naked boys." The Senator then proceeded to hold up the pictures his staff had provided him the night before. The Chairman rigorously banged his gavel with contempt and Vanderbilt's staff member lunged across the desk before the TV cameras could catch sight of the innocent boys about to be victimized by a dunce of a U.S. Senator.

"Senator, your time has expired," the Chairman said, shaking his head in disgust.

After the confirmation hearing had been completed, the Democrats were in no mood to fight. They were in the minority in the Senate and several members on the left side of the aisle indicated their intention to vote for Judge Lincoln. No sense digging a hole when you're already down at the bottom of the well.

The next day on the floor before the whole body, the question was then asked of the members: "Shall the Senate advise and consent to the nomination of John A. Lincoln to be Associate Justice of the Supreme Court of the United States?"

Judge Lincoln was confirmed on a vote of 62 to 38.

CHAPTER 26

Fort Dupont Park – Washington, D.C.

Hassani and Mularah met again at Fort Dupont Park on the east side of the District of Columbia. In a rented windowless van, four men exited and approached the two sitting at one of the picnic tables away from the road. Traffic in the park was light, and the solitude would give the men an opportunity to set out their plan. They all hugged like brothers, but the smiles on their faces quickly vanished when they got down to business.

"Rasoul has modified the garbage truck by cutting a five foot long strip down the right side," Hassani said, pointing to the truck sitting across the way. "The strip is about six inches in height. We have placed a removable piece of plywood in the space and painted it to look like the rest of the truck."

Mularah and Hassani had spent the previous evening in an abandoned industrial park outfitting the garbage truck with everything needed to carry out the attack. They jacked up the right side of the truck to make it look like they had a flat even as the welding torch cut a hole in its side. The RPGs and AK-47s were hidden inside and ready to go.

The four men sat opposite of Hassani and Mularah. Each was under the age of thirty five and their athletic look was the result of intense training at the Pakistani camp.

Abu Nasra was an American citizen who succumbed to the poisonous rhetoric of an extremist imam in Detroit and for the last ten years had taken a vow to bring jihad to America. He trained in Afghanistan and then moved to Pakistan after U.S. airstrikes scattered the terrorist camps. He recruited his brother, Nouri, and both provided much needed intelligence about American targets.

Mustafa al-Kandar, the third homegrown terrorist, had studied in Boston and then in Paris, where the increasing Muslim population was growing disillusioned by the French Government and its crackdown on militant mosques and the burqa-covered faces of Muslim women.

The fourth man hailed from Afghanistan and was known only by his first name of Omar. He was the son of an Afghan diplomat who worked both sides of the political spectrum in Afghanistan – whether it be the resurgent Taliban-led regimes and their opium fields or the U.S.-backed government trying to weed out the former. Omar, who decided he liked the life of an international opium dealer, decided to work against any American intrusion into his country. He had made a nice living for himself, but now he was ready to die for the cause.

Mularah took the lead and laid out the plan. "Omar will drive the garbage truck down Constitution Avenue with Abu and Nouri hanging off the back end. We have coveralls for all of you, just like the garbage collectors wear. Mustafa, you will be inside the belly of the truck."

Three of the men nodded their heads, their minds envisioning the attack. The only one who looked mildly quizzical was Mustafa.

"Rasoul," he said, interrupting. "You said Constitution Avenue. Did you mean Pennsylvania? That is the avenue of the White House."

"No, we are not attacking the White House," Mularah chided. "Such a plan would be foolish. The White House is a fortress."

"But I was told we were going to strike at the very heart of the President."

"We are," Mularah shot back. He did not like people questioning his plan.

"His heart is at the National Archives," Hassani added.

"The Constitution!?" Abu exclaimed. He was knowledgeable enough about American history to know the treasured contents contained within the walls of the Archives and the suicide mission it would result in if they tried to harm the documents. "We are to destroy the Constitution? Its protective vault is impenetrable. We could not put a dent in the case even with the RPGs."

"No, we are not after the Constitution," Hassani said, although it would provide a great story in light of their belief the President was himself destroying the Constitution with his war on terror.

"We are not after the Declaration either." Hassani then handed over his iPhone. "This is what we are after."

There, under the e-mail from Sharif al-Rashad and its subject line labeled "Constitution Pics," were the pictures of Anna Schumacher.

"The woman?" Omar asked.

"Yes," Hassani replied. "But not just any woman. The President's very own daughter."

The eyes of the four men across the table widened. Two of them smiled at the possibilities. All of them thought they were going to attack the President, and all of them knew the chances of success were slim. That would be a suicide mission. But now. Now they were presented with a plan that could succeed and could have damaging effects on not only the President but America as well.

Hassani played the video shot by Sharif before he was nearly arrested by the Secret Service. All four men peered into the screen to look at the beautiful blonde. Their heartbeats were beginning to rise.

"The President's daughter is the target?" Omar asked, making sure he heard correctly.

"Yes."

"And she has Secret Service?"

"Yes," Mularah said, pulling out a map of the National Archives.

"It is a smaller crew?"

"Yes. We have been watching the building for the past week. There are at least four Secret Service agents inside and one, sometimes two, in an SUV parked outside on the west side."

"Where do we enter?"

Mularah pointed on the map to the south side of the building. "Omar will drive the truck and pull it to the curb. When everyone is in position. Abdullah will give the order."

Hassani nodded in agreement.

"Mustafa will then remove the plywood and fire the RPG at the main entrance. The bronze doors weigh over six tons, but they will be open. The blast will most likely stun, if not kill, everyone near the entrance. Abu and Nouri will then proceed into the building and find the girl. Mustafa will have the second RPG ready to take out the Secret Service SUV if necessary. Omar, who will also be inside the truck, can cover the plaza with the AK-47 and take out any police that respond."

"Where will you be?" Omar asked of Mularah.

"I will be outside surveying the scene just in case the Secret Service manages to get the girl out of the building."

Hassani piped in. "You must be quick," he said, then pointing at the map. "The Justice Department is across the street and the FBI Building just north of it. Once the first RPG hits the front entrance, you must get inside quickly and find the girl."

"And we are to take her alive?"

The four men looked at Mularah and Hassani. The group knew a kidnapping would be more difficult to pull off, but the reward of holding the President's daughter hostage would be tremendous. The world would be transfixed with the news – pictures of the crying blonde with a knife at her throat and the gut-wrenching audio of her begging Daddy for help would be played and replayed on every station for days on end. The men knew their every demand would be met.

Hassani, however, wanted none of the hassles of getting the President's daughter out of the building and through the streets of D.C. It was an added element of risk that did not need to be taken.

"No, you are not to take her alive. I want her dead."

The White House – Washington, D.C.

The day after the Senate vote on Judge Lincoln, the President held the swearing-in ceremony in the East Room of the White House. Lincoln attended with his wife, his son and daughter, and his ninety-year-old mother Orvetta. Chief Justice Shannon had already administered the Judicial Oath at the Supreme Court earlier that morning. Before executing the duties as a justice of the Supreme Court, each justice must take two oaths – the Judicial Oath, which originated in the Judiciary Act of 1789, and the oath to support the Constitution mentioned in Article VI.

With the President looking on in the East Room, Judge Lincoln stepped forward and placed his left hand on the Bible.

"Would you please raise your right hand and repeat after me."

Judge Lincoln then repeated the oath taken by all federal employees excluding the President of the United States.

"I, John A. Lincoln, do solemnly swear that I will support and defend the Constitution of the United States against all enemies, foreign and domestic; that I will bear true faith and allegiance to the same; that I take this obligation freely, without any mental reservation or purpose of evasion; and that I will well and faithfully discharge the duties of the office on which I am about to enter. So help me God."

The President made a few gracious remarks congratulating Justice Lincoln on his appointment. The newest Supreme Court justice thanked the President for his confidence in him and his abilities. He stated he looked forward to working with his new colleagues and hearing oral arguments when the Court started its new term in October.

Following the ceremony, the President held a reception in the State Dining Room for Justice Lincoln, his family, and the Supreme Court and justices' staffs. It was a small affair, one where the two branches of government could come together and mingle. Orvetta Lincoln regaled those in attendance with wonderful stories of her "little Johnny" growing up on the farm in Indiana. In one corner, Rickenbacker's Lockhart held court with the other law clerks and tried to convince them all that he was more conservative than the new justice. He claimed to have case law to prove his point. The President also posed for photographs with Justice Lincoln and seven other members of the Court.

One justice, however, decided not to show up.

CHAPTER 27

The National Archives – Washington, D.C.

The statute establishing the Secret Service was signed into law in 1865, ironically by the first President to be assassinated – Abraham Lincoln. At the time, the Secret Service was created to catch counterfeiters, a burgeoning industry during the Civil War and one that threatened to undermine the Union. It wasn't until after President McKinley's assassination in 1901 that the role of the Secret Service changed to protecting the life of the President of the United States, a responsibility that seeks the preservation of the Union still to this day.

Federal law provides Secret Service protection to the President and the Vice President, as well as their families. Former Presidents are entitled to a protective detail for ten years after leaving office. If necessary, the President can issue an executive order granting Secret Service protection to a protectee.

A security detail on the President's children may not have the complete package of SUVs and counter assault teams but the agents are no less vigilant. No agent wants to lose a protectee, and the greatest fear for a security detail of a presidential offspring is a kidnapping attempt. A successful kidnapping would not only paralyze the President personally but would also hold the country hostage until the kidnappers' demands were met. Or worse, until the protectee was killed. It was something the agents worried about every minute of their shifts.

"Strawberry is in the conference room," Agent Sessions said into his microphone.

The Friday afternoon sunshine was beginning to bake the capital on this late June day. The stifling humidity of July and August was right around the corner. Members of Congress would soon flee to escape the heat only to be replaced by scores of buses bringing hot, sweaty tourists to the museums and monuments.

Anna was preparing for another day on the job as "First Docent of the United States." The *Post* had run a story on her the day before and it was surprisingly complimentary given the paper rarely said anything positive about her father. It mentioned her love of American history and contained a glowing review from Archivist Daniels. Her father and mother were very proud.

Before she headed to Roberta's office to see if she had anything for her to do, she stood in front of the mirror and took a deep breath. She made sure her light pink shade of lipstick was perfect and she brushed her hair back just so. She looked beautiful as always. The late Justice O'Malley would have hired her in a heartbeat. This should be easy for her, although she rarely had to do it. But when she did, the response was always the same. She turned to the partially opened door and smiled.

"Jason," she whispered loudly. She waited without a response for a good five seconds. Take two. "Jason." Still a whisper but a little louder.

Special Agent Sessions appeared at the door. "I'm sorry, ma'am," he said. "Did you say my name?"

She nodded and whispered, "Come here." The index finger on her left hand beckoned him inside.

Sessions entered the room and scanned it from end to end. Nothing out of the ordinary. What the hell could she want? And why was she whispering?

"Yes?"

"I want to ask you something." Again in the whisper.

Agent Sessions leaned in closer. Obviously it was a matter of great importance to her. He felt the need to whisper too. "Okay."

Her cheeks were as red as the stripes on the American flag in the corner of the room. It wasn't this awkward when she practiced it last night.

"Would you like to go out to a movie sometime?"

Agent Sessions started to chuckle, which miffed Anna to a small degree. He thought she must be pulling a prank on him. "Is that what you're being so super secret about?" he whispered back to her.

She was twenty two and looked twenty six. He was thirty and looked twenty eight. Both were single. She, however, had trouble getting dates. Not because of her looks but because of her father. The handful of guys she liked at school were scared off by having to deal with the Secret Service. Making a move on a girl has its risks when her armed guards are standing nearby. The guys that did ask her out were the rich country club types who erroneously thought they could impress her with a ride in a shiny BMW. She was a country girl from Indiana. They were way off base. But now she just wanted to find a boyfriend to hang out with or go to a movie on a Friday night. Even though her dad was President of the United States, she wanted to believe that she could still be a normal twenty-two year old.

"Or dinner. Or ice cream. Or running." She was practically begging him.

"Ma'am."

The response caused her to cover her mouth with her right hand, her shoulders slumping in sadness. She was afraid this would happen. Her eyes began welling up with tears. "My name is Anna," she sniffled softly.

Agent Sessions racked his brain trying to remember the protocol for handling tearful protectees. He must have missed that day of instruction.

"Anna," he said smiling. "I can't." He at least made it sound like he wanted to if it weren't for those pesky rules. "I'm not allowed to get involved with somebody I'm protecting."

The thought hit both of them that she might be able to ask the President to have him removed from her detail. Her thoughts went even farther. Maybe she could get Walter back, and then she and Agent Sessions could go out.

"Maybe you could come over to the White House movie theater sometime. Or bowling! They have a bowling alley in the White House!" Her enthusiasm told the room that it was a great idea. It could work!

"I don't know." He was genuinely flattered. He was also genuinely worried that he might lose his job. He worked damn hard all his life to make the cut at the Secret Service.

"Don't you like me?" Her beautiful brown eyes were pleading with him.

He decided to break protocol, or probably some unwritten rule, and put his arm around her. "Anna, let me see if we can work something out."

She liked what she was hearing, and he could smell the strawberry-scented conditioner that was befitting her code name. She then took the lead and made her move. The lipstick was scented strawberry too.

The garbage truck headed north on Third Street, the occupants glancing quickly to the east at the Capitol Dome on their right. A part of them was wishing they could target it. At the light, the truck turned left on Constitution Avenue and pulled to the side of the curb in front of the National Archives.

Omar exited the driver's seat and searched the sidewalk. A handful of tourists were busy looking at their maps and pointing in all directions. Others were taking pictures. A garbage truck was not on their radar screens. Omar crawled in the back of the truck and behind the false wall covered on the outside with rumpled plastic garbage bags. Mustafa was removing the plywood from the side of the truck and readying the RPG. He gave Omar a nod.

"Standing by," Omar said into his walkie-talkie.

Abu and Nouri walked south on the Seventh Street sidewalk. They had parked their van three blocks north. They wore their bright orange vests and matching hard hats over their blue coveralls. Upon approaching the idling truck, they hoisted two barricades each from the hooks on the side. They then walked to the southern corners of the National Archives Building that front Constitution Avenue.

Abu took the farther corner and placed his barricades facing the sidewalk used by those coming from the Department of Justice. Nouri placed his two on the opposite corner. They both spread the barricades apart – yellow caution tape filling the gap.

The signs on the barricades read "Hollywood Movie Set – Filming In Progress – Keep Back."

Abu and Nouri then took two forty gallon trash cans out of the back of the truck. The garbage had been emptied and replaced with an AK-47 in each one. The pockets of their coveralls were filled with two Glock handguns. They walked separately to the sides of the Archives Building and waited for the mayhem to begin.

The walkie-talkies squawked to life. "In position," both men reported.

Watching the proceedings from the steps of the Museum of Natural History on the opposite corner of the Archives was Abdullah Hassani. The tourists making their way outside had no idea the history they were about to witness.

"Action!"

The smoke trail from the grenade made a beeline for the front entrance of the building. It whistled through the open doorway and exploded five yards from the security checkpoint. The booming concussion shook the ground outside. The smoke bombs were rolling down the sidewalks filling the air with heavy white smoke. Abu and Nouri were up the steps in seconds and fired their AK-47s inside the smoke-filled entryway. They were not taking any return fire. They stepped inside and swept from left to right. They did not worry what was coming up behind them because Omar was ready to gun down anyone who tried to enter.

Tourists began to gather behind the barricades, some taking pictures or video with their cell phones. A few asked who was starring in the movie. Hassani was across the street watching armed men fall to the ground as they made their way up the steps.

Agent Sessions was tasting the strawberries when the blast shook the building causing Anna to fall into his arms. The lights flickered off and then back on. He instinctively knew it wasn't an earthquake or anything natural in origin. He spun Anna around, his big muscular right arm across her chest and his left hand grabbing the waist of her black slacks, his fingers in between them and her underwear. He was ready to move. The unmistakable sound of gunfire could be heard echoing off the walls in the cavernous Rotunda.

"Control, Sessions. Advise," he said into the mike in his right hand and over her left shoulder. He could feel her heart beating through her chest and against his forearm.

Abu and Nouri had worked their way past the security perimeter and into the Rotunda, the marble floors now filling with blood from tourists, volunteers, and security guards gunned down in the hail of bullets.

"Find the girl!" Abu yelled over the wail of fire alarms.

"Abu, over here!"

They had been told to turn left upon entry and look for the sign marked "Employees Only." That's where Anna was seen coming and going before and after her guided tours.

Sessions did not go for his gun. Its use was only a matter of last resort. His job was to cover the protectee and evacuate her as soon as it was safe to do so. He activated his mike for a second time. "Control, Sessions. Advise."

Agents Tony Mason and Rachel Carpenter were not responding to the radio traffic being yelled into their earpieces. Both were dead. Agents Shawn Franks and Talon Mays were holding their ground in the rear hallway. Through the ringing in their ears, they could hear "Find the girl! Find the girl!"

Agent Franks activated his mike. “AOP! AOP!”

The word was sent out. This wasn’t an attack on the Constitution or the Declaration of Independence. This was an attack on a protectee – an AOP.

The SUV on the west side of the building rumbled to life, the reverse lights catching the attention of Mustafa in the garbage truck. The SUV backed up and drove onto the sidewalk and closer to the west exit. The white streak of the RPG ended at the rear bumper, the SUV exploding into flames.

Agents from FBI Headquarters located northeast across the intersection from the National Archives were running to the scene, their suit coats flailing in the wind and their holsters empty. Traffic had stopped as police vehicles were blocking the streets with their lights flashing and sirens blaring.

One man in a suit, however, was not running. It was Mularah. He was walking south toward the Archives and scanning the scene behind his dark sunglasses. Smoke could be seen rising over the southern front of the building. From his position he could see Archives staff running out of the north exit and then left and right down Pennsylvania Avenue.

Some of the women were holding their shoes and sprinting barefoot to get as far away as fast as they could. One woman poking her head out the door caught his attention. It was the blonde hair. She was wearing dark slacks and a white blouse. Her attire and the ID hanging from her neck made it obvious she was an Archives employee and not just some tourist in the wrong place at the wrong time. The men in suits were running with her. Mularah gritted his teeth and placed his sunglasses on top of his head. This is why Hassani wanted him on the team. To take care of business and clean up the mess in case the hired help from Pakistan failed to hold up their end of the bargain. They had at least chased her from the building, he thought.

Mularah walked directly across the street, almost oblivious to the chaos happening around him. FBI agents were hustling Archives staff out of the area. People were running everywhere. Mularah, however, never took his eyes off the blonde. He raised his handgun from his side, and when he got within five feet he fired one shot into her head. She crumpled to the ground never knowing what hit her. The four men around her looked on in horror, wondering what was going on and why the guy in the suit was firing at them.

What the hell was happening!?

Mularah proceeded to put a bullet in each of their brains. With his dark eyes ablaze, Mularah walked to the bodies to savor his victory. He stepped over the dead men and turned over the blonde. He grabbed the ID hanging from around her neck. This would be his finest moment. It might be his last but it would be the moment for which he would be forever remembered. He also wanted to put an exclamation point on his great deed by putting another bullet in the First Daughter's skull. The gory autopsy photos would surely haunt the President for the rest of his life. First, however, Mularah flipped over the card and looked at the perky blonde in the picture.

His heart then sank and his eyes widened, his clenched teeth showing in his jawline. The sweat on his brow now rolled down the side of his face.

The name on the ID was Britney Waterson.

"Freeze! FBI! Put the gun down!"

Mularah turned and raised his gun but he had no chance. The bullets struck him in the chest and he hit the sidewalk.

Abu and Nouri reached the hallway and were trading fire with Agents Franks and Mays. They could not get the agent in the SUV to respond. The Secret Service Joint Operations Center issued an alert from its H Street headquarters that there was an AOP in progress at the National Archives and the perimeter was not secure. The Joint Ops Center also issued alerts to all security details that a terrorist attack was in progress and emergency evacuation plans should be implemented. Automatic weapons were drawn. Barricades were raised. Combat air patrols launched from Andrews.

"Say again!?" Agent Franks yelled into his mike.

"Perimeter not secure!" came the voice on the other end.

Other than taking on the terrorists at the end of the hall, Agent Franks only had one viable option.

"Sessions! Evac! Evac! Route two! Route two!"

Agent Sessions still held Anna by her belt line. She was five eight. He was six four. And her feet weren't touching the ground. They moved toward the door.

"Strawberry is in position."

"Clear!"

Agent Sessions carried Anna across the hall shielding her body with his as they barreled into the door. "Route two!"

The stairs went down four flights and he stopped on the second floor. He could hear Agents Franks and Mays bounding down the stairs above them. Anna was breathing hard and her big brown eyes did not blink. She said nothing but the trembling was noticeable.

"You're gonna be all right," Agent Sessions whispered into her ear. There was no sense of fear in his voice. His granite-like arms held her tight.

Agent Franks took the lead followed by Sessions and Anna and then Mays guarding the rear. They stopped at a heavy steel door in the sub basement of the Archives some sixty feet below street level. Franks whipped out a plastic key card and swiped it through the reader. When the light turned green he pushed on the door and the quartet hurried in the tunnel.

"Strawberry is in the route two tunnel."

Sessions carried Anna like an intercepted pass with the goal line fast approaching. They moved so quickly Anna could feel the cool subterranean air on her face, the streaks of tears running down her cheeks a few degrees cooler. The only sound was of the thumping of their rubber soles echoing off the cinder block walls. At the end of the tunnel, Agent Franks swiped the card again and opened the door.

What Anna saw next took her breath away. Ten men, automatic weapons, tactical gear. The letters "FBI" plastered across their chests in bright yellow letters. The good guys. Five men entered the tunnel and the door locked behind them. They were going after Abu and Nouri. The other five stayed with Anna's group and hustled them into the hardened bunker of the Department of Justice with Sessions carrying her all the way.

Once inside, Agent Sessions, only slightly out of breath, made the call. "Strawberry is secure."

The AOP had failed.

CHAPTER 28

The White House – Washington, D.C.

The President and the First Lady had been whisked away into the White House bunker during the attack, and the Vice President was on her way to a secured undisclosed location. The Secret Service didn't know whether this was a more coordinated attack with the National Archives simply being a diversion to a more devious plot. The perimeter of the White House, as well as its roof, was occupied by every available agent with every available weapon ready to take on all-comers.

The President was in constant contact with Director Stubblefield, who went to the Justice Department's bunker following the attack to personally escort Anna back to the White House in an armored caravan. Anna's mother wouldn't let go of her when she returned as Anna cried for an hour over the ordeal and then another one after she learned her friend Britney had been killed in the attack.

After a few moments of family time, the President huddled in the Situation Room with his homeland security team.

"Sir, we can confirm that twenty five people are dead," Director Stubblefield announced solemnly. "That's not counting the five terrorists who were killed – one on the street, two inside the Archives, and two inside a converted garbage truck parked to the south of the building. I believe we also have ten to fifteen people wounded in several hospitals across the city. I'll get that information to you as soon as I can."

"Do we have surveillance tapes?" the President asked.

"Yes, we are analyzing them now."

"It was a well coordinated attack?"

"Yes, very well coordinated."

"And you believe they were after Anna?"

Stubblefield shook his head. "Yes. From what we have seen so far on the tapes, the terrorists who entered the building made no move toward the Documents. Agents Franks and Mays heard them shout to each other to find 'the girl.'"

"What about the identity of the terrorists?"

"We are analyzing the tapes with our facial recognition software. They had identification on them but the names are fake. We'll know more when the fingerprint results come back."

"Do you believe this was connected to the information passed on to the FBI by your informant?"

"It's very possible. Four men apparently came to the United States within the last two weeks. If it's them, we believe we know the location where the plan may have been hatched along with two other training sites."

When the Chairman of the Joint Chiefs of Staff heard Director Stubblefield talk about terrorist locations his ears perked up. He was itching to take the fight to the terrorists and waiting around didn't suit him well.

Joint Chiefs Chairman Huey L. Cummins had been appointed by the prior administration and President Schumacher held him over to keep the military running like a well-oiled machine. Cummins was six-eight and two hundred and eighty pounds of pure kick ass military muscle. He had been involved in every war back to Vietnam and had been decorated for his service many times over. As he aged, the stars on his shoulders increased in number. He now had four and some thought he deserved another so he could join the ranks of such military luminaries like MacArthur, Marshall, and Eisenhower. He, unlike the justices on the Supreme Court, knew how to run a war and was highly successful. The President relied on him greatly.

"If you give me the location of those camps, Mr. President, I'll obliterate them by noon tomorrow," he said.

The President smiled. That's what he liked to hear from his military leaders.

"General, I want you to start thinking of a plan to attack these camps," the President said. "Once we have some actionable intelligence then I'll give the go ahead if you recommend it."

"Yes, sir." Chances were pretty good the General was going to recommend it. He added, "I will have the plans drawn up by Monday morning. I can have Predator and Reaper drones in the air by tonight."

"Good. Do it."

With the meeting over, the President headed for the Oval Office where Wiley and the TV cameras were waiting for him. It would be his second address to the nation from the Oval Office, the first one after he took office under trying circumstances. The address was short, and the President took one last look at it.

"Mr. President, we have the speech all ready to go in the TelePrompTer."

"Did you take out the references to Anna?" he asked flipping to the second page.

"Yes," Wiley nodded. "I still think you ought to keep her in there."

"I don't know if I can make it through the entire address if I have to mention her."

The cameraman with the head set interrupted and gave them the three minute warning.

Wiley looked the President over. Hair fine. American flag pin in place. Red tie straight. "You're good to go," he whispered.

The President situated himself behind his desk and said nothing.

"Thirty seconds."

When the countdown reached ten seconds, the President took a deep breath and cleared his throat.

"Good evening. I come to you tonight as your President with a heavy heart. Today, our way of life was once again shattered by an evil act of terror. In the very repository of our republic, terrorists in the pursuit of their radical ideology brutally attacked innocent men, women, and children. Sadly, twenty five of our fellow Americans lost their lives in the attack. Many more were injured and need your prayers.

"Inside the National Archives today were parents bringing their children to view the Declaration of Independence and volunteer guides showing excited tourists the United States Constitution and the Bill of Rights. This maniacal act of terror sought to strike at the freedoms those historic documents espouse and protect – life, liberty, and the pursuit of happiness.

"I have spoken with Mr. Barry Daniels, the Archivist of the United States, and he assures me the Founding Documents are safe, secure, and unharmed. In remembrance of those who today lost their lives viewing, enjoying, and protecting the Charters of Freedom, I ask tonight that mothers and fathers across this great country read to their children the documents our Founding Fathers created, even under the threat of death, and our fellow Americans since then have sought to preserve and protect, even to their death, so that we might continue to cherish the unalienable rights bestowed on us by our Creator and thereby preserve for our future generations a land that is free.

"In the coming days and after our investigation is completed, those who helped plan and facilitate this murderous atrocity will be held responsible. The United States of America will not back down in the face of terror and any one, any group, and any foreign power found harboring terrorists connected with this attack will be held to account for their actions.

"May God bless those who lost their lives today and be with their families in this their time of need. And may God bless the United States of America."

With tears running down his own cheeks, Wiley hit the cameraman on the arm signaling him to cut the feed. The cameraman worried the picture might have gone blurry, but he realized it was just the tears welling up in his own eyes. The President sat at his desk, his head buried in his left hand. The tears began to fall when his Elle and his Anna Julia wrapped him in an embrace.

Georgetown – Washington, D.C.

The terrorist attack wreaked havoc on commuters heading home at the end of a long day. Large sections of Pennsylvania and Constitution Avenues were shut down as law-enforcement authorities searched for clues, evidence, or maybe some dumb bastard sitting in a getaway vehicle. The metro station on Capitol Hill was overflowing as riders who were forced to skip their normal stations clogged the closest one open. Those with cars were rerouted either north or south of Capitol Hill and flashing signs warned drivers to steer clear of anything near the Federal Triangle.

Sharif al-Rashad finally pulled his car into the space at his condominium on the Potomac River in Georgetown at a quarter til eight. He had watched the horrific aftermath with his cohorts in the office. Justice Hussein was in New York to give a speech at the United Nations that evening and had made no public comment on the attack. He called the office to talk with Sharif and only Sharif. Both were angry and feared the President would soon ratchet up the war on terrorism. Their brothers in the Middle East would once again be under the fire of that "bully in the White House."

Justice Hussein also asked Sharif to run some errands for him before he returned to D.C. so Sharif spent a good part of the evening driving down blocked off streets to pick up the Justice's dry cleaning and a new black robe, the old one, the Justice complained, had become too small.

Although stoic in the office, Sharif was beside himself thinking what was to greet him once he got home. Hassani had been staying with him the past two nights after he got kicked out of his fourth hotel. Hassani promised he would be leaving soon to return to Illinois.

But Hassani overstaying his welcome was the least of Sharif's worries.

For the past five hours, his mind replayed the incident at the National Archives when he had been accosted by the Secret Service. He remembered he handed over his ID to an agent who radioed the information to headquarters. His name was probably in some log book somewhere. Then there were the phone calls from Hassani and the meetings that somebody might have witnessed. But there was an even more worrisome issue. He had e-mailed the video and pictures of Anna Schumacher at the National Archives to Hassani. His mind was clear enough to know he could be looking at a conspiracy charge, one that would be hard to win an acquittal once the pictures of the victims were put before the jury. He kept telling himself that he had no knowledge of the attack or even if Hassani was involved.

From the parking lot he could see no lights on in the second floor condo. He had given Hassani a key, and the man had been in and out at all hours of the day. Sharif approached the unit cautiously. The door had not been battered in by SWAT teams, the windows were intact, and nothing else seemed out of the ordinary. The lights were on at his neighbors – the two coeds on his left were probably studying while the young professional couple on his right were most likely glued to the TV. With a quick glance down the balcony that ran in front of his unit, he pressed his ear against the door. He heard nothing. He then did something he had never done before.

He knocked three times on his own front door.

The lights in the living room didn't come on, the curtains didn't move, and nobody answered. Sharif gave another glance down the length of the building. He looked back over the balcony into the parking lot. The cars looked familiar. He didn't see any obvious looking government vehicles containing armed men set to pounce when he showed up.

He inserted the key into the lock, turned it to the left, and then took the key out. His heart was thumping in his chest, not knowing what might be lurking on the other side of the door. He turned the handle and nudged the door open with his foot, his body moving to the side of the doorjamb. Nothing. Just the cool breeze from the running air conditioner. He reached in with his left hand and turned on the lights to the entryway. A quick peek revealed nothing out of the ordinary. The furniture was upright, the phone was on the hook. He gave one last look in the crack of the door to see if someone was hiding behind it. Nobody. He walked in and quickly shut the door behind him.

"I'm home," he said to no one in particular. It was his way to alert anyone on the inside as much as it was to calm his own nerves.

Hassani was nowhere to be found. His suitcases, however, were still in the guest bedroom. A letter had been placed on the bed. Sharif took it and sat down. The stationary was from the Holiday Inn, the words at times in cursive and then in print. The letter read:

Sharif,

I have gone off to fight the infidels who seek to bomb our countries, our cities, our people. Those who seek to impose their lifestyle of drunkenness, debauchery, and homosexuality on the nations of the world must be stopped. And they will be stopped. They will soon understand the greatness of Allah and how their government of sin will lead them all to hell. I have lived a full life but it is lacking in service. Soon, I will give the ultimate service.

You, my friend, must continue to fight the battles that will come after me. You have the power, the intelligence, and the will to beat back the infidels and destroy their country from within. And it will be a glorious day when you succeed. And you will be richly rewarded for all eternity. Bless you, my son. Goodbye.

The letter was not signed. Sharif probably would not have been able to read it anyway what with the tears dribbling down his cheeks. He would most likely never see his mentor again. Unless it was with bars in between them in an attorney-client relationship or at his mentor's funeral.

The ringing of the bedroom phone startled him, the bed shaking along with the rest of his body.

He knew it had to be Hassani. Perhaps he had been watching from the parking lot, afraid to come to the apartment for fear the authorities might have Sharif under surveillance. Sharif's trembling hand grabbed the phone.

"Hello."

"Sharif!" The voice was female. Early twenties. "Where have you been?"

Sharif recognized the voice as that of Pam Williston, his neighbor. He licked his parched lips. "I just returned home."

"We were worried about you."

"The traffic was very bad."

"Well, come over and we'll fix you some dinner. We want to know what you saw downtown this afternoon."

The girls had been in classes most of the day and had only heard about the terrorist attack when they returned to their condo after a run in the park. They had become friends with Sharif ever since he moved in after taking the job with Justice Hussein. Both girls were very impressed with the dapper young professional, and he regularly attended their cookouts and spirited games of volleyball in the condominium sand pit.

"I should be getting to bed," he said, not really wanting to be around people interested in his thoughts on this day.

"Sharif, it's Friday night. You don't have to go to work tomorrow." She then stopped to consider what hours a law clerk might put in. "Or do you?"

"No, I don't have to work tomorrow."

"Well, if you don't come over we'll come over there and drag you out."

"Okay, okay," he relented. "Give me ten minutes."

Sharif hung up the phone and looked again at Hassani's note – the handwritten anger of a determined terrorist staring him in the face. He took it to the kitchen and flipped on the light. He found a match in the drawer and held the letter over the sink. With tears in his eyes, he lit the letter on fire and watched Hassani's words crumble into charred pieces of history. When the flame reached the Holiday Inn at the top, Sharif threw the remnants down into the basin, stirred it around with the end of a wooden spoon, and turned on the water to wash it all into the garbage disposal. Hassani the terrorist was out of his life.

For now.

CHAPTER 29

FBI Headquarters – Washington, D.C.

Five hundred FBI agents were hard at work tracking down leads, readying search warrants, and asking for court-ordered wiretaps. By late Saturday afternoon, federal agents had concluded their evidence recovery at the National Archives, finding the remnants of the two RPGs which they sent off for testing as well as 450 fired rounds from various weapons. Archivist Daniels was determined to reopen the building, believing the ability of free people to observe the Founding Documents would be the ultimate act of defiance in the face of terrorism. Daniels conferred with the President who conferred with the Vice President, the Speaker of the House, the Senate Majority Leader, and Director Stubblefield. The decision was made to reopen the Archives on Sunday afternoon after a short memorial service to remember those whose lives were lost in the attack.

Director Stubblefield also had more news for the President. The video conference call with the President and his national security team began at six p.m. The President, Vice President, the Director of Homeland Security, the National Security Advisor, and the Secretary of Defense had spent the entire day on the phone or in meetings trying to figure out who committed this heinous act of terror and who would be receiving a wake-up call from the United States military in the near future.

"Mr. President, we have identified all five of the terrorists who were killed yesterday. Four of them slipped into the country recently from Pakistan."

"Ty, what do you mean by slipped in? Like an illegal entry?"

"No, sir. They had proper papers. Three were American citizens and the other had a temporary visa. Their names weren't even on any no-fly lists. They were already in the country before we knew something was going down."

"All right."

"We have identified the fifth terrorist who was killed on the street as Rasoul Mularah, also an American citizen."

Everyone in the Situation Room mouthed the words "Rasoul Mularah" to themselves. They didn't recognize the name. It hadn't been on the FBI's Ten Most Wanted List or plastered on the walls of Post Offices across the country.

"Details on his history are sketchy. He does not show up in any of our databases. He had at one time ten years ago been on the payroll of Hassani Enterprises, a construction firm south of Chicago with offices in St. Louis and Kansas City. We have had that firm under surveillance for almost six months and we believe the owner Abdullah Hassani has gone missing."

"Do you believe this Hassani is involved?" the President asked.

"It's very possible," Stubblefield said pressing a button on a remote control. Up popped Hassani's Illinois driver's license photo. The face was definitely Middle Eastern. The eyes were dark. The eyebrows furrowed in perpetual anger.

"Our source on the inside had heard some harsh words against you, Mr. President, but nothing definitive. He is definitely a person of interest."

"Okay."

The video feed from Director Stubblefield's end showed an FBI agent handing over a short stack of papers. He quickly shuffled through them, then placed half the stack next to the other. His finger began tracing back and forth across the pages.

"Mr. President, I have just been handed the phone records from Mularah and Hassani. They had obviously been in contact with each other over the past several days." Stubblefield stopped and flipped to several of the pages below. "Actually, they've been in contact with each other for a long period of time."

"Any other numbers jump out at you?" the President wondered.

Stubblefield looked at Hassani's list of numbers. Half went to Mularah. The other half wasn't so clear.

"Mr. President, this Hassani has multiple calls to a number listed as 'unavailable.' Sometimes seven or eight times a day."

"When would this 'unavailable' show up?" the President asked. "Is this something we can ask the phone company to reveal?"

"I don't think so. Our search warrants would have covered that. It could be an encrypted phone. We're going to have to do some more digging."

"Who could get their hands on this encrypted phone technology?"

"Techno gurus could figure out a way to do it. Other than that it could be a phone of a foreign intelligence service or of a state sponsor of terror. Perhaps the terrorist network has figured out a way to encrypt their calls."

"Well, I guess we should find this Hassani guy."

"I agree."

"And find out who this 'unavailable' person is."

No sooner had the video conference ended when Director Stubblefield picked up the phone on the table and punched in the numbers.

"Mac, it's Ty. I need you to find Abdullah Hassani."

"My old boss?"

"Yes. Go get him."

Georgetown – Washington, D.C.

Sharif al-Rashad had slept most of the day following the attack. The girls next door didn't call him because they were off visiting friends in Mount Vernon. They said something about being back in time to have a going away party for Pam's roommate on Monday night. When he was awake, he lied on his back in bed looking at the ceiling. He couldn't bear to watch TV, not wanting to see that smug President or his bitch of a daughter or the First Lady bawling her eyes out again.

As he walked around the apartment in silence, he stopped in the doorway of the guest bedroom. Hassani had left the spare key on the night stand so Sharif knew he wouldn't be coming back. He didn't even think he would call. He opened up the closet and noticed Hassani didn't even take his luggage. Sharif looked for suitcase tags just in case he needed to burn it and wash it down the garbage disposal. He thought he should probably throw the luggage into the Dumpster once nightfall hit.

He decided to open up the suitcases, for one out of curiosity and the other wanting to properly dispose of anything that might connect Hassani to the attacks. The big blue suitcase was an American Tourister. It looked brand new and it wasn't locked. He grabbed its handle and hoisted it onto the bed. With a couple of clicks, Sharif opened the top and peered in. The sight brought a smile to his face. The left side of the suitcase was filled with five crisp white dress shirts with the Hassani Construction logo on the right hand pocket. The right side contained five nicely creased black slacks. Put them together and you had Hassani's daily uniform. A search underneath revealed five pairs of underwear and black socks. Nothing inside would indicate anything belonged to Hassani. Sharif decided to keep it as it was and put the suitcase back in the closet. Just in case.

The cell phone buzzing at his hip gave him a quick jolt. Perhaps it was Hassani himself. Before the third buzz, he decided he would offer Hassani any help he needed. He picked the phone off his clip and looked at the number on the screen.

"Justice Hussein, hello."

"Sharif, how are you doing?"

"Hanging in there."

The Justice was still in New York and would return Monday afternoon. They had little to do at the Supreme Court given the summer recess.

"Did you hear that bastard President is going to have another address before a Joint Session of Congress on Monday?"

"I did not hear that."

"He's probably going to parade his wife and daughter into the chamber and cry some tears for the victims. It'll be a pathetic display."

"Will you be attending?"

"I will probably have to. The Chief Justice has been jumping down my throat lately and wants us to show respect for the other branches. I might just go to flip off the President."

The conversation lasted for ten minutes, and both men were in a foul mood at the end.

"I will see you on Monday, Sharif."

"Okay. I will drop off your robe and dry cleaning at the office tomorrow in case you need them," Sharif said before hanging up.

The second suitcase was just as big as the first but with a harder shell. It had a place for a key but it was not locked. The top came open and Sharif noticed the contents were covered by a black towel. He ran his fingers over the towel and around the sides. He pulled off the towel and shook at the sight.

Two fishing vests loaded with tubes of Tovex – the construction company's dynamite – and detonator cords with buttons resembling a morphine injector. The pockets were filled with ball bearings and children's jacks, sharpened at the tips, along with fishing hooks straightened into mini-arrows.

He had hoped his mentor was only remotely involved with the attack but the contents of the suitcase proved he was in it to the death. Both vests were ready to wear. Notes labeled "Remove Cap, Then Push" gave the user the instructions that would end their life as well as kill or maim anyone within twenty-five yards.

Sharif held up one of the vests. His hands were shaking, his mind disbelieving he was holding such an instrument of death. The thoughts of Hassani strapping the vest to himself and blowing himself up started to steel his own nerves. His mentor would have put his right arm through the opening and his left through the other. Sharif did the same. The ten-pound vest hung loosely over his slim frame. He moved to the mirror over the dresser. He buttoned the vest together and smoothed it out.

His eyes ran up and down the vest and then stopped to look at his face in the reflection. His face had changed over the years. The eyes seemed darker, the brow more furrowed, the anger within blossoming.

"It feels good," he whispered to himself. This was how it would feel to the Muslim soldiers who offered themselves as a martyr for their brothers around the world, who gave their last breath in support of Allah.

Sharif inspected the second vest. It was the same size and loaded with the same explosives and shrapnel. He walked to his own room and opened his closet. He tried on a white dress shirt over the top of the vest. The shirt was too small to fit over it, the buttons unable to reach the holes. He tried on his suit coat. The combo was doable.

He began to wonder if Hassani had another vest with him. Maybe the ones in the suitcase were extras that had been part of the initial plan to attack the National Archives. He desperately wanted to call him but he could not take the risk. There was a good chance he would see his mentor's face on a TV soon.

CHAPTER 30

Union Station – Washington, D.C.

The D.C. Metropolitan Police, the FBI, and the Department of Homeland Security had officers and agents manning the train and metro stations all over Washington. The automatic weapons were drawn and ready for use. Bomb-sniffing dogs prowled the streets and buildings. Backpacks, bags, and purses received a thorough inspection and unattended ones sent people scurrying for cover and explosive-detecting robots to the scene.

The upcoming Fourth of July holiday had everyone on edge. The investigation of the terrorist attack indicated another man was involved and he was still on the loose. The FBI had enhanced security camera footage from the National Archives, the Department of Justice, and the Natural History Museum, which showed a man, believed to be Hassani, holding a cell phone to his ear immediately before the attack and then filming the attack as it happened. Hassani's driver's licence photo had been shown on TV and the Internet as a person of interest and anyone who saw him or knew his whereabouts was directed to call law-enforcement authorities immediately.

An undercover Mac Carter was himself patrolling the subway stations and bus depots. He was the only FBI agent that had met Hassani and actually looked into his eyes. Carter had a feeling Hassani was still in the area. The attack on the National Archives was not one in which the terrorists would just give up if it didn't go as planned. If someone who planned the attack was still alive, they would fight to the death. They did not want to live. They wanted to die for Allah.

Foggy Bottom – Washington, D.C.

Hassani had spent the previous evening in the underground parking garage five blocks west of the White House. His beat up station wagon had not caught the eye of law enforcement as the garage was often used by visitors staying long term. The darkened garage provided some respite from the stifling summer heat. Always the master planner, Hassani had loaded the wagon with enough food rations and bottled water to hide out for a whole week. A covering over the rear storage area provided a place where he could lay his head and stay hidden from prying eyes.

He had ventured out once late that Saturday afternoon when the tourists would most likely be filling the sidewalks on their way to the Mall or the White House. The Nationals ball cap was pulled down near his eyes and the white dress shirt had an American flag sticker covering the Hassani Enterprises logo. He knew he didn't need to go far – the paper box was only twenty feet from the exit door of the parking garage. He was dying for news on the attack – the radio reception being worthless in the underground garage. And he desperately wanted to call Sharif but he did not want to use his phone or even make a call to him for fear the feds might be listening.

He fed seventy-five cents into the machine and pulled out the window copy, its headline blaring:

Attack on the National Archives

The photos, some professional, others reader submitted, showed the building in various stages of the attack – the billowing clouds of smoke, the dead bodies on the front steps, the bloody aftermath with yellow police tape, and a makeshift memorial of flower bouquets and teddy bears on the southeast corner.

Hassani scurried back into his hole and hid under the plywood cover of his wagon. His eyes followed the flashlight as its crisscrossed the page.

"Twenty five killed . . ."

"Scores injured . . ."

"Five terrorists also killed . . ."

"Capital in lockdown . . ."

"The Constitution and the Declaration of Independence were undamaged and are secure."

He skimmed the article again skipping over the parts he had already read. He wasn't finding what he was looking for. Above the fold, below the fold, front page, back page, he wasn't seeing it. It should have been front and center.

"Come on, come on," he grunted, the sweat sliding down his face.

The second page finally had the picture he was looking for. It was only a file photo but so what. The headline nearly stopped his heart.

President's Daughter Safely Evacuated; Unhurt

"Damn!" he screamed at the top of his lungs. "Damn! You bastard!" The next headline fueled Hassani's rage even more:

President Vows "Immediate and Forceful" U.S. Response

"Damn him!"

The station wagon was rocking in step with his anger. Hassani beat the side of the wagon cursing the President and his own failure.

"He must die! They all must die!"

With his chest heaving, he crawled out from under the plywood and stepped out into the darkened garage. There was no one else around. He wiped the sweat drenching his face and ripped off his dress shirt. He reached behind the back seat, pulled out a backpack, and unzipped it. His hand pulled out a fishing vest – the third and final suicide vest that had made the trip with Mularah. But this vest had more than the sharpened jacks and ball bearings. Four glass test tubes topped with caps and containing the anthrax smuggled in through Mexico were taped two to a side. When Hassani detonated the vest, the blast would send anthrax spores on the wings of the prevailing winds. Thousands of lives would be at risk.

Hassani reached into his overnight bag and pulled out another white dress shirt. He had a whole closet full of them and never wore anything else. Before putting it on, he did make one major adjustment to his usual wardrobe. It being ninety degrees outside, he cut the sleeves off at biceps level. Long sleeves and profuse sweating would look suspicious. He put the shirt on and it fit nicely above the vest. He ran the detonator cord under the vest so the button came out at the belt line allowing it to be stashed in his right-hand pocket.

The drive to the Capitol would take ten minutes.

Georgetown – Washington, D.C.

Sharif had not slept the night before and the dawn found him pacing the floor of his condo. He would often look out his window and then east down the Potomac to the Washington Monument and then the Capitol. He kept looking at the vest and wondering whether Hassani had his on. Sharif also wondered whether he had the balls to put it on himself. He could put it on and walk down to the Mall and mingle with the tourists enjoying a summer afternoon at the Washington Monument or Lincoln Memorial. That would make Hassani proud.

He had the TV on but the sound down. The media had put Hassani's picture in a small box in the right-hand part of the screen with a flashing banner telling viewers the man was a person of great interest to the investigation. Sharif had actually dialed Hassani's number within the last hour unable to stand the pressure of not knowing where he was. He quickly hung up not knowing what to do.

His cell phone buzzed at ten minutes til two in the afternoon. He figured it would be Justice Hussein since the only other person to call that number was Hassani. He let out a yell when he looked at the caller ID.

"Abdullah!" he yelled into the phone.

"Sharif, my son."

"Where are you?"

"I cannot tell you. . ."

Sharif cut him off before he could finish the sentence. "Please, Abdullah, let me know where you are. Let me help you."

Hassani had parked his car on Second Street on the east side of the Library of Congress and just to the south of the Supreme Court Building. He had checked the flags flying at half-staff and determined the wind was blowing toward the northwest.

"Where are you?" Hassani asked. He was worried Sharif might be in his office at the Supreme Court and wanted to make sure he was well away from the blast and out of the direction of the wind.

"At my condo," he said nearly out of breath. "Come stay with me. You will be safe here."

"No. You must leave your condo and head south toward Arlington, Virginia. Stay away from the downtown area."

"Will you be in Arlington?"

"No, I will be in heaven." With that the phone clicked off.

"Abdullah! Abdullah!"

Sharif dialed Hassani's number but the phone had been turned off. In fact, it was now resting in the bottom of a trash can.

Hassani was making his way to the Capitol.

FBI Headquarters – Washington, D.C.

The flurry of movement through the hallways in the FBI command center startled even Director Stubblefield who was overseeing the manhunt for Hassani.

"We got a hit on the number!" came a voice from the corner of the room.

A military spy plane flying circles above the capital intercepted the call after waiting and waiting for Hassani to make the mistake of contacting someone.

The FBI agent in the corner looked at his screen and made the announcement. "Second Street and East Capitol in D.C.!"

Stubblefield whipped out the cell phone from his holster and punched the red button. "Mac! Second Street and East Capitol! He's heading for the Capitol!"

Off went the phone and Director Stubblefield started barking orders to his command team. "All agents in the vicinity descend on the Capitol! Now!"

The heads of Homeland Security, the Capitol Police, and the Metropolitan Police Department sent similar orders to their men and women in the area. Stubblefield motioned for his security detail to move – they were heading to the Capitol too.

"Shoot Hassani on sight!"

Capitol Hill – Washington, D.C.

Hassani joined a group of fifty Japanese tourists, their tour guide directing them to follow the red umbrella she was holding in the air. They dressed conservative – lots of white shirts and black slacks – and some of the Japanese men wore red Nationals caps and big tourist smiles. They planned on attending the "great American pastime" later on that evening at "big American ballpark." They each posed for pictures with the Capitol Dome over their left shoulders.

Mac Carter was sprinting from the south side of the Capitol after exiting the Capitol metro station. He stopped at the edge of Capitol Plaza and scanned the throngs of people strolling the grounds, heading to the Visitor Center, and taking pictures on the Capitol steps. There were whites, there were blacks, there were Hispanics, there were Asians.

There was a red umbrella popping up and down. And Carter was looking for a needle in a haystack.

The Capitol Plaza slowly began swarming with police and SWAT team members. A loudspeaker on top of an armored personnel carrier announced that all visitors must exit the Capitol Plaza in an orderly fashion. Police officers were seen spreading out from the Capitol steps yelling at people to get back.

"Let's go, folks! We have to evacuate the area! Move to the sidewalks and away from the Capitol! Move!"

Carter moved his way toward the Library of Congress and the stream of tourists walked down the sidewalk facing him and looked to cross the street. He searched their eyes, their clothing, anything that might catch his attention, anything that might be suspicious. He knew Hassani was out here somewhere. The red umbrella kept bobbing up and down as its handler approached.

"Follow the red umbrella," she instructed, hoping the foreigners understood what she was saying. The itinerary hadn't called for an evacuation of the Capitol grounds.

Carter was glad when the umbrella passed him by. It was distracting. But something had caught his eye. The male Japanese tourists wore clean dress shirts that were all white. They had no outer insignia – no Nike Swoosh or Izod gator.

But one man's shirt had a green moon on it.

In his haste to exit the parking garage, Hassani had forgotten to place his American flag sticker over the logo when he put on the clean shirt. Seeing the crescent moon, Carter spun around and noticed the line of Japanese tourists had one glaring abnormality. The man near the end was four inches taller than the rest of the group.

"Hassani!"

Carter whipped out his Glock 9mm and sprinted toward the red umbrella.

"Hassani!"

Hassani turned around. This was his moment. It would have to be now. In the split second that it took for him to turn back to the east, he could not believe his eyes. He recognized the face of Mac Carter coming toward him. His mind raged with the thought that someone had infiltrated his inner circle and lied to him. The man he trusted, the man he reached out to, now had a gun pointed at him. Hassani's right hand reached into his pocket for the button. This would prove his worth.

But the detonator button never came out.

The bullet ripped through Hassani's right wrist from behind, blasting his hand out of the pocket. He had time to look down to see his right hand now hanging by a frayed strand of tendons. The gun that fired the bullet was in the hands of none other than the Director of the FBI, Tyrone Stubblefield.

The red umbrella was on the ground and those from Tokyo were diving for cover faster than a Zero on a kamikaze run.

When Hassani reached his left hand over to his right pocket, Mac Carter fired a shot into his left wrist. A shot from the north capped Hassani in the left knee and he crumpled to the ground.

Sirens filled the smoky air as tourists screamed in horror. The FBI moved in and cuffed what was left of Hassani's wrists and hogtied his ankles. A removal of his shirt revealed the suicide vest and the suspicious white substance.

"The President must die," Hassani whispered under the pressure of an agent's boot on his neck. "America must die!"

"Get me a bomb disposal unit here right now!" Stubblefield yelled to his team. "And get these people farther away! Get 'em back!"

When the disposal SUV arrived, Stubblefield told the agents to get Hassani in the vehicle ASAP and out of the area just in case the vest would happen to go off. Four men in full explosive protection gear carefully moved Hassani to the SUV.

After the vest was removed, Hassani would be transferred to the hospital under heavy guard.

With a river of sweat running off his forehead, Director Stubblefield holstered his weapon on his left hip and took his cell phone off his right. He held the phone to his ear and smiled for the first time in two days.

"Mr. President, we got him."

CHAPTER 31

The White House – Washington, D.C.

On Sunday evening, the President stepped into the press room to make a statement. He had been huddled with his advisors throughout the day. On the domestic front, Stubblefield stated his belief that every terrorist that had been at or near the National Archives had been captured or killed. The investigation revealed the anthrax found on Hassani was of the same type found stolen from a Mexican university within the last six months. It was most likely smuggled over the southern border along with the RPGs. Stubblefield told the President the investigation was ongoing.

On the military side, Chairman Cummins brought his top generals and presented the President with a plan to strike terrorist hideouts and training camps in the mountainous regions of Afghanistan and Pakistan. The Predator and Reaper drones had been in the air for the past two days gathering intelligence, and Chairman Cummins strongly believed the targets were of high value with little chance of civilian casualties. The President gave the go-ahead and no one objected, although a livid Wiley mumbled angrily under his breath that they ought to add Mexico to the bombing list based on that government's failure to stop illegal drugs and weapons smuggling that had a hand in the recent mayhem. The President decided to worry about Mexico and the border after the U.S. response.

The President stepped to the microphone and read his prepared statement. The press had been told he would not take any questions.

"Good evening. I want to start off by saying the FBI is continuing its investigation of the Archives attack. I want to commend Director Stubblefield and his fine work in hunting down those responsible for committing this dastardly act.

"I also want to announce that, within the last hour and on my orders, the United States military has launched a strategic offensive in Afghanistan and Pakistan to hunt down terrorist hideouts and training camps in those areas. Intelligence agencies in the United States and

Great Britain have confirmed that the terrorists who attacked the National Archives were trained in these camps. When I first took office less than eight months ago, I stated that if the United States was attacked, we would travel to the ends of the earth to protect our national interests. Tonight, we have done so."

FBI Headquarters – Washington, D.C.

Director Stubblefield was probably the most hands-on FBI Director the Bureau ever had. As a former agent, he knew what those who served under him were thinking and how seriously they were taking the investigation. But no one was taking it more seriously than he did. The mental image of Anna Schumacher and her flowing blonde hair was constantly popping up in his mind. He had known her since the day she was born, and his close friendship with the Schumachers made him a part of their family.

Ty was not one to enjoy a nice five-mile run to ease his mind or play a round of golf for relaxation. His way of letting off steam was to open up his ready arsenal of firearms and head to the basement at FBI Headquarters. There, he could fire away at the unlucky silhouettes at the end of the firing range. But on this Monday morning, even ten minutes of pumping hot lead into the paper sheet did not help his anxiety.

Something was still bugging him about the attack. It was the "unavailable" number Hassani was calling. There was somebody out there that knew Hassani and the odds were good that person knew what was going down at the National Archives. He put down his gun and pulled out his phone.

"Mike, it's Ty."

Mike Carson was the head investigator on the numbers' front. He had been working the FBI computers hard for the last several days.

"Are you in your office?"

"No, I'm in the basement."

"Ah, thinking with your gun, are you?"

"Yeah. I want you to start looking at the government numbers to find out who Hassani was talking to."

"I've been trying every trick I can think of to break the codes of at least twenty foreign governments."

"No, I don't want you to look at foreign government numbers. I want you to look at our own government."

Georgetown – Washington, D.C.

Sharif al-Rashad had spent his Sunday morning watching the TV reports of Hassani's arrest. Cell phone videos from a handful of tourists around the Capitol showed law-enforcement officers carrying a hog-tied Hassani to the bomb disposal van. It looked to Sharif that Hassani had spit or mucus falling from his nose. They manhandled him into the van like a piece of slaughtered beef, he thought.

The descriptions of Hassani by the FBI and the Schumacher Administration were one of an intelligent Arab-American who had bought into the radical wing of his religion and brought death and destruction to the streets of the United States. Sharif cursed the TV and the President for the ignorant characterizations they were making. Hassani, he believed, was a man of honor and integrity. And one who was willing to give his life to show "the Great Satan" the error of its ways. But now, Hassani would spend the rest of his life in prison, if he was not sentenced to death for his crimes.

After watching the President's announcement of the military offensive, Sharif drove to his office at the Supreme Court Building. The place was empty on Sunday evening, and the quiet stillness was quite a contrast to the chaos that had taken place the day before on the Capitol Plaza.

In his office, he picked up a pocket-sized copy of the Constitution and his Koran. He also took a picture of him and Hassani that was taken on the day he graduated from Northwestern. He put the items in his backpack and walked to the door. Before he turned out the lights, he turned around to look at his office. He once thought a clerkship at the Supreme Court would bring meaning to his life, as if to somehow propel him to greater stature or give him more self-worth. But now it felt meaningless, like no matter how good the opinions or dissents he drafted would ever mean much in the grand scheme of things. He decided it was time for him to join the crusade.

On his way out, he delivered Justice Hussein's robe to his chambers and wrote him a note that he was resigning his clerkship in the near future. With his eyes filling with tears, he hid the letter under the Justice's daily planner and hurried out of the office. He was so upset he forgot his backpack. On Monday morning, he called Justice Hussein's secretary and told her he wasn't feeling well and was taking a sick day. He then paced the floor wondering what he should do. The anger in his heart only deepened when the cable news programs would show Hassani's picture and label him as a terrorist animal.

When the phone rang at 5 p.m., Sharif wondered if he should answer it. He didn't want to talk to Justice Hussein in case he was calling to try and talk him out of quitting.

"Hello."

"Sharif! You need to come over!" It was Pam Williston from next door. "We're having a going-away party for Michelle. Burgers and beer!"

"I don't think I'm in the mood."

"Not in the mood! Michelle is not going to like to hear that!"

His mentor was sitting in an eight-by-ten cell after he had been shot by the FBI. He was also facing charges of conspiracy to commit a terrorist act on United States soil. So forgive me, Sharif thought to himself, for not being in the mood.

"I have things to do."

"You're not going to spend your Monday night watching the President's speech to Congress, are you? That's for old people."

Sharif had forgotten all about President Schumacher's address to Congress. Watching it would just make him more angry.

"No, I won't be watching it."

"Well, we've got a lot of people coming over. You should come and meet some of our girlfriends from school. They would be very impressed with you."

Sharif had no desire to meet any American women right now. He told Pam what she wanted to hear but he had no intention of following through. "Give me some time to take a shower and I'll be over later."

"Great! Don't be late!"

Sharif didn't take that shower. He just stared out from behind the blinds and stewed in silence. When the black SUV showed up in the parking lot, the gap between the blinds got a little wider. His eyes did too. He could not believe what he was seeing. It was the blonde hair that he recognized. The same that he had filmed for Hassani at the National Archives. And there was no mistaken identity. The four men in suits following the blonde indicated it could be only one person – the President's daughter.

Anna Schumacher knew Pam and Michelle from her political science classes at Georgetown. They had become fast friends and even had an old-fashioned sleepover at the White House over the Christmas holiday break. Now with Michelle leaving for her new job in California, Anna wanted to make a quick stop at the party before she headed to the Capitol to watch her father give his address to Congress.

The calming sensation over Sharif's body indicated he knew what to do. Hassani's unfinished work could now be completed.

He went to the closet of the guest bedroom and pulled out Hassani's hard shell suitcase. He hadn't thrown it away, and his beating heart indicated he was glad he hadn't. He removed the towel and took out the last remaining suicide vest. He ripped off his shirt and placed the loose hanging vest over his chest. Since his own white dress shirts were too small, he grabbed one out of Hassani's other suit case and buttoned it up. He then cut off the sleeves at the biceps because of the heat outside. Of course, he didn't think he'd be out there long enough to attract unwanted attention. He decided on a pair of dress shorts. As he glanced at his reflection in the mirror, he smoothed out the shirt over the vest. He grabbed a towel from the rack and wiped the sweat pouring down his forehead. He then ran the detonator wire under his shirt and placed the button in his pants pocket.

Now it was time to party.

FBI Headquarters – Washington, D.C.

Ty Stubblefield was sitting around the conference table in his office with six agents who were discussing the investigation as it then stood. The President wanted an update before he went up to Capitol Hill in less than two hours. Mike Carson was the last agent to show up and it looked like he had been sprinting up from his office two floor below.

"Director, I think you need to look at this again," Agent Carson said. He turned on the computer and then lowered the video screen from the ceiling. He then inserted the flash drive into the slot. With a few mouse clicks, everyone seated around the table was looking at what looked like home video inside the National Archives.

Director Stubblefield instantly recognized the object of the camera's gaze by the blonde hair. "That's Anna Schumacher."

"That's right. I haven't been able to figure out who had been calling Hassani. But this video was sent to him. So I've been trying to work backwards. If we roll the video a bit, you'll see an Archives volunteer asking the man to stop photographing as it is prohibited by rule."

Those around the table then heard the stern but sweet voice of Britney Waterson and glimpses of her could be seen on the screen as the camera man tried to keep filming above and around the pesky volunteer. The next thing the audience saw was the camera phone shaking back and forth before falling to the ground, courtesy of someone grabbing the man's wrist and not letting go. As the camera continued rolling, three men in suits could be seen confronting the man and hustling him out of the building.

"Those are Anna's Secret Service guys."

"That's right, and the Secret Service would most likely have logged that confrontation into their books."

Director Stubblefield didn't need to hear anymore. He picked up the phone and barked orders into the receiver. "I want to talk to Director Defoe at the Secret Service. Tell them it's urgent."

It only took two minutes for Director Allen Defoe to come on line. He was currently stationed at the Joint Operations Center preparing for the President's departure to the Capitol. Director Stubblefield put him on the speaker phone.

"Allen, your detail guarding Anna Schumacher had a confrontation with a man at the National Archives."

"Yes, I remember."

Stubblefield whispered over to Carson asking when the video was shot. "It appears it happened several days before the attack."

"The man checked out I think. Nothing ever came of it."

"Allen, that man sent an e-mail of the video of Anna Schumacher to Abdullah Hassani."

"You're kidding?"

"No. I want to know his name."

The agents sitting around the conference table could hear Director Defoe yelling to those around him to bring up the log book involving Anna Schumacher and the National Archives.

"It's coming up here right now," Defoe said into the phone. "The man's name was Sharif al-Rashad." He then spelled it out for the benefit of those writing the name down. "He had no warrants and no prior contacts with the Secret Service. The log states he is a law clerk at the Supreme Court."

"Law clerk?"

"Yes."

"To which justice?"

"Let me see here," Defoe said as he scrolled down the screen. "It doesn't say."

"Allen, I think this guy might have something to do with the planning of the attack. Do you have an address at your fingertips?"

"His home address is 1100 Potomac Circle in Georgetown."

"Georgetown?"

"That's right."

Stubblefield had gone to an early dinner at the White House not two hours before. The Schumachers had asked him and his wife to come over for a light meal, the President thinking Ty could use a break from all his hard work. Ty remembered Anna coming in to the private dining room, giving both Stubblefields big hugs, and then excusing herself saying she had to hurry to make an appearance at a going-away party.

In Georgetown.

"Where is Anna Schumacher's security detail right now?"

Director Defoe thought it was an odd request from the Director of the FBI but he wasn't going to simply disregard it or engage in any turf wars in light of recent happenings. Defoe looked up to the massive screen listing the location of all protectees under the watch of the Secret Service. The President and First Lady were in the White House. Four former presidents were in their residences. Ashley Schumacher was at her home outside Indianapolis, and Michael Schumacher was at the family home in Silver Creek.

"Anna is currently . . .," he said looking at the screen, "in Georgetown."

"What address?"

Director Defoe's jaw suddenly hit the floor. "1100 Potomac Circle."

"Get her out of there!" Stubblefield yelled into the speaker. "Get her out of there!"

The coats were flying off the back of the chairs at both the Joint Operations Center and at FBI Headquarters. It was time to move.

CHAPTER 32

Georgetown – Washington, D.C.

The Potomac Circle condominium complex was home to a horde of festive young twenty-somethings, half of them trust-fund students whose parents sprang for an upper-end apartment and the other half a collection of professionals who didn't worry about putting anything away in a savings account at this stage of their life. The pool area was a happening place, the spot the young women came to show off their hot bikini-clad bodies after a long day of studying or on the job and the young men came to ogle at and flirt with said bodies. Tonight was no different. And the alcohol was flowing as going-away Michelle was getting the royal send-off complete with gifts and Jell-O shots.

Anna Schumacher arrived wearing a modest pair of jean shorts; modest in that they only went half way up her very tanned thigh. The spaghetti-strapped red tank top was her invitation to Agent Sessions to enjoy the view. He, however, had on his slacks and suit coat in the eighty-five degree heat. The other three agents wore the same. They had been promised this was going to be a quick visit and then they could towel off and get Anna back to the White House to change and then to the Capitol. The lucky agent who drew the longest straw sat in the air-conditioned SUV and waited with all the patience in the world.

Anna walked around the pool to greet all the guests. She knew most of them from school, others looked familiar but she didn't know their names.

"Anna, I'm so glad you came," Michelle gushed. "Thank you so much."

"I can't stay long, but I just wanted to wish you well."

Agent Sessions had already scanned the entire crowd of twenty – eleven females and nine males. His attention was drawn to one male in particular. The young man had obviously been partying since early that afternoon. His face was beet red and a glazed curtain hung over his bloodshot eyes. He wore a T-shirt with a bulldog on it and had his sleeves rolled up to show everyone his massive pipes. He was loud and obnoxious and it was obvious to everyone that he got into Georgetown on the strength of his parents' political pull. It sure as hell wasn't his intelligence. Sessions dreaded the confrontation that was headed Anna's way.

"Hey, good looking," the man bellowed. "Where you been all my life?"

Anna took a step back and her head went back even farther. The cheap beer on the man's breath along with what appeared to be two packs' worth of Camels could make a person puke from ten feet away.

Agent Sessions sighed under his breath. This wouldn't be happening if he had been assigned to the President's security detail, he thought to himself.

"Take a hike, pal," he said quietly, putting a hand between the man and Anna.

The drunk swiped at the hand but missed. "Who the hell are you!? Her bodyguard!?" The guy obviously had no clue who she was other than a hot blonde he could hit on.

"Yeah, I am," Sessions said, holding his Secret Service badge two inches in front of the man's eyes.

"I don't give a fuck who you are!" the man slurred.

Sharif walked slowly out his front door and onto the walkway facing the parking lot. The heat of the evening would show up in his shirt in no time. He wiped his upper lip with the back of his hand and headed for the sound of the revelers in the back. Grabbing a half full beer can on a railing so he would blend in with the crowd, he noticed three agents standing near the entrance of the pool away from the party. This was going to be easier than he thought. It was going to happen and his name would be written in the history books forever. Even in prison, Hassani would receive word of the suicide bombing killing the President's daughter. He would then praise Allah at the joyous news and know that his "young son" Sharif had served him honorably.

"Sharif!" Pam yelled upon eyeing him. He waved back.

Sharif made it beyond the three agents with barely a second glance. The target was sixty feet away, just a short few steps to his right and then a left turn down the length of the pool. He could have pushed the button now but he waited. He wanted to take the bomb right to the target like the Hezbollah guerillas do when they blow themselves up inside the bus or in the disco. That way he could make sure the bombing succeeded. The result he wanted was instant death, a gruesome maiming of the President's daughter would not be enough. As his eyes scanned the pool side, Sharif could not believe what he was seeing. The man who had accosted him in the National Archives had his back to him. He would never know what hit him. He would now return the favor to the man who had disrespected him.

Anna stood off to the side growing redder by the minute. She had caused a scene with her bodyguards and everyone was staring. She thought about telling Agent Sessions that they could leave but she just put her hands up to her mouth wanting the commotion to end.

When Sharif made the left turn he noticed out of the corner of his eyes that the other agents surrounding the pool were beginning to close in to help Agent Sessions. With all the yelling, those three were the only ones who heard the urgent radio traffic in their ears. Sharif grabbed the button from his pocket and broke into a full sprint.

"You don't own her, you fuckin' jarhead! She's going home with me tonight!"

When the drunk reached his hand out to grab Anna, Agent Sessions went all Dick Butkus on him. He grabbed his right wrist with a bone crunching grasp with his right hand and clamped on to his belt with his left. He then picked the drunk off his feet, spun him around three feet off the ground, and hurled the man straight into the path of the oncoming Sharif, hitting him square in the upper chest, the drunk's head colliding with Sharif's lower jaw. The drunk and Sharif let out two vicious grunts as they went ass over tea kettle into the pool, the giant cannonball of a splash drenching those within three feet of the pool.

The drunk, who apparently thought Sharif was Agent Sessions, now proceeded to show off his manhood by beating the man underwater and cursing him at every waterlogged punch. Those top side would later report they could faintly hear the man yelling something about "kicking jarhead's ass." On the wrong end of the repeated blows, Sharif had no clue where the detonator button was and the pummeling he was taking indicated he wasn't going to find it either. When the drunk finally had enough, he pulled Sharif up for air and almost wet his pants at what was staring down at him.

There, standing around the pool weren't any of the hot chicks he was sure he was impressing with his great underwater jujitsu display. But ten men with automatic weapons pointed at his and Sharif's heads. Even through his glassy eyes, the drunk could see the red dots coming from the laser sights on the weapons and they were all focused on him. Anna Schumacher and Agent Sessions were nowhere to be found. They were already hightailing it back to the White House.

"Don't move!" the armed man closest to the drunk yelled. "Don't you move a muscle or you're a dead man!"

Two agents jumped in and rescued Sharif from the grip of the idiot. They then led Sharif over to the side and handcuffed him. The drunk was left standing there to ponder what they were doing. Whether he would ever sober up enough to realize he had a hand in saving the life of the daughter of the President of the United States, only time and a handful of Tylenol would tell.

The wailing police sirens and heavily armed men surrounding the complex indicated the party was over. Directors Stubblefield and Defoe hustled to the pool area and checked on Sharif. He was bleeding from the mouth and his eyes were beginning to swell. His jaw might have been broken.

"Another suicide vest," one agent explained. "Same as the one Hassani had on him."

"Good work," Stubblefield said.

Director Defoe looked at his watch and it read 7:45. He radioed to the Joint Operations Center that it was all clear to move the President to the Capitol at 8:30. The last known person involved in the planning of the attack on the National Archives had been apprehended. Since Anna was out of danger, he said her detail could bring her down to Capitol Hill once she was ready. A collective sigh of relief went out among the law-enforcement personnel in the capital. Defoe then left to oversee the President's arrival on Capitol Hill.

Director Stubblefield, however, was not going to the Capitol to watch the speech. The President already told him what he was going to say anyway. Stubblefield wasn't going to be able to sleep that night either so he instructed his agents to hurry up on the search warrants for Sharif's condo and car. He wanted to see if the evidence finally put him at ease.

At ten minutes to nine, the FBI entered Sharif's condo very carefully. He and Hassani obviously had knowledge of explosives and could have rigged the doors, the cabinets, or the microwave to surprise the authorities when they came snooping around. Once the "all clear" was given, Stubblefield and his men entered and set their FBI-trained eyes on anything that might be of evidentiary value. It didn't take long.

"Hey, here in the bedroom!" an evidence technician yelled after only five minutes of inspection..

On the bed were Hassani's two opened suitcases. His folded clothes were still in the soft one and the harder one only contained the towel that had surrounded the suicide vests. Nothing really out of the ordinary.

"What do you got?" Stubblefield asked.

With his latex-gloved fingers, the technician held up to eye level a plastic cap with a broken seal attached to its bottom. "It's the cap that goes on top of the detonator button. When you're ready to push the button, you twist off this cap like the top of a milk jug and it leaves this little piece of plastic hanging by a thread." He bent back the piece to demonstrate.

"Yeah," Stubblefield said, nodding his head. "You showed me the one yesterday that you recovered near Hassani's vest on Capitol Hill."

The technician looked straight into Stubblefield's eyes. "I know I showed you that one." He then held up both of his hands. "But there are *two* here."

Stubblefield stared at the two plastic caps. There was a cap for Hassani's vest. There was one for Sharif's vest. And now another cap without a vest. Something just didn't feel right, like a piece of the puzzle was missing. And in this line of work, a missing piece could cost lives. He thought of the President and then the First Lady and Anna. The latter two would be sitting in the First Lady's box in the gallery. Stubblefield reached for his phone and called Director Defoe who was now intently monitoring the situation at the Capitol.

"Allen, it's Ty," he said as he started pacing back and forth across the carpet. "We've been sifting through al-Rashad's stuff at his condo and I'm worried about another suicide vest being out there. We have recovered three detonator caps but only have two vests to go along with them. I think you should check everybody in the House Chamber."

Defoe almost choked. "What? Are you nuts? The President is set to enter the chamber in ten minutes."

"Was everybody screened going in?"

"Yeah, even the members of Congress had to be screened," Defoe said quickly so as to dispel any more thought of clearing the House

Chamber. It was as secure as it was going to be. "About the only people who weren't were the Vice President and the Speaker of the House." He stopped before adding. "And the Supreme Court justices, but I don't even know how many of them are showing up."

"All right, thanks Allen. Just checking." Ty clicked off his phone and turned to the technician. "Well, there's got to be another vest around here somewhere. Be careful when you're opening up any drawers, closets, or boxes."

The conversation was interrupted again when Ty's phone started buzzing on his hip. It was Special Agent Mac Carter providing a quick update on Sharif at the station.

"He's been booked and fingerprinted," Carter said. The FBI had transported Sharif to the hospital and he was quickly released with a bag of ice that FBI agents held onto his head on the way down to interview him. The jaw wasn't broken, but he might have sustained a concussion. "He's refusing to talk and lawyered up."

"No surprise there."

"That's all I got from down here," Carter said before remembering one last thing. "Hey, I found out that al-Rashad works for Justice Hussein."

"Okay."

"Should I put a call into the Justice tonight?"

Ty looked at his watch. "He's probably getting ready to go into the House Chamber. Just wait until after the speech to break the news to him."

"Ten-four."

Once Ty hung his phone back on his hip, the technician reentered the bedroom and spoke up. "Director, the guys haven't found any other vests in the condo. Nothing in al-Rashad's car either."

Something wasn't adding up. Stubblefield ran through all the evidence in his head. None of the terrorists had suicide vests on at the National Archives. Hassani only had the one on him, no other vest was found in his car.

"Here's al-Rashad's wallet."

The technician handed it over and Stubblefield started laying out the contents on the bed so a photograph could be taken for evidence. Driver's license, Supreme Court ID card, CLA membership card, Visa, MasterCard, American Express, and eighty-five dollars in United States currency. No pictures.

There were, however, two receipts – one from the Old Ebbitt Grill and the other from Executive Brothers Clothiers. Stubblefield looked at the date and then threw the restaurant bill on the bed. The Clothiers receipt was from three days ago. Three hundred and fifty seven dollars and sixteen cents was the charge, paid with Sharif's American Express. It wouldn't be out of the ordinary for someone like al-Rashad to wear a suit of that price. But the charge wasn't for a nice tailored suit.

It was for a size forty eight judicial robe.

"Why would a law clerk buy a judge's robe?" Stubblefield asked the technician.

"Maybe he's a dreamer and thinks he might need it in the near future. You know those law clerk types, they all think they're going to be a Supreme Court justice by the end of next week. Maybe it's for his boss."

"What size suit does al-Rashad have in his closets?"

"Forty. He probably has ten of them. He's not that big of a guy."

"What size suit do you think Justice Hussein wears?"

The technician thought for a second. He had never met the man, only saw him on TV. "I'd say he is a forty four." The technician then looked at the receipt. "Why would al-Rashad or the Justice need a size forty eight robe then?"

Stubblefield's heart sank. The larger than normal robe. The extra plastic detonator cap.

"Oh shit."

CHAPTER 33

The United States House of Representatives – Washington, D.C.

"Mr. Speaker, the President of the United States!"

The presidential motorcade had traveled down an empty Pennsylvania Avenue thirty minutes ago. A separate decoy motorcade went south from the White House and headed east on Independence Avenue. Three Apache attack helicopters roared above each one. With the prior use of RPGs, the Apaches were "white-hot" and ready to respond with more hell-fire than any terrorist could ever imagine. Behind each armored limousine rumbled a Humvee with a .50-caliber machine gun on a swiveling turret, its gunner ready to put a softball-sized hole into a person's chest if the idiot so much as looked at him cross-eyed.

After a brief period in a holding room, the Senate majority leader and a handful of his Senate colleagues met the President to escort him to the House Chamber. Now, following the introduction from the House Sergeant-at-Arms, the President was moving down the aisle to thunderous applause. The media had gotten wind of the arrest of the last suspected terrorist and all in attendance were breathing a welcomed sigh of relief. Maybe now the Republicans and Democrats could get back to attacking themselves – at least that was nonviolent warfare. The President shook every hand of every House member lining the center aisle and even had a few smiles for the Democrats. As he approached the end of the aisle, he shook the hand of Chief Justice Shannon and the other eight justices and then headed left. He made his way along the line of the Joints Chiefs of Staff and even reached out a hand to Wiley standing off to the left side of the Speaker's rostrum waiting to hear his boss's speech. He gave a quick nod to Agent Craig who was ready for this night to be over. He longed for a quiet weekend assignment to Camp David. With a quick hop of the steps, the President was atop his perch and the applause grew louder.

Director Stubblefield and his entourage were roaring down Pennsylvania Avenue in a manner befitting a drag strip. He had yelled for all available agents to meet him at the Capitol and tires could be heard screeching to a halt on the East Front. Stubblefield had been fiddling with his walkie-talkie all the way east and he was yelling into it as soon as the doors opened.

"It's the Justice! It's the Justice!"

The commotion was reaching a crescendo in the House Chamber as the President raised his left hand to the First Lady's box in the gallery and the assembled throng whooped and hollered for the First Lady and Anna Schumacher, both of whom nodded and waved in thankful appreciation after these trying times.

Stubblefield took the Capitol steps two at a time and entered the Senate side. "It's the Justice! It's the Justice!" He knew this was the Secret Service command channel. Why weren't they responding?

Agent Craig could barely hear over the adulation in the chamber and put a finger in his ear. "Control, Craig. What's he saying?"

The voice over the command channel was clear. "It's Stubblefield and his men. I think he's saying it's 'Just us.' It's just Stubblefield and the FBI."

"Copy that."

When the President raised both hands, the crowded chamber relented but only until they received their next cue. The Speaker banged his gavel and brought the House to order.

"Members of Congress, I have the high privilege and distinct honor of presenting to you, the President of the United States."

Stubblefield and his team of four agents were sprinting through the Rotunda of the Capitol, their shoes thumping the marble floor, their guns drawn and ready for battle.

"It's Justice Hussein! Get the President out!"

When the President was finally able to calm down the members of Congress enough to get started he began his speech.

"Thank you, Mr. Speaker. Madame Vice President. Members of Congress, Mr. Chief Justice and members of the Supreme Court, distinguished guests, and last but not least, my fellow Americans."

The President continued on as Justice Hussein made his way left in front of his colleagues and to the center of the aisle. This was highly irregular. A Supreme Court justice walking out in the middle of a President's speech to a Joint Session of Congress would be seen as a great insult. But Hussein had waited for the moment of highest drama, the time when the curtains would have been pulled high on this grand stage and everyone in the audience was at full attention. The TV camera from the rear of the chamber caught both the view of the President of the United States and an associate justice of the Supreme Court. With the detonator button in his right hand, Hussein stopped in the middle aisle and turned to face the President.

"Mr. President! Allahu Akbar!"

The House Chamber grew eerily quiet as those in attendance wondered what in the world was going on. None of them had ever seen such a thing. One Representative managed to get the words "Get down!" out of his mouth. Agent Craig was already on his way up to the rostrum when the rear doors of the chamber opened.

"Allahu Akbar!" Justice Hussein yelled again. He held up his right hand, the cord showing outside the sleeve of his larger than normal robe.

The bullet flying out of the smoking barrel of Tyrone Stubblefield hit the backside of Justice Hussein's palm, blood splattering on the Chief Justice's shocked face in the front row. Another shot hit Justice Hussein in the neck and he fell face first into the aisle. The nationwide TV audience then saw the Chief Justice of the United States diving to the floor to grab the button in Hussein's hand.

Agent Craig had tackled the President and now had him by the belt on his way out the door. The House Chamber was in complete chaos. Screams and shouts echoed off the walls. The Secret Service cleared the First Lady and Anna out of the gallery. Two Democratic Congresswomen fainted into the center aisle and were nearly trampled by Representatives and Senators who were climbing over their seats and their colleagues trying to reach an exit. The smell of gunfire filtered throughout the chamber. Stubblefield pushed his way through the melee to get to Justice Hussein and found the Chief Justice and Chairman Cummins holding him down. The Justice wasn't going anywhere.

Agent Craig and two other agents were carrying the President by his belt and his armpits through the halls of Congress, the automatic weapons from fellow agents on full display.

"Move! Move!" the agents yelled in full sprint.

Heavily armed men seemed to appear out of nowhere – from congressional offices, behind pillars, from empty stairwells. Helicopter gunships took position over the Capitol. The whole facility was on lockdown, the steps and sidewalks were empty, and no one was exiting except the men carrying the President.

"Get him in the limo! Get him in the limo!"

The drive to the White House was made in record time. With guns drawn, every available Secret Service agent ringed the property. Newsmen intent on catching sight of the President or grabbing a sound bite from an administration official were seen sprinting down the sidewalks of Pennsylvania Avenue not wanting to wait for the police to reopen the roads. The view from the Washington Monument showed a patriotic collection of red, white, and blue flashing lights encircling the White House complex. The cacophony of sirens could be heard for miles.

Yet another AOP had failed.

Although the last plot to kill the President had now been thwarted once and for all, he and the First Lady spent the night holding each other tight in the White House bunker. Anna was there too, with Agent Sessions standing guard right outside the door. Some day life would return to normal, they all thought.

At least they hoped.

The White House – Washington, D.C.

The President just finished up his third Oval Office address to the nation, his first one to take place at noon on a Tuesday. The early hour was meant to assure the American people and the world that he was unharmed and in command. After the cameras were removed, the President shuffled the papers in his chair behind the desk. Commentators and pundits were already discussing who the President might pick to fill the newest Supreme Court vacancy. The President decided he would take his time replacing the now-deceased Justice Hussein. The Democrats, of course, would want another fight. He picked up the paper to continue the story he had started earlier.

Wiley fell into the chair next to him holding an ice bag on his head. In the chaos of the previous evening, the Secret Service agents in charge of protecting the President's chief of staff carried Wiley to the waiting limo only to hit his head on the roof when they were throwing him in. Wiley had a huge red bump on his bald dome and two black eyes to go along with it. He looked like a cartoon raccoon who had been hit on the head with a sledgehammer.

"Did you see that last night was the first time there was a shooting in the House Chamber since those Puerto Rican Nationalists shot up the place in 1954?" the President asked, his eyes fixated on the articles as he recapped the events from the previous evening.

"Uh huh," Wiley replied, his head still aching.

"They have a nice picture of you being wheeled into the ambulance after the limo made it back to the White House." The President tried hard to suppress his laughter.

"Great."

The President then scanned down to the meat of the story. "'Initial reports indicated William Cogdon, the President's chief of staff, had suffered a heart attack and he was rushed to George Washington Medical Center. The reports turned out to be unfounded, as Cogdon only suffered a slight head injury after being hurried into his car by the Secret Service.'"

"'Hurried into?'" Wiley mumbled. "Try thrown in like a bag of garbage. I think they meant to do it. My security detail hates me."

The President could not help but laugh at his chief of staff's plight. He decided to keep the article for future ribbing so he folded up the paper and placed it in his top drawer. With his reading done, the President moved on to the next item on his agenda. "Well, I guess we better get started."

"Oh how I long for my Indiana home," an exhausted Wiley moaned.

"What are you talking about?" the President said with a smile. "Go get yourself a Red Bull. We've got an election to win."

THE END

Rob Shumaker is an attorney living in Illinois. *Showdown in the Capital* is his second novel. He is also the author of *Thunder in the Capital*, *Chaos in the Capital*, *D-Day in the Capital*, *Manhunt in the Capital*, *Fallout in the Capital*, *Phantom in the Capital*, *Blackout in the Capital*, and *The Way Out*.

To read more about the Capital Series novels, go to

www.USAnovels.com

••• •••• ••—

Made in the USA
Middletown, DE
08 December 2020

26836989R00144